SLIPSTREAMERS

THE RISE OF CASSIDY CANE

ENGEN
BOOKS

Published in Canada by Engen Books, St. John's, NL.

Library and Archives Canada relevant to this title can be found online.

ISBN-13: 978-1-77478-016-9

Distributed by:
Engen Books
www.engenbooks.com
submissions@engenbooks.com

First mass market paperback printing: December 2020
Cover Design: Ellen Curtis
Slipstreamers Committee:
Amanda Labonté
Ali House
AJ Ryan
Ellen Curtis
Erin Vance
Lauralana Dunne
Matthew LeDrew

NEW WORLDS! NEW ADVENTURE!

MATTHEW LEDREW & JD RYOT

CHAPTER ONE

Cassidy slammed chest first into the stone ledge, letting out both a long gust of air and a curse so strong she wouldn't have said it on any continent that her mother might have been in. She paused briefly before gravity began to take hold, tugging at her quickly and dragging her down towards the gaping maw below.

She dug her nails into the crevasses of the stone, sliding until she found purchase and ground to a firm halt, her nails pulling against their beds and threatening to break. She turned, red hair whipping and clinging to her sweat-laden face as she looked down the embankment she dangled from.

Intellectually, she knew that no pit was bottomless. But when her feet kicked and dangled over a chasm so deep and dark that it disappeared beyond her focal point, it was hard to find any other word for it.

The walls around her began to shake and vibrate. Dust and silt that fell between them, making a distant rumbling that she knew was coming closer with every passing second. She ground her teeth together and pulled, her jacket protecting her from the coarseness of the stone as she pulled her body back onto solid ground.

Behind her, the ledge she'd leapt from cracked in two with the shifting of the temple's foundations. It stayed that way for a moment, as through the split would be the worst of it, before several quick jolts made it snap apart and fall into the abyss below.

She let out a long, deep breath and laid on her back before bringing her right hand up into her field of vision. She still clasped the lead disk she had taken from the tomb, the small ringlets along its edge spread between her fingers. There was a square hole in its center, through which she could only just see the gash that had been sliced through her palm. Despite the pain that ebbed from it, she smiled as she looked at the artifact.

"At least I've got my tetanus shot," she smirked.

The ground beneath her moved and she laid her hands flat to steady herself. As if on cue a large, lightning-bolt shaped crack opened in the stone beneath her, splitting from the mouth of the cavern to the ledge she'd just crawled over. She turned quickly, scrambling onto her feet as dust and sand kicked loose. She bolted for the exit, slipping twice on loose grains before finally making it out into the humid air of the Nubian sun. She gasped as the cloud of dust followed her, outrunning it as the temple door slammed shut behind her.

"Are you okay?" her Guide, David, said, running over to her. He laid his hands on her shoulders and she laughed: a full, honest laugh. He took out a pouch of water and handed it to her. She leaned back her head and doused herself with it, revealing the freckles that had been hidden under the dirt and grime of the enclosure.

She drank from the skin and handed it back to him, then turned over and pressed the pointer and middle finger of her right hand into her neck. "Come on..." she huffed, still stifling her laughter. "Come on..."

"What're you--" David started. She held up a finger to stop him.

"Sixty-four, sixty-five... sixty-six." She paused, waiting. "Sixty-six." She cursed. She looked down at her hands, ignoring the slice along the right palm and spreading her fingers wide. She turned her palms down and then up, examining them as if waiting for them to do something.

Cassidy cursed again, then rose to her feet and started the long trek back to her camp. David followed close behind.

***

"And that's how I retrieved the Amulet of Ra, one of the ten fabled Amulets of the Ok'Tid," Cassidy said as the lights came up and the projector wound down. The absence of the bright light made the lecture hall visible, with all two hundred seats of it filled with students and still more standing along the back wall.

She smiled with showmanship, turning and spreading her arms towards the iron disk, which now rested comfortably in a glass display case. She felt like Vanna White while doing it, her smile wide and forced, pushing her cheeks up so far that they obscured her vision.

"Once thought to be a myth, this relic was believed to be a part of a set that, when combined together, possessed the ability to make their wielder *immortal*." She turned and stepped closer to the case, the fake smile fading. She tugged at the edges of her coat, the same brown leather she'd been wearing in the temple, but now clean, until it fit around her shoulders properly. "This legend stems from the region, going as far back as three *thousand* B.C., and is thought to be one of the precursors to modern healing myths. Your fountains of youth, your holy grails." She turned sharply on her heel and pointed to the case, her fingers clicking like a gun. "It all starts right there, and until last month we thought it was lost to time."

Several of the students in the front row leaned forward, as if trying to get closer -- if only by a few inches -- to the artifact. To Cassidy's right, near her entrance to the hall, came a loud cough. There were four men standing in the door -- three large and one much older and shorter.

Cassidy nodded, turning to address them. "And it is of course being handed over, with appreciation, to the Plainsfield Museum, who have agreed to fund the Archeology and Anthropology departments for a further three years." She brought her hands together to lead the applause, and most of the students followed. She did so gingerly: her hand had healed, but a pink line of tender flesh remained.

The men stepped forward until they flanked the display case. It looked at first as though they were about to step forward and speak, but instead they turned their backs to the student body. Two of the larger men picked the case up off of its podium, and the lot of them walked back the way they'd come with it.

Cassidy coughed, and her feigned smile returned. She clicked a button on her remote and the projector whirred back to life, displaying an image of the amulet on the screen behind her. "Were there any questions?"

Fully half of the students present raised their hands immediately.

She smiled and pointed to a tall blonde girl in the third row. "Yes?"

"I guess the thing I have to ask, it sounds silly... but with all that going on, weren't you scared?"

Cassidy paused. She looked down at her hand, splayed out with her fingers wide, not shaking in the slightest. When she looked back up again she had resumed her public smile: that broad, too-wide and too-bright expression she put on for others. "I must have been, mustn't I?"

CHAPTER TWO

"That," Cassidy said, making a big circle with her red pen on the page of text in front of her, "is not how a preposition works."

The stack of papers in front of her was large and oppressive, a tower that shifted and swayed whenever the air conditioner kicked in. Which was often. They teetered near a framed photograph of an older couple and two young women: the photo was old, but the frame was new.

Her office was small and cluttered, only six feet across but a full ten feet long, with the door at one end and her desk on the other, near a window that barely opened but let in the heat of the sun all throughout the day.

The space between the door and the desk was packed tight, so tight that she had to squeeze and maneuver to make it through. There was a wide wooden chair of the sort that came with any University office, she felt. Against either wall was a bookshelf stacked with reference materials, most of which now gathered dust -- a byproduct of a digital age. Atop the stacks of books and along the ridge of each shelf were trinkets -- artifacts from different regions that hadn't been needed by the University or the museum. There was a fat doll made from hollow wooden balls and catgut. There was a plate gold-plated disk with a hollow center and small shards of shimmering metal dangling from it.

Stacked beside the bookshelf against the west wall was a box overflowing with maps, each of which looked well used. Several were on the floor around it, and one was spread over a corner of her desk like a tarp, a days-old yet full cup of coffee weighing it down. Next to the box of maps was a large globe, upon which all the landmasses were a light tan color and the oceans were a deep, chocolate brown.

Cassidy found that she'd been staring at a spot on the globe with the sort of trance-like boredom that she sometimes found herself doing -- especially when correcting papers. The place she was staring at was deep in the center of Mexico, a section of Mesoamerica she'd marked long ago with four red stickers she'd never been able to remove. She forced herself to look away from them and back to the work in front of her. "And that is a comma splice connecting a faulty argument," she said aloud, circling the splice and then striking out the problematic sentence.

She sighed.

On the page, the words began to blur and jumble, and before she knew it her head had lolled up towards those red stickers on the globe again. She sighed again, then reached over the stack of papers and gripped the map that hung over the edge of her desk. She inched it forward until the coffee cup was in reach, then picked up both cup and map and brought them down in front of her. She took a long sip of the ice-cold liquid, slurping it as she spread the map out over the essay she was correcting. She took her red pen -- no longer for correcting -- and marked a spot quite near the center of Mexico.

"It's the boredom, isn't it?" came a firm, hoarse voice.

She looked up from her map and saw a man standing in her doorway, his heels in the hall and his toes firmly in her space. He was a short, portly man in a suit that looked expensive but hadn't been fitted properly, a sign of a man who had money but hadn't had it long. He had a smattering of incidental facial hair and was balding, with glasses so thick they were what her grandfather's generation would have called 'Coke Bottles.' They rested atop a small nose and a kind, wry smile that traveled up one side of his face. Despite the fact that Cassidy was sure she'd never seen the man before, he still looked familiar.

"Pardon?" she asked, straightening a little. She wasn't sure yet if he was even entering the room. Some people -- especially men of a certain age, she'd found -- thought of open office doors as an excuse to step in and make a comment. It was typically a comment that the speaker considered to be in good humour, regardless of the fact that nobody ever laughed.

"The boredom. It all seems good, it seems like maybe this time you'll be able to stay... catch up on your office hours, maybe binge the latest season of that show that's on your DVR... but the moment you sit down, the boredom hits. And suddenly it all feels the same, and the office feels too small." He stepped in on the word 'office', looking around at the books that lined the walls. "Quaint."

"Is there something I can help you with?"

"Yes, I dare say so." He turned to one of the shelves, examining a long row of volumes on Papua New Guinea with his hands clasped behind his back.

Cassidy waited a long, pregnant moment for a further response. "And that is?" she said finally.

He smiled, almost unknowingly. "I need help with my latest project. The project is... well it's your cup of tea, actually." He turned to her. "I need your help finding a cure, for more than just boredom."

He said the word *cure* with the U sound drawn out, inflecting up at the end as though he were saying the word *demure*. It was slight, but enough that it triggered a dormant part of her memory. "Are you..." she paused, glancing at the photo on her desk again, at the only male in it. He was smiling with broad, full cheeks. The man in the photo was not the man that stood before her, but one had saved the other, even though they'd never met. "You're Dr. Gamgee."

He grinned. "Herbert."

"You cured McMillon disease." Her cheeks were flushed with warmth.

"And, potentially: boredom." He smirked, running a finger along her books and coming back with a thick layer of dust on the digit.

She stared for a moment, then forced a smile. "I just got back from Nubia. Brought back one of the ten Amulets of the Ok'Tid. It's priceless. Literally, without price. Once in a lifetime discovery. History book stuff. I'm not..." she paused, leaning in and smiling for dramatic effect, "*bored*."

He turned to her and smiled that knowing smile. It was

the sort of smile people had when they'd known you your entire life and could see the culmination of everything in your every statement. "Then I suppose your pulse got up above seventy beats per minute?"

She opened her mouth to answer before she'd really processed the statement. Once she'd heard it she stopped short, her finger hanging in the air.

He nodded. "Join me for a meal. I hear your cafeteria is horrible." He turned and stepped out of the room without looking to see if she was following.

She narrowed her eyes, watching him go until he was out of sight. Finally she cursed, pinned the map back to her desk with the still-full coffee mug, then grabbed her coat.

CHAPTER THREE

The cafeteria at Plainsfield University was wide and open, with the sort of flat white tiles that used to be only found at cell phone carrier storefronts, but had in the years since been utilized anywhere that desired to look modern. False glass walls divided and herded the traffic from the kitchen, lined with USB outlets and creating a false sense of privacy while still making everyone visible.

Gamgee took a bite of his taco. Lettuce fell from its lower half onto his plate, tumbling out like water over a falls. He laughed at it, trying to catch it at first and then giving up. As he swallowed he said, "It's been years since I had one of these."

Cassidy squinted at him from across the small, round table. She had a plate of fries in front of her that was largely untouched, a healthy smear of spicy ketchup next to the mound. All around them students moved and shifted, bustling from tables to classrooms and back again. Her vision was locked on the man who sat before her in an ill-fitting suit, letting everyone else move in and out of her peripherals.

"You cured McMillon disease," she said finally and

declaratively.

He paused, let his head warble from side to side, then nodded.

"You are one of the world's most celebrated medical doctors, so I feel like I owe you the time here. But I didn't come to talk about tacos. So let's get to the point before I get--"

"Bored?" he smirked.

She lowered her eyes at him. "*Distracted.*"

He nodded empathetically, wiping his mouth with a paper napkin. "Physicist, actually," he corrected, waggling a large finger at her.

She raised an eyebrow. "Pardon?"

"You said I was a world renowned medical doctor. I never got my MD. I'm a physicist, world renowned for an advance in medical science." He took a long drink from his soda through a straw.

Her eyebrows scrunched together, but she said nothing.

"But I understand. You're a busy person, I'm a busy person," he took another sip of his drink, "we all have places to be, so I'll approach my point. Or attempt to." He took the salt and pepper shakers from the edge of the table and pushed them closer to the center, between Cassidy and him. He paused, laid his hands flat on the table, then looked at her. "Do you know what McMillon disease does?"

"I know the effects."

"Yes, but how does it do that? McMillon disease affects the... oh, I can never remember the term. The *garbage collector* genes. Things build up in our bodies, our lymph tissue, on our nerves, etcetera. Your body has functions that remove that gunk and let it pass."

Cassidy nodded.

"McMillon disease inhibits those functions. The gunk builds up on the nerves and synaptic fibers, and things get... things get bad. Slowly, in stages. Sometimes in stages so slowly that people don't realize it's happening. Most people know it for the loss of the senses." He took another bite of his taco. "That gunk, it builds up on the nerves around the eyes and around nerve endings... people lose their sight, their touch sensitivity, their hearing... everything."

Cassidy's right hand touched the finger on her left uncomfortably, before she forced them apart again.

"In the end it mimics Alzheimer's, but by then with McMillon... well, by that point with McMillon most of the sufferers have already died, if we're being honest."

She nodded.

"It's an awful disease. Truly. So ten years ago I found a treatment, which I turned into a cure." He sipped his drink. It was nearing the bottom of the cup and made a slurping sound through the straw. "That's the thing that people don't get: McMillon disease isn't something you get, it's not HIV. You're born with it. It might stay dormant or inactive, but if it was going to activate in you it's going to activate. No amount of healthy living or good life choices will circumvent it. It's genetic." He shrugged with one shoulder. "So apart from gene therapy, which we don't yet have for it, there's not strictly a 'cure.'" He used air quotes when he said the last word.

Cassidy shifted uncomfortably, her gaze shifting around the room briefly.

"There's just the treatment. You treat McMillon disease, and eventually with rigorous treatment the affects can reverse. In the best of cases it can reverse totally, to the point that the treatment is no longer necessary on a daily or even monthly basis... but the underlying cause, it's still there." He took the pepper shaker from the table and held it up at eye level, like a token. "But you know how some people are." He moved the shaker to the other end of the table, then gestured at it. "People don't take their prescriptions as doctors prescribe, and doctors don't take human behavior into account. All around, people are dumb. They take their treatment until they feel better, or until they can't afford it or..." he shrugged. "Any number of reasons. But the point is they don't take it as instructed. So the gunk builds up again, but in new ways. *Resistant* ways. It builds up on some nerve types more than others."

He tapped the pepper shaker on its head. "So now we've started to see McMillon disease Stage Two."

Cassidy felt gooseflesh break out across her arms in one long wave.

"Stage Two is... different. You don't see the same sort of nerve damage to the senses. That still gets managed with treatment. Where you see it worst is cognitive function. The gunk, it starts to line the nerves in the brain. And once it starts there, it's hard to get at. The treatment, it doesn't chip away at it like it does the nerve endings outside the brain."

"What does it do?" she asked, her voice hurried.

"It causes degradation of brainwave activity. Some in the field liken it to Alzheimer's, but honestly as we learn more and more about Alzheimer's... the comparison is less and less apt. But, broad strokes, sure." He paused, wetting his lips. "Not many are to that point yet, but we're starting to see it. The early signs actually resemble split brain patients."

She furrowed her brow.

He brought all his fingers up to the middle of his head. "There's this bundle of nerves called the corpus callosum that connect the right and left sides of the brain. We used to sever it in seizure patients... we don't anymore, don't worry. But those that did -- split brain patients -- whoo man, you'd see wild things. You see the left hand arguing with the right about what snack to pick up, or what shirt to wear. The left hand will just... reach out, and slap the right hand choice away." He paused. "It happens because the left brain is mute. It usually communicates across the corpus callosum, but when that's severed it has to communicate in different ways." He sipped his drink. "It's deeply distressing."

Cassidy nodded.

"As McMillon disease Stage Two progresses, there's more and more gunk on the corpus callosum, to the point that it hinders communication. So we start seeing behavior like split brain patients. Benign stuff at first... clutter on one side of a desk but not the other. The left hand picking up things to answer a question and then the right-brain controlled mouth making up a reason why it's holding it. Over time... over time this gets worse. Eventually there's nothing to be done."

There was a long pause between them, where all that could be heard was the gentle sway of the crowd moving to and from their classes.

She swallowed. "What does this have to do with

me?"

"The treatment -- Duplionyl -- it doesn't work for Stage Two. Or it works, but it just doesn't work on the most destructive elements." He paused, taking a deep breath. "I never told anyone how I found the cure."

She squinted. "No. But then... aside from penicillin, how many medicines do we know the story behind?"

He waggled his finger at her again and smiled: a big, toothy, honest smile. His teeth were too far apart, a slight gap between each one. "Quite right. I think that's why it's never been questioned, not really. But now we're here and we need the cure for Stage Two... and I'm too old to get it."

She straightened. "Get it?"

He smiled. "Let's just say... there was more to finding the treatment than leaving some bread out to get mouldy. Like I said, not just a cure for McMillon... but for boredom, too."

"Why me?"

Gamgee looked at her for a long, slow minute. "You're Dr. Cassidy Cane. *The*. It honestly didn't take a lot of research."

She fidgeted again. "I'm in the middle of planning a new expedition right now. I can't just get up and--"

"You're correcting papers and thinking about maybe going to Mexico for the fourth time before something else sidetracks you, and you go do that instead. Before you chase that buzz." He said this with less levity than he'd spoken with up to this point, his voice becoming serious. "That feeling, that excitement... when you can feel your pulse throb, not just in your neck but in your earlobes. In your fingertips. That big, defining surge of excitement."

She stiffened, her back ramrod straight and her elbows cocked at ninety-degree angles.

"That feeling, I guarantee, you will not find in Mexico."

"I have to go," she said, standing up from the table. "I have papers to correct."

He frowned, then nodded and dismissed her with a wave of his hand. She turned without saying goodbye, making a bee-line away from him to the hall that led back to her office. When she was gone, he reached over and touched her plate of fries, sliding it across the table until it was in front of him.

***

Cassidy returned to her office, her face flushed and tinged with green. She made her way to her desk to resume correcting her papers, then stopped and pushed them to one side. She closed her eyes and took several long, deep breaths, then opened them.

The old photo in the new frame was directly in front of her. She tisked and picked it up, tracing first the edge of the glass, and then the familiar lines of the man's face. She pursed her lips, then fished her cell phone out of her pocket.

"Hello, Mom?" she said when there was an answer. She forced a smile: you could hear a smile over the phone, she'd been told. "Yes... yeah I am back, actually. A week or so now." She ran her fingers through her hair, gripping her scalp. "No... sorry no, I've been busy. Yeah... so hey, I was wondering..." She looked back at the photograph on the desk. "I was wondering if I could come over for a meal."

CHAPTER FOUR

"Can you pass the mash turnip?" Preston Cane asked, holding his hand out with the palm up and fingers splayed, ready to receive the bowl. Cassidy smiled. Her father's idiolect was something that had never ceased to bring warmth to her face. The way he said 'mash turnip' instead of 'mashed turnip,' 'Chicargo' instead of 'Chicago,' or any number of other small inflections that were uniquely him, always brought a fresh grin to her face.

She raised the blue swirled bowl of mashed turnip high as though it were a prince she was presenting to the Pridelands, then set it down with great weight on his waiting hand.

He laughed.

The dining room of her childhood home shrank more and more every time she returned to it, to the point that she wasn't sure if she'd be able to get out to go to the washroom without asking her sister Margo to scootch in. Even then she would have bumped her shoulder-blades along the edges of the vinyl paintings that lined either side of the room, threatening to crash them to the floor and eliciting a series of disgruntled tisks and rasps of air from her mother.

Her mother, Kayla, sat at the far end of the table, eating edamame that had been drizzled in olive oil and topped with fresh black pepper. Every time she bit into one Cassidy could hear it across the table, even above the chatter and laughter of her sisters, Margo and Rica.

Margo was twenty and had been a theatre arts student at the local community college for the last year. She'd been Margaret all her life up until she'd graduated high school, but upon coming home from that first day of college she'd been asked to set the table by her given name and had corrected them with one spinning, erect finger: "Actually, it's Margo now I think." She said it in such a way that she had expected it to be questioned and was ready to start something over it. It hadn't been. Cassidy and her parents had just shrugged, gotten the carrots ready, and asked *Margo* to set the table.

Rica was a year younger and had always been Rica, as far as she could remember. Whenever her full name, Frederica, was said over the loudspeaker at school, it always took her a moment to realize they were talking to her. It was a name that sounded foreign to her ear, despite being technically hers. Rica was the more quiet of the two. She hadn't graduated yet, but was planning on attending Plainsfield University when she did, and had politely asked Cassidy not to put herself into the process, one way or the other. Cassidy had respected that, as had their father, when she'd told him.

Her father finished scooping the mash turnip, which was now a hefty mound on the right side of his plate. He put the bowl back onto the table in front of him, then picked up the gravy boat and added a healthy dollop to the pile, turning it into a volcano just as he had when they were little. She had thought at the time that it had been just for their benefit, but it was clear now that it was not.

"Eruption on mount turnip," he said under his breath, his grayed eyebrows high and exaggerated.

Cassidy and Rica laughed, more at the memory of the joke than at the joke itself.

Across the table from him, her mother smiled wanly, then took a long sip of her wine. "How long did you say you'd been back, dear?"

Cassidy turned, as if suddenly realizing there were more people in the room than just she and her father, and pushed her hair back behind her ear. "A little over a week," she said, then took a bite from her pork roast. After a moment of eyeing the sheen on the cutlery, she forced herself to return her mother's steadfast gaze. "Sorry I didn't call to tell you."

Her mother smiled naturally and shrugged. "You're a grown woman, Cass. You don't need to tell me every time you come into the country." She paused, letting her grin slide up over her cheeks after a scant moment. "Did you bring back anything with you?"

All parties at the table turned to Cassidy at the question. Margo wiped sauce from her mouth.

Cassidy grinned. "There was this ah... yeah, there was this thing." She grinned, laying down her fork so that she could talk with both of her hands. They formed a loose sphere in front of her, as though she were trying to conjure whatever she was talking about. "This Amulet... thing." She laughed. "Until a few years ago everyone kind of assumed it was a legend, but I kept seeing this circle in different texts and glyphs and stuff. This symbol, at the end of a lot of really portentous and pretentious religious and cultural texts." She smirked. "This one guy out of Cambridge, he'd found references to it that he thought meant it was punctuation, like a really emphatic form of a Full Stop," she laughed.

"And it wasn't, I assume?" her father egged warmly, poking her elbow with his own.

"No, yeah... no. I mean I see why he thought it was. He kept seeing it as this reference to 'everything ending with this'. Like a sentence, or a paragraph. Just one of those 'you have taken this too literally' moments." She took a sip of her water. "And I was looking at it and I realized it was a thing. Like it wasn't a concept, it was a visual representation of a thing. A thing that ends everything."

Margo raised an eyebrow.

"It doesn't really," Cassidy laughed, waving off the implied criticism with some jazz hands. "But when we kept digging I found these ancient texts and references, remnants from a bunch of different cultures. Like some sort of original template for all the end of times myths we have today. And it was these Amulets, the ten of them. And so I followed the patterns and, well..." she shrugged, leaning back on her chair. "I found one."

"Nice," Rica nodded. Cassidy lifted her hand as if to say it was nothing.

Her mother hummed in agreement from the opposite end of the table. "Was it valuable?"

Cassidy cocked an eyebrow and looked sidelong at her mother. "It was thousands of years old. Possibly one of the original devices used to tell stories, ever. I had to fish the thing out of a temple that was rigged to crumble if it was removed from the place, which it did. Like something out of an old adventure serial or something," she drawled.

"Is that a yes or a no?" she asked, as though Cassidy had said what she'd said without emphasis.

"It's *priceless*, mother," she said finally, putting both her palms face up in the air in front of her, as if displaying a large tray of money.

"I think what your mother wants to know is," Preston smirked. "Is it priceless as in expensive, or priceless as in worthless?" He shoveled the last of his mash turnip into his mouth when he was done his dad-joke.

Cassidy laughed. "The department is funding me for a further three years off of it."

"Oh darling, that's fantastic," her mother smiled. She lifted her wine glass to toast her, then took a long sip.

"Yes, wonderful," her father returned, clasping his weighty hand on her shoulder and patting it heartily.

Her smirk faded, and she picked up her fork again, the gleam of it catching her eye as she looked back down. "You're right," she said, forcing a smile. "It's fantastic."

Preston clapped her once more, laughing proudly. "That's really great, Cass. Really. Can you pass the mash turnip?"

Cassidy raised an eyebrow at the repeated request, but picked up the bowl and handed it to him, this time without humour. He took it graciously and started pulling more and more orange mush from its depths. When he was done he put the bowl back where she'd gotten it from, just to his left and well within his reach.

"Thank you," he said, smiling sincerely.

"You're welcome," she returned. "You must really love Mom's mash turnip. They must be your favorite."

"They are," he smiled, his left hand picking up his fork and plucking a carrot with its spears. "I can't get enough of them. I'm sorry, has everyone else had enough?" He looked down and switched the utensil from his left to right hand, ate the carrot quickly, then resumed scooping up his mash turnip.

"I'm fine," she smiled, almost blushing. She narrowed her eyes, and when she spoke again it was with trepidation. "Would you say they're your favorite though? The best ever vegetable?"

"Hands down," he laughed, as though the question itself were laughable. "It's the brown sugar, gives it this extra zing." He picked up his dessert fork in his left hand, plunged it into a carrot again, then switched both to his right hand.

She cocked her head towards the bright orange root vegetable. "Why do you keep doing that?"

He paused, then looked down at the fork in his hand. After a moment he smiled. "Well you haven't had enough, clearly. Kayla, are there any more carrots in the kitchen for Cass to have?"

"I'm good, thanks," Cassidy said, raising her hand politely. She took a deep breath that nonetheless failed to fill her. She stood from the table. "I have to visit the restroom, if I can be excused?"

Margo scootched in to let her pass.

***

Cassidy stepped from the restroom into the crowded main hall of her childhood home, still wiping her hands on her pant legs. She heard her family downstairs, still laughing over something her father had said, their voices already seeming unreal and far away. She swallowed, then made her way down the hall, away from them.

She passed her former bedroom without looking into it, closing the ajar door as she passed. When she reached the end of the hall she turned and entered her father's study, either side of it occupied by a bookshelf piled high with texts, just like her own. Unlike hers, his office was wider and much less claustrophobic. Also unlike hers, his books were well read and never had the chance to form dust. Most were paperbacks, and they were either kept and reread often or donated to goodwill, but they never stayed in one place for very long.

His desk was cluttered, as hers had been. But rather than covering the entire desk, it was confined to the left side. The right was clean, undisturbed, and reflecting the light from the window back at her.

On the shelf next to her was a picture of she and her father on a fishing trip, many years ago. He leaned over her and she into him, pressed cheek to freckled cheek. Their hats had hooks on them that they never used, and they were getting tangled in one another. There was a man on her arm opposite her father with a square jaw and kind eyes, smiling right along with them and holding a large bass.

She looked behind her, into the hallway and then,

swallowing hard, stepped around the desk and moved her father's seat out of the way. She opened the second drawer down without looking and reached inside, pulling out an orange prescription bottle. The label across it read 'Duplionyl' in its cold, sans serif font. The dosage period was from well over a year before, but she could see five pills still rattling around in the bottom of the bottle.

When she looked, there were seven other bottles in the drawer.

She cursed, bringing her hand up to rub her furrowed brow.

CHAPTER FIVE

Herbert Gamgee's lab was a warehouse with a walkway that went all around it, spreading into smaller offices that could be occupied by other people in the field, but weren't. The space was wide and open, cold both in temperature and emotionality, the light off the stainless steel instruments giving it an unearthly clean glow. It had been used for testing deep sea equipment at one point. He'd bought it once the site was decommissioned and used it to house his work.

Echoes were a constant fact of life in the space, so although he heard Cassidy Cane enter the building long before she reached him, he'd made no effort to put down his newspaper and address her until she was within ten feet of him. When she was, he lowered one corner of his paper and looked up at her, his face sallow and without expression.

"The cure to the next stage of McMillon disease," she said breathlessly. "I'll help you find it."

He nodded, taking his feet down off of a mini-fridge that was marked with a biohazard sticker on one side. "You changed your mind fairly quickly."

"Yes well... I went home and looked up how many people suffered from it. You can't just do nothing, in the face of that many."

He eyed her for a moment, then smiled. He stood up and walked with her to a large table on an adjacent platform. It had a dozen seats around it, each one bathed in a blue hue from above that disguised the fact that they were black leather. When he reached the opposite end as her there was a keyboard waiting, the cord of which connected to a small bobble in the center of the table. He pressed four buttons and the bobble began to glow blue, and before she realized what was happening his computer screen appeared as a hologram hovering above the desk before them.

She was taken aback for a moment, then smiled.

With two more clicks, a map of Plainsfield, Massachusetts faded into view.

"Did you ever wonder how a physicist cured a biological problem?" Gamgee asked, eyeing her mischievously from between the glowing lines of the map as he zoomed in further. The University retreated to the side as the map continued to zoom into the coast.

She watched him for a tense moment, then shook her head.

"I thought not," he tisked. "No one does, really. I had a whole story planned, a whole thing. I never once got the chance to use it. I blame the media. Whenever there's a scientist character on a team, they just have them be good at science. In general. All fields." He laughed, then turned back to her. "Does that happen in your field? People expect you to know about every culture? Every historical period?"

She smiled and nodded. "Yes."

He bobbed his head. "I thought as much. Good to know it happens to everyone." When the map had zoomed in so much that it focused only on the state's rocky coast, he pushed both his hands to the right. The screen responded by shoving the entire map away. What was left was a blinking blue cursor in the middle of a star-field. He moved his hands forward and small dots appeared, corresponding to each of his fingers... then he stopped. "How to explain this."

She squinted.

He drew two glowing blue circles in the air, one with each hand. "Have you ever heard of the Mandela effect?"

She shook her head. "I've heard of Nelson Mandela, is that--?"

"Yes. Well no, but: yes." He smiled, waggling his finger at her again. "Nelson Mandela was a prominent political figure up until his death in the mid 2010s... and yet there are some who vividly remember reports of him dying in the 80s. Hundreds of people, in fact. Tens of hundreds." He smiled, perfecting the edges on the circles he'd drawn. "And there are yet more oddities. The spelling of a popular children's author's name. Different versions of movies that have come out. Deaths that didn't happen, others that did. Slight variations on reality." He paused. "It led some to postulate that they'd come from another world."

Cassidy laughed, bringing her hand to her face to quash it.

Gamgee looked back at her from between the two circles, without humor.

"You can't be serious," she said, letting her hand fall to her side.

With one quick motion he pushed the two circles together, making a Venn diagram of them. At the points where the two diagrams intersected, they glowed red. "Imagine two worlds, two *dimensions* stacked on top of one another, nearly identical save for a few small changes. And over time, those changes grow and diverge."

"The Butterfly Effect."

"*Exactly*. But in this, both can coexist. Both matter. But there still remain... links between them." At the world 'links' he motioned to the red dots, and they began to blink a soft, ephemeral hue. "Spots in reality indistinguishable to the naked eye, but if one should stumble through one, they would find themselves in another world. Likely without even realizing it."

Cassidy squinted. "Without realizing it?"

Gamgee nodded. "Unless the traveler looked for the differences, they would have no clue. None. They might even come back, if they hit the same spot in just the same way, by chance. Imagine it: people able to walk in and out of reality with the ease of air flowing in and out of an open window." He smiled broadly, pushing his cheeks back and showing all his teeth. His glasses glowed blue in the light from the projection. "Now imagine if you knew where that doorway was."

He swiped both hands to the left, minimizing the diagram of the two circles and returning to the map of the Massachusetts shoreline. Now, in one small spot along the bluffs, was a red oval dot blinking with a soft, ephemeral hue.

"That's where I discovered the cure," he said, his voice now almost a whisper.

Cassidy stared at the blinking red oval, and for the first time in what felt like years, she felt the heat of her pulse rise into her cheeks.

CHAPTER SIX

"There may be some disorientation when you step through," Gamgee said as he navigated his way past a large, smooth boulder.

Cassidy stopped in her tracks just a little down the slope from him, turning to him with narrowed eyes that pushed her freckles up towards the crest of her nose. "You said people managed to walk through this and not even realize it." She paused. "You said that people could step through this thing into another world and not even realize what they'd done -- that they'd just keep living their lives and think the changes were lapses on their part."

"And that's true. For most."

They were five miles from the outer edge of Plainsfield, in an area populated by dense evergreen trees and brush that continued to the very edge of the continent before suddenly dropping off into large, tanned boulders. They came together haphazardly and yet with great purpose, laid there like toys a toddler was done playing with and yet firmly in place after an age of time and pressure. They formed caves that dotted the shoreline, lined with kelp and small shellfish. The tide was out, but it was clear that at another day or time the caves might have been hip deep with crashing waves.

She continued to squint up at him, the late evening sun behind him making him into a dark silhouette. Without thinking about what she was doing, her hand drifted to the pouch on her hip. She unclasped its button and let it hang open like that, ready. "I'm warning you, if this is a con, you will live to regret it."

"There's no con," he said. His Adam's apple bobbed when he said it, descending to the furthest pit of his throat before rebounding to the middle. It stayed there, quivering in the cool air coming off the water.

She narrowed her eyes more, then turned and continued down the embankment, along the path he'd marked. She kept her pouch unbuttoned. "Watch your step."

They came off the steep boulders onto the relative flatness of the shore, a brief edge of ten feet that bordered the last edge of her world before disappearing into the oblivion of the sea. The waves were such a deep blue they were nearly black, like ink pushing its way towards the unspent parchment of the forest. They crashed and rolled, leaving creamy foam in the crevices and cracks of the stone.

She turned back towards Gamgee as he finished his descent. His back no longer against the sky, he came out from the silhouette he'd been in and seemed the kind, portly man again: less sinister by circumstance. Behind him the trees were thick and black with the shadows of evening, but she scanned their expanse with a weather eye she'd trained over many, many years of action.

Unexpectedly, they found a bear walking along the edge of a steep ridge of the cliff, its fur barely visible between the trees but clearly there all the same. It ate berries the way only a bear could, entire branches of the bush finding their way into its mouth and then being strained through clenched, sharpened teeth when it pulled back. It ignored them, far enough away that neither party was a danger to the other. It was used to humans. Even this far into the wild, there was no wilderness.

She sighed, then turned her attention to the caves and parts of the rock face they'd scaled down. They were slices in the cliffside, holes that came to sharp points at the top and bottom, widening into foot-long gaps at their middles. They gaped like maws, small breaks in reality where light had no place. There were several of them in varying shapes and sizes, some appearing more inhabitable by an adult human form than others.

"Which one were you talking about?" Cassidy asked, looking from one to another with a tense, analyzing gaze. Her eye found a mark along the right side of one, a set of two identically-curved squiggly lines that were nested into one another, spooning. She tilted her head.

Gamgee moved to stand alongside her, his head roughly adjacent to her squared shoulders, and surveyed the same cracks in the wall that she did, as though he'd not been the one whose instructions led them here. He waited, not making a sound or gesture, letting her continue to scan the ice-flow remnants.

"It's not that one," she said with decisiveness, gesturing towards the cave with the squiggles carved next to it. "You're trying to keep it hidden. So..." she trailed, letting her eyes fall over it again. The lines were slanted right and she followed their path to a gap in the rocks that was elevated slightly above the rest, wide at its bottom and curving dramatically at its peak. With imagination, it looked like a wizard's hat. "It's that one," she said finally and with certainty.

"Very good," he smiled, nodding. He started towards the break in the rocks she'd motioned towards. "Symbology is something that must come in handy for someone in your line of work."

"It has its moments."

"It will have many more, I think," he smiled.

Again, she squinted at him.

They reached the edge of the cave in near unison. Now that they were closer the black depths looked less black, with some light filtering in from the setting sun. She took out her phone and activated its flashlight with several deft, familiar motions of her thumb, illuminating the cave in iridescence. It was deep and damp, the sides slick with condensation and castoff from the sea. It was too narrow for Gamgee to fit into by half, and barely wide enough to squeeze even her hips through.

"Homey," she said under her breath, even as her light caught something shimmering and reflective along the cave's curved interior peak. Her eyebrows came together as she moved the light to see it better, revealing a small shaft of metal, no wider than a tube of lipstick. Her nose crumpled as she turned her light to fault points in the rock on the left and right sides of the cavern, and then finally at the lowest edge as well. She turned back to Gamgee. "Nice try, but--"

"They're explosive, be wary of them," he admitted, gesturing to the metal items.

She stopped mid sentence.

"It's dangerous, I know. But as I said, these doors work both ways. Never too careful." He looked down the length of the cave as he spoke, as if expecting something to be waiting for him in the dark of it.

She squinted at him, then turned her gaze to the cavern. "It's empty."

"If it were glowing blue, everyone would find it." He almost laughed. "Look again."

She scanned the interior of the cave again, trying hard to not focus on the metal shafts that kept attracting her attention, as dangerous and obvious as they were. The shimmer of the walls reflected back at her and the very back of the cave could not be viewed, but other than that there was... "Nothing," she said. "There's nothing."

Gamgee tisked. "You disappoint me," he smiled, without disappointment. He took her phone from her gently, then aimed it at the rock floor. A small stream of water trickled from it, down past their feet and out towards the sea.

She watched it go, finding its way down the stone shore and generating the same cream-colored froth as the sea as it tumbled. "It's a stream. All running water heads towards sea-level... if I'm meant to be impressed by something, I'm not."

"Look at where it comes from."

Cassidy sighed, then took her phone back and aimed it towards the cave's wall, looking for the split in the stone the water was produced from... and found none. She frowned, shining the light down at the stream and then following it back to a large piece of stone a foot into the cave, where the water appeared from the stone's mid-point, as if from nowhere.

She tilted her head curiously, then smiled. "I've lived on this coast my entire life. A stream can seem to come from nowhere, but there's always a source of--"

"Taste it then," he said, his voice devoid of all humour for the first time since they'd exited his vehicle.

She paused, then leaned down and cupped her hand under one of the water's crests. It took a moment to fill to her knuckle, then she brought her hand to her lips and sucked back. She spit immediately, cursing.

Gamgee laughed.

"Salt!" she said, still sputtering. "Salt water."

"Where it should be fresh," Gamgee said, bending to squat and watch the water that flowed, as if from nowhere, from the rock in the cave. "The tide is different there. Low here when it's high there, and vice versa. The water, it just laps at the edges of the portal when it's at high tide... a little bit of our world into theirs, a little of theirs into ours, with every push and pull of the tide."

Her eyes widened, and without doing it consciously, she backed up from the cave a single step. She reached for her thermos, took a long glug from it, swished it around her mouth, then spit it onto the rocks below to get rid of the last of the saline taste. She repeated this twice more until the taste was gone. "This is impossible," she said finally.

"I recall saying the same thing when I first found it," he nodded. He was still watching the salt water from another world as it trickled down over the rocks, past his feet and into the sea. When his voice returned it was wistful and faraway. "Years looking for a thing, trying to prove it exists, only to find it and your first thought be to deny it." He smiled wryly to himself, pressed his hands to his knees, and pushed himself up. "We're odd, aren't we? Humans?"

She nodded, glaring not at Gamgee for the first time but past him, into the dark of the cave. She said nothing. She straightened, arched her back, then stepped forward until she was at the mouth of the cave again. She shone her light in one last time, turned it off, then turned and handed it to him. "I don't suppose there's cell service there."

He smiled. "None that we'd pick up, anyway."

She nodded, gently pushing her head and shoulder into the cavern.

"As I said, you may feel disoriented," Gamgee reiterated, tucking her phone into his pocket. "I find once you think you're through you feel the need to breathe in, but it's actually better to exhale. But don't hold your breath stepping through, you want to--"

Gamgee's voice cut short in mid syllable, and a sharp snap of pain erupted from the back of Cassidy's head. The mouth of the cave became blurred suddenly.

Cassidy lost consciousness with his words ringing in her ears.

CHAPTER SEVEN

Cassidy woke up with salt water splashing on her face. It was light at first, but was then accompanied by a roar and splashed down on her with force. She jolted upwards, coughing, her hair clinging to her neck and cheeks in fiery red clumps. She gasped, then cursed.

Above her, she could see metal shafts embedded in the rock face, sputtering blue sparks and illuminating the cave. She cursed again, rising to her feet and bolting through the mouth of the cave. She found herself shin deep in salt water, the tide trying to pull her back towards the sea. She turned and fought it, making her way back up onto dry slate before catching her breath.

She cursed again, so loud and with such vulgarity that she was almost glad no one was around to have heard it. After a moment to catch herself, she felt for her keys in her pouch and located them. She sighed with relief. "He best not have hotwired my car," she fumed, even as she began to pull herself up over the ridge. "Never should have trusted that little madman."

She pulled herself up onto the ledge by the tufts of grass that grew there, the midday light warm on her neck as she ascended. Even when she reached the top, there was no one in sight. She sighed, then started to make her way west towards the start of the treeline.

***

Her car, just as she'd worried, had been missing.

She had been walking the Massachusetts back highway for almost three hours, feeling the oppressive heat of the sun on her neck and shoulders the entire time. She hadn't packed her sunscreen, she'd realized after the first hour. She hadn't packed for travel, a rookie mistake she chided herself for, and not Gamgee. She had her water, but it was running low.

Sweat billowed down over her freckled cheeks. She'd considered retreating into the shade of the forest on several occasions, but the memory of the black bear she'd seen on the bluffs reminded her every time that she'd left unprepared for danger.

"Stupid," she said to herself, though her tongue was a dry slug in the center of her mouth. "Of all the stupid things to believe. He probably knew about your father... wasn't he in the town paper last year, for the fundraiser? And every time there's a Birthday Charity on social media, you give to McMillon disease. Every time. Doesn't take a genius."

She huffed. "You are a stupid, stupid person sometimes, Cassidy Cane."

Behind her, far in the distance, she heard the soft drone of an engine.

At first her brow furrowed, thinking it was Gamgee returning in her car to end his great prank. Then her brow softened: it could be help. It could, in fact, be anything. She turned and raised her arms high into the air as she did, ready to flag down the (hopefully) Good Samaritan.

There was nothing on the road.

But still, the sound grew.

She furrowed her brow again, slowly lowering her hands as she stared out upon the hilly, dry landscape she'd just hiked over. There was no movement save for the dust and grass in the breeze. She waited to see if the car was hidden in one of the dips and valleys she'd come over, but even after waiting longer than should have been needed, there was nothing. And yet still, the engine whir increased.

Her hair began to flutter, even despite being weighed down with perspiration, and dust began to swirl in clouds around her as the sound became louder. She looked up and saw it at last: the long, rectangular body of a car, travelling past her and over the embankment at high speed. When it flew overhead the gust was such that it almost pushed her down, and from within she heard screams and yelps of praise.

Red streaks followed in its wake, caught in the vapor trails left by the vehicle's passing and slowly ebbing out of sight.

She covered her mouth to block the sand, trying to catch her breath as she watched it disappear over the peak of the hill. "What in the world?" she gasped, bolting forward with new energy. She climbed and climbed despite her arches aching, finally mounting the summit of the blind hill.

There was a city in the valley, where there had never

been any such city before. In all her travels, she'd never seen a city anything like it. Blue and green skyscrapers lifted into the sky, so high that they pierced the clouds, coming to sharp points. Their windows shimmered against the sun, each one shining natural light back at her. The tallest building was dark blue with a symbol at its apex, a red man with a white cross on its belly.

Cassidy's eyes went wider still as she saw the flying cars -- not just the one she'd seen, but *dozens* -- making their way in and out of the city. There were no suburbs, just skyscrapers that travelled for miles and miles, and yet she saw no hint of smog or pollution. It looked like it had grown out of the landscape, like deep forest trees that had been alive longer than man and rose up to heights that boggled the mind. It shimmered and glowed, casting off so much heat that it had a mirage effect on the air around it.

She found the strength to swallow, then continued down the highway towards it.

CHAPTER EIGHT

As large as the skyscrapers had seemed in the distance, they were much, much more so when standing among them. Cassidy had spent a month in Dubai last year on an expedition, and had stood at the very foot of the Burj Khalifa and stared straight up its mass. It might have been merely situational, but she thought it now paled in comparison even to the average of these towers.

She bumped shoulders with people who didn't obey the laws of traffic. There didn't seem to be laws of traffic here: no right lane forward, left lane back. Somewhere in the back of her mind, she wondered if that was a consequence of perfecting flying cars: rules of the road ceased to be the law of the land. She tried to adjust but found it impossible, and so tried to avoid getting within arm's reach of anyone.

Despite the height and cluster of the buildings, somehow she still felt the heat of sunlight. She squinted up at the buildings, and saw that their edges were lined with what she would have called retroreflectors, but weren't, that shone the sun's rays down to street level. "Clever," she said to herself.

Behind her, several heads cocked suddenly at the sound of her voice and watched her as she continued down the street.

There were no street signs, but the buildings were alternating shades of blue and green, and never quite the same shade twice. The greens were getting lighter the more blocks she walked, she noticed, and the blues lighter. She remembered the presentation Gamgee had given about the divergent timelines and wondered just how far back the timelines would have had to have diverged to make it so that street signs had never been thought of, and instead color coordination used. *A hundred and seventy years at least,* she thought, struggling to remember her history. *Unless they had them once and have since outgrown them?* That detail change, although small and benign, seemed incomprehensible. She tried to remind herself that she'd thought the same about foreign cultures on her own world on some of her early expeditions, and that this alternate Earth was under no burden to be more familiar than her own.

I wonder if they even call it Earth?

She passed by a blue region into one of aquatic green, where there were canopies hanging from the edges of the tower, each with its one symbol on it. She did not recognize them, but each had the plump silhouette of a man with a different symbol somewhere on his body. Many were on his stomach, at least the majority, she estimated.

Steam wafted into the air from under the canopies, sending smells foreign and yet familiar churning towards her nostrils: food. Suddenly she remembered how hungry she was from her journey and started to look from side to side. She knew where she was suddenly, the cultural differences melting away as the rose-colored glasses of her point of view finally faded: she was in a market.

There was a grill that let out hot hisses of steam as she walked by, a motor rotating what she would have called beef kabobs along its edge. The fruit on it was charred strawberry and pierced fresh lime, a strange combination she'd never heard of and yet, in many ways, could not wait to try. The man serving it had a long mustache, of the sort she associated with travelling salesmen from the wild west. His apron was made of denim and he held onto the straps proudly as he surveyed for customers, only furthering the association. She stifled a rude laugh, not wanting to offend in this strange place, and quickly stepped away from the booth.

There were five women wearing what looked to be shaylas, but the edge framing their faces was bright gold and the main fabric was a bold, dark red. They stood out against the greens and blues of the architecture. They carried pouches of dried fruit in their hands that they'd bought from the vendor behind them, and were trying to get the young children that ran around their legs to ingest some. One, the one closest to Cassidy, was holding dried peaches out in front of herself and making a series of cooing noises, as though trying to coax an animal to do what she wanted. Cassidy thought at first glance that they had been family, but realized now that there was not a common trait between them: not hair colour, eye colour, body type, face shape... not even tone of flesh. They spoke a language she couldn't recognize -- and she recognized many -- that to her ears was made of too many vowels and hard

Rs. She had trouble distinguishing where one word ended and the next began.

The woman selling the dried fruit smiled at her with her arms wide, and Cassidy smiled back. There were many vats of dried goods -- most of which Cassidy recognized at a glance -- each with its own plastic shovel wedged into it, and she recognized it as a kind of portable bulk depot.

The next booth had a man and a woman behind it. Each wore solid colors -- one green and one blue -- and stood with their hands behind their backs like military personnel awaiting orders. Their faces were expressionless, yet menacing, and their eyes seemed to watch Cassidy as she passed. They were armed. They were the first weapons she'd seen since entering the city limits.

The table in front of them was lined with pill bottles, almost exactly like the ones she'd found in her father's drawer, right down to the child-proof cap. The only difference that she could see was that instead of orange, this world's bottles came in sharp greens.

The pills inside even looked the same. There was writing on the bottle in a language she couldn't understand, but there was also a symbol like the one she'd seen on the building from the horizon: the outline of a plump male figure in red with a white cross on his stomach.

She lingered by the table for a moment, then looked to the attendants -- who were looking back at her -- and then to their weapons. They continued to stare at her.

In front of the pills were pamphlets, though hexagonal and oddly shaped, with the same white-crossed man symbol on it. She took one and held it up to them, nodding politely. They did the same, a regimented motion, not a social one.

She moved on quickly.

The next three stations sold prepackaged tubes of fried meat, and the proprietors talked among themselves as if they knew each other quite well. She couldn't follow the conversation they were having, although their language seemed different from the one she'd heard the women using. There were still too many vowels, but the hard R sounds had been replaced by elongated Ks. Even their laughs sounded like Ks, and they laughed often. Even without context, Cassidy could recognize people engaging in locker-room talk, by the body language and laughter, if nothing else.

One of the men was emptying pills from a green bottle into his hand, even while laughing with his friends. He took out an imprecise amount and popped them into his mouth mid sentence, and the other two showed no signs that this was odd behavior.

Cassidy moved on the the next vendor, a tall woman with purple hair and a broad smile selling hot sandwiches. They were pork and Cassidy could smell what must have been horseradish swirling up from them, and salivated. She made eye contact with the vendor and smiled, only noticing at the last moment the top of a green pill bottle sticking up out of her breast pocket.

Cassidy's smile fell. She turned back to the street she'd come down, now looking for something specific.

There's no way... she thought, even as she scanned the crowd. Several shoppers had pill bottles in their hands, the green plastic color showing through their fingers. Others had bulges in their pants pockets, the right size and shape to be them. Still more were stopped at the pill vendor, purchasing them in varying stages of a transaction.

The man with the large mustache and denim apron had a bottle peeking out his front pocket.

As she watched, the woman in the dark red shayla that had been coaxing a child forward with a dried peach was now wedging a small pill into the flesh of the peach, feeding it to the child, and patting him on the head.

Cassidy stammered, unable to speak, and almost tripped as she turned back to the sandwich cart. She forced a smile at the vendor, who smiled back. She sighed. Each of the sandwiches rested on thick squares of parchment paper that one was clearly meant to wrap around it to hold. She plunked her finger down on the largest of them and slid it forward, the smell from it somehow intensifying as she did.

She reached into her pouch and began to withdraw her compass. "Look, I'm sorry I can't pay at this exact moment--"

Behind her an old woman's head spun towards the source of her voice, and her formerly relaxed gaze devolved into a hateful scowl. She let out several hard R words with very few vowels in them, each word having a distinctive bite and single-syllable cadence to them. A man near her -- her son, perhaps -- tried to coax her away but looked back with the same darkened expression.

The purple-haired woman behind the booth, whose smile had been so sweet before, had changed her expression to one with a slackened jaw and wide eyes. Her cheeks had even lost some of their color. She opened her mouth to speak, and from her lips came a series of soft vowels that Cassidy could not tell from each other, strung together with hard R sounds.

"You don't speak English," Cassidy sighed, nodding. "Of course you don't. Why would you? That's... that's silly of me, really."

The purple-haired woman leaned in, her teeth bared and hands outstretched. It was the motion an adult did when trying to stop a child from touching something hot.

Cassidy squinted, then slowly turned her head. She no longer had to force a bubble of personal space around herself in the crowd: the crowd was providing it all on their own. She swallowed, then lowered her voice and extended her hand with the compass in it. "Listen I'm... I'm hungry, okay? I need food. This is gold. I hope... I hope that's worth something here. If you could just--" She reached out for the woman's hand to place it in. The woman pulled away.

Cassidy sighed, then lay the compass down on the table roughly and slid it forward. "Thank you," she drawled under her breath, taking the sandwich off the table.

Several other vendors called after her as she left, a volley of hard R and long K sounds following her until she turned the corner and escaped the market square. The purple-haired girl did not call after her: she picked up the compass with the same amount of awe and reverence as Cassidy had had when she'd found her first artifact.

CHAPTER NINE

Cassidy sat on a small concrete ledge near the mouth of an alley, five streets removed from where she'd parted with her compass. The blue buildings were darker here, and the reflective strips on the side of each was less and less effective and bringing the sunlight down to street level as a result. She ate the last of her pork sandwich, the wax paper crinkling and popping as she brought it to her face.

The pork had been infused with the horseradish somehow. It had been pickled with it in layers, and the flavor combination -- though surprising -- was strangely magnificent. The best of it by far had been the bread. She didn't think she'd ever tasted bread so soft and so warm, and it had remained so even now, right to its last bite. It fell apart in her mouth like butter.

She chewed the last of it absently, staring out past the frame of the alley into the street beyond. She was well past the market now, and into an area she could only have assumed was a business district. Men and women walked back and forth on the street wearing suits that were similar enough to the ones she remembered, except that they were always in exacting shades of green and blue. There were several different shades, like the buildings, but only so many. They walked and talked on cell phones and smiled and cursed and laughed, all in that same too-many-vowels language she'd heard back in the crowded market. As much as she tried, she still couldn't ascertain where one word ended and the next began without an obvious, emphatic tell.

It was like watching people pantomime western behavior. Like AIs stepping from one fixed point on a map to the other, each time yammering gibberish that she tried not to think of as such.

A green suited man with an extreme widow's peak of black hair stopped at the corner. He took an equally green bottle of pills out of his pocket and poured them into the cup of his hand. He separated two, dry swallowed them, then pushed the rest back into the bottle. He straightened his shirt, stood up straight, and stepped back into the chaotic pace of traffic as though it were nothing.

Across the street there was a woman in a red gown that stood out from the rest, walking slowly among the crowd. She carried a small pail of change with her and a sign -- which was written in an alphabet that Cassidy was also completely unfamiliar with -- affixed to it. She didn't appear to be derelict or in need. *Collecting donations for a religion, maybe*, Cassidy thought, her eyes following the woman as she passed. She spoke little and had a sweet smile, the ways nuns on her world often had.

How far back must this world's divergence point be that we aren't on a Latin-inspired alphabet? she wondered, as the sign and its holder faded from view. *At least 400, but prob-*

ably more. Probably far, far more now that I think on it. That is, assuming I'm not on a part of this globe where my alphabet just isn't in use.

Across the street, a sallow woman with long dark hair shook as though she were having a panic attack. Her hands were curled up beside her in a way that transcended spoken language -- it was body language that one would have to go back past the beginnings of human history to root out. She was shivering and shaking, although she didn't otherwise appear cold. She fumbled with her purse, rummaging about in it before finally emerging with a dark green bottle of pills. She popped open the top with great effort, looked inside with one eye closed, then downed the remainder of the bottle in one smooth motion. Her shakes lessened, and as Cassidy watched, she put the bottle into what on her world would have been a small biological waste bin, but which she suspected was recycling for those perfectly uniform glass bottles. After a moment, the shaking girl had fully straightened, righted her blouse, and started walking out of sight.

Cassidy squinted. Near the edge of the street, a mother pulled on the arm of a fussy toddler. Her cheeks were flush and frustrated. After a few feet of trying to drag the obstinate child, she stopped and withdrew a green bottle of pills. The boy stopped immediately. He waited while the mother produced a single pill from the bottle and laid it on his waiting tongue with a smile. The child beamed, suddenly well behaved.

"It's addictive," she said under her breath, as she watched the child and mother leave her field of view.

A man on a cell phone stuttered in his stride when she

spoke, turning just briefly in her direction with a scowl before continuing on.

Cassidy wiped her mouth of any remains of her sandwich with her sleeve. She licked her lips -- still spicy from the horseradish -- as she bent back and shoved her hand deep into her pants pocket. She withdrew the hexagonal pamphlet she'd taken from the medical vendor and unfolded it into seven adjacent sheets. Each had writing on it, that same strange cursive font that had been on the woman's donation sign, but each page also had accompanying *pictures*.

Every society that's advanced to this point has learned pictograms, she nodded to herself. Symbology predates language.

The pictures were alternatively of a man and woman wearing light, inoffensive blues and greens. They looked like mannequin people or the figures that enacted safety procedures in air travel safety videos. In the first, the man was sitting at his desk. His hand was against his forehead, which was furrowed. Lightning bolt shaped lines exclaimed from the top of his scalp.

The second picture was a woman with her hands and fingers splayed out before her as she stepped down a busy street. There were squiggly-tornado swirls around her head, and her eyes had been drawn without irises.

Back to the man, who was attempting to eat but had a sullen look on his face. For emphasis, a tongue floated above his head and had a blue X through it.

The woman sat at a desk as coworkers yelled behind her. Her expression was calm and serene, while theirs had the squiggly-tornado swirls and lightning bolts of anger and cursing.

The fifth image was the man, sitting behind his desk again. The left side of the desk was cluttered while the right was clean. The left hand was in the air, and the man had turned to look at it with some confusion.

Her mind couldn't help but go back to her father, his left hand picking up things he was completely unaware of.

The sixth image was of both the woman and man taking doses from a green pill bottle. The final was of both smiling directly at the reader, their faces beaming like cartoon suns. There was a symbol in the bottom right of that image, the same red human with the white cross on their stomach.

She looked back over it from the start, her mind playing her own audio in a cheesy infomercial-style voice: *Do you get headaches? Have trouble seeing, tasting, or hearing properly? Do you experience split brain symptoms or other neurological problems? Then Duplionyl is right for you! May cause addiction and aggression, do not consult a physician.* She sighed, then closed the pamphlet again and slid it back into her pants pocket.

She rose up off the concrete step and straightened herself and her shoulders. The people still walked by -- and she'd still seen no colors other than the greens, blues, and reds -- talking on their cell phones and stuttering through their vowels, with hard Ks and hard Rs punctuating every third syllable. She stepped out into the street between two men looking at their phones for directions and weaved throughout the flow of traffic, making her way across the street when it seemed as though everyone else was going up and down. There were no cars, just people. Hordes and hordes of people, so many that she wondered where the city fit them all.

Cassidy reached the other side of the street and stepped onto the sidewalk, turning right to follow the flow of traffic for several meters, trying not to bump or crush anyone. When she reached the edge of where the shaking woman had been, she turned right suddenly, her right arm splaying left. The hand motion was so quick and exaggerated that it drew the eye, making everyone in a five foot radius pause to avoid striking her, grumbling.

She nodded in retreat, pushing back into the alley opposite the one she'd been in and stepping out of the flow of traffic. From beneath her jacket, she produced the recycling bin for the pill bottles. Just as she'd thought, it was filled with the green bottles. No one had noticed her swiping it with that quick, left motion, the right one had been so dramatic.

Once again she thought of her father, and the illustration of the man whose left arm disobeyed.

She shuddered, pushing the thought from her mind as she tipped the receptacle over and dumped it out into the alley. Two dozen translucent green bottles clattered onto the pavement. She started to pick them up one by one and shake them, tossing them back over her shoulder as she did so.

"Come on, come on," she said through gritted teeth as the pile of bottles became less and less.

A hard R sound followed by a long string of vowels came from the mouth of the alley, and Cassidy's head jerked up suddenly, her hand out in front of her defensively.

The woman with the kind smile and the red robe

stood in the mouth of the alley, staring down at her with kind, squinting eyes. She'd placed her donation jar and sign down and had both her hands clasped before her. Her tongue rolled out another long series of hard Rs and vowels, and though Cassidy couldn't understand them, the tone and intention was kind. She sounded like a nun imparting wisdom or giving aid.

Cassidy looked down at the barrage of empty bottles around her and sighed.

The woman in red nodded knowingly, then reached into her pocket and pulled out a half-filled green bottle. It had the symbol on it, the little man with the white cross on his stomach. The Red Nun held it out with long, thin hands that were pockmarked, placed it into Cassidy's palm, and then closed Cassidy's fingers tight around it.

Cassidy sighed, then nodded appreciatively. She almost teared up, not from her own need, but for what she gleaned the sacrifice must have meant to the Red Nun. She stood up as the Nun turned to walk away, and placed the bottle deep into her jacket pocket and zipped it closed.

She exited the alley just as the Nun did, heading left as the Nun headed right, then stopped and touched the woman's arm. The Red Nun turned, smiling softly, her ears perked.

"I know you can't understand this," Cassidy said, "but thank you."

At once the Nun's eyes filled with shock and then, as Cassidy stepped away: rage. Redness rose to her cheeks and she stepped forward, letting out a bellow of loud, harsh vowels. Cassidy stumbled back as the crowd around her turned their heads, and then bolted into the crowd.

CHAPTER TEN

This is now becoming a problem, Cassidy thought to herself. The pills weighed down her jacket pocket just as she could feel the pamphlet bunching in her pants. Both had the same symbol on it, that plump red stick-figure man with the intersecting white lines on his belly: like crossed bandages or an addition sign. Despite it looking like those things, she'd known from the second she'd seen it that it looked most like the Red Cross, just inverted. *Symbology goes back further than language, she reminded herself again.*

She ran down the street, making a hard right and then a left at the end of the following block. She didn't think she was being followed but wanted to be sure. She wasn't just running from something though, she was running towards something. The greens of the building windows got lighter and lighter, and the blues got darker and darker, as she made her way into the heart of the city that she'd seen from the highway.

She turned the corner one last time and at once it was there, the amazingly tall blue behemoth skyscraper that she'd first laid eyes on while she'd still been crawling towards the city: the tallest building she'd seen in this world or any other, with the stories-high symbol of a plump red man with a white cross on his stomach emblazoned proudly across the top twenty floors.

She looked up at it. She'd seen many things in her life, but somehow this building was still one of the wonders. It was so tall that even from its base, its peak was unfathomable, rising past the focal point of her vision. The towers around it were tall too, but they paled in comparison.

She palmed the bulge in her bomber jacket where the pills were, making sure they were still there in a moment of paranoia. "Got the goods," she whispered to herself. "Now we need the formula."

She clicked her tongue against the roof of her mouth, then peeled off the bomber jacket and tucked it into a square that she lopped over one arm. She withdrew an elastic from her pocket and drew her uncooperative tangle of hair up into a bun. She crossed the road and looked into the reflective side of the building, producing a wide, toothy, happy smile and seeing a version of herself that she hadn't seen in nearly a decade, and didn't miss. She called this person 'Résumé Cassidy.' She tucked her shirt in.

Cassidy took another deep breath, then stepped inside the building.

Behind her, a woman in a blue skirt pointed towards her, and a police officer with a red man emblazoned on his hat followed the line of her gesture.

***

At the far end of the long, blue main floor hallway was a desk that looked like every security desk she had ever seen. It was broad and thick and high to accommodate the tech that went behind the lip of it: monitors and keyboards and radio equipment. It was almost reassuring: not everything was different here. This, at least, Cassidy could take for granted.

The hallway was nearly empty. One lone woman sat on their cell phone next to a fern, scrolling through text absently. She looked like someone waiting for a ride. The only other person was the guard, a stout fellow who was on the phone when she approached, with his eyes on the security camera. She planted one foot directly in front of the other with each step as she approached, doing so quicker than she would have preferred, to make sure her boots were out of his eye-line before he looked up at her.

When she reached the desk she held onto its lip with both her palms, strumming them as though she were playing a piano. She smiled that broad, fake ear-to-ear smile that she'd plastered on outside, her head tilted just to one side and several wisps of hair that had escaped the elastic falling to her face.

The guard looked up, at first only glancing and then looking back in a double take that she took to be encouraging. He said something low and final into his phone then turned to her, his own wide grin on his face, his hands clasped before him. He opened his mouth and let out a short series of vowels, enunciated by a hard K sound, gesturing to her calmly.

Cassidy smiled back. She waited a moment longer than a response to a greeting, rolled her pupils towards the uppermost edge of her sockets, as though she were thinking of something, then spoke slowly, as if considering each syllable: "AeiRy EouiR Riuao Oa-RiR."

The guard paused, raising an eyebrow into the air. He frowned, shifted uncomfortably in his chair, then steadied himself and gestured politely again. The words he spoke were slower and similar to the ones he'd spoken before, but with more emphasis. At the end he pointed to a directory that was placed to his left, each section of which was written in the swirling cursive font she assumed he was speaking in.

She leaned forward again, keeping her smile broad. "AeiRy EouiR Riuao Oa-RiR." She then reached into her pocket and pulled out the octagonal pamphlet. She turned to the last page and held it out to him, pointing to the fine print at the bottom -- which she could not read.

Out of the corner of her eye, she saw the woman who had been waiting on her phone glance over at them, roll her eyes, then get up to leave the room. It was a look she'd seen often, both at home and abroad. *Nobody has patience for people who don't speak the language*, she thought dismally.

The guard looked at the fine print, then back at Cassidy, then back at the fine print again. She'd understood from the context it was placed in -- assuming that corporate culture was the same in this world as in hers -- that it was either a call to ask questions or a call to apply for a position within the company. She hoped it was the latter, but either would do.

He looked up at her from the pamphlet and sighed, his smile gone. He spoke to her again with a voice that was now short and curt, and was only vowels. She was taking note that the more vowels that were in a phase, the less welcoming it tended to sound in this language. She stared at him blankly for a moment, not having to pretend that she didn't understand him but having to pretend that she was trying to decipher it, then nodded enthusiastically.

An instant after she'd done it, she hoped that nodding meant the same thing in this culture as it did in her own. Her moment of hesitation was unnecessary: he nodded back, then picked up his phone and turned away from her, pressing a blue button on the base. He spoke into the receiver cordially -- with lots of K sounds and less vowels than than when he'd snapped at her -- then nodded and hung up. He gestured towards the hall behind his left and smiled, saying another long string of polite K sounds.

She smiled and nodded politely. "EouiR Riuao."

He smiled and nodded back, but shook his head with dismay as she walked past his desk.

The hall he'd pointed her down was short. She turned at the first right and found herself at a wall of elevators. Two had no panels, only key locks, while the third and farthest from her had a single green button and an arrow pointing up. She walked to it, pressed it, and yanked the elastic out of her hair, sliding it around her wrist and letting her nest of red hair fall free.

***

Elevator music was the same no matter the dimension, she thought, unsure if this was a positive or a negative thing. In any event, pleasant, inoffensive tones played over the elevator's speakers to a tune she thought she might have recognized, but didn't fully. It was not unlike the experience of hearing a remixed cover of a song you'd only heard twice twenty years prior: familiar, but uncannily so.

To the right of the elevator door was a long panel of buttons, taking up the entire length of the frame. They were in three columns, and she was mathematically aware that there was no way even that amount of buttons could represent the entire building she'd seen from the front. She imagined the very top floors were accessible only from the locked elevators. When she'd gotten in she'd pressed the highest button she was able to and started her long ascent up.

She didn't know how long she'd been in the shaft, only that the auto-tuned songs had started and stopped three times. Her ears had popped twice since the climb had started, and the pressure was building to threaten to do so again. She had heard the elevator's motors switch gears four times.

I'm half a kilometer up, she thought to herself, doing her own mental calculations. *Half a kilometer up with no idea how to read the words or the numbers around me, and no idea how to speak the language. But I'm supposed to come out of this with a formula to cure a dangerous disease. She licked her lips, which were suddenly dry. All said, I've been in tighter spots.*

The elevator made a dull tone and she felt the motors slow. She prepared herself, planting one foot in front of the other and turned to provide the doors with the slimmest target possible, her fists not raised but also ready, hanging in the null space between her waist and shoulders.

The doors opened, revealing a large blue room with dull, dark shadows. She could see the outlines and silhouettes of furniture -- and possibly people, though she thought not -- against the blue tinted windows that surrounded her field of view.

She squinted, then stepped in. The lights came on when her boot touched the floor, revealing a penthouse lounge that had been used recently, but not currently. There were couches around a large television set, each with a mini fridge next to its arm. There were game tables -- one that looked like pool and another that looked like air hockey, but both of which were slightly wrong. To the left was an open-concept kitchen. To the right were several cubicles, each hosting a screen-saver that had the red plump man and white cross logo on it, bopping around from one corner of the screen to the next.

Out of the windows was sky, and the barest tips of building tops beyond that.

When Cassidy moved again she moved quickly, turning swiftly and heading to the cubicles. It hadn't been exactly what she'd been hoping to find, but it was close. She squat down and pushed the rolling chair away, grabbed the computer tower by its back edge, and hauled it out of its space. Cables pulled out of their housing and the screen it was attached to switched itself off, but she didn't take notice. Instead she pressed the clamps that held the side of the tower in and yanked on them, hard, peeling off its side and revealing the mess of fans and wires within.

She stuck her tongue into her cheek as she pulled back the wire bundles, finally finding a thin purple rectangle that was nestled carefully at its middle. She pulled it free, disconnected the connecting wires from their clamps, then tucked the hard drive into her breast pocket.

Suddenly the room lit up with blue and green, in

rapid alternation. She stood and turned and there were lights blazing in from the windows. It took her barely a moment to recognize them as headlights before the windows smashed in and she was confronted with the roar of a half-dozen flying car engines.

Cassidy cursed, stepping back and shielding her face from the glass that came in. There were sirens as well, she could hear them now. *Flying police cruisers*, she thought, cursing again.

There was a hard '*tunk*' sound at her right as a zipline anchor imbedded itself into the wall. From the nearest cruiser a man in what looked like tactical SWAT gear came in on the line, letting go when he was above solid floor and drawing a rifle so large that it took both his hands to hold it.

She raised her hands, hoping that it was the correct response to being arrested in this dimension.

Tunk. Tunk. Tunk. Three more ziplines snapped into frame and officers accompanied them, each with their own rifle, each one aimed in her direction. The first was closest and the other three stayed back. He kept his sights on her, opened his mouth, and yelled a long string of vowels, the tone of which were commands. There were no K sounds she could articulate. He pointed the gun at her as he barked orders.

"I don't know what you're asking me to do," Cassidy said as calmly as she could. She kept her eye level down and was lacing her fingers together behind her head, hoping that the procedure was the same on this world as it was on hers.

He screamed at her again, this time with more K

sounds, but still with edge. His tone was guttural and hard.

"I'm sorry, I don't... I don't know what you're telling me to do." She got down on her knees.

His face turning red, he adjusted an earpiece on his helmet, then barked again: "Jeni nën arrest për dimensionin e dyshuar të ndalur."

She raised an eyebrow and cocked her head up, looking up and making eye contact with him for the first time. The words were unlike any she'd heard spoken since she got here, but were still familiar. "Pardon?"

"Ant qayd alaietiqal bsbb qafz albued almushtabah bih."

She squinted. "That's... that's Latin based."

He yelled again, each time with more anger: "Vous êtes en état d'arrestation pour un saut de dimension suspecté."

"That's French. Um, I know this you said, uh... you said..."

"You are under arrest for a suspected jump of dimension! Please stand and place your hands on your face!"

She froze, then started to stand.

"English?" He asked, astonished.

She nodded.

"English!" He called to the others around him. The three adjusted their headsets. He turned back to her, his voice thick with contempt: "*Slipstreamer*."

CHAPTER ELEVEN

Her Father held his hand out with the palm up and fingers splayed, ready to receive.

"Slipstreamer!" the Officer bellowed, holding his gun high, its sight obscuring his eye. "Put your palms and knees flat on the ground. You are being taken under arrest for the crime of knowingly traversing the multi-verse. Do not resist!"

Cassidy fell to her knees, her hands still flat with palms out next to her head, her elbows bent at ninety degree angles. She swallowed, her mouth suddenly dry; a cold breeze coming in from the shattered windows and pushing her hair back.

The three officers that had held back raised their weapons to mid height, following the speaker's lead.

"Place your palms flat on the ground!" the Officer-in-Charge yelled again, his voice cracking from doing so. He was red in the face and looked as though his blood pressure had spiked.

Cassidy let out a breath she had been holding, out through her mouth until her lungs were empty, then took a long, slow intake through her nose again.

Her Father held his hand out with the palm up and fingers splayed, ready to receive.

"Hands! On! The! Floor!"

"You may want to see someone about your blood pressure," she smiled. "Seems unhealthy."

He shot her a quizzical look.

She lowered herself as if to obey his command to fall forward onto her palms, but broke the momentum into springing to her feet instead. She bolted past them, her legs moving like pistons as they turned and tried to track her with their weapons. One of them opened fire, and distantly over the gunshot, she heard the man giving orders bellowing at them to stop. She felt the shattered glass crunch and give beneath her feet.

When she reached the edge of the ledge she leapt, her arms pressed forward. For a moment there was nothing between her and the ground below but a mile of thin air, and she felt gravity begin its hungry tug.

She landed with a yelp in the seat of the flying police cruiser, her knee slamming into the stick shift as she made impact, sending the craft spinning towards the ground.

"Tailspin!" she yelled, scrambling to sit up despite the centripetal force thrusting her about the cabin. It pushed her back towards the passenger door she'd come through and almost hurled her out. When it pulled her back the other way she snagged its handle and pulled it closed, then righted herself behind the steering wheel.

She pulled the wheel to the right with great force, centering it, and the car stopped spinning. It was still heading down though, the ground coming towards her at an alarming rate.

The controls were in that same cursive script, filled with blue and green lights that were not intuitive.

"Come on," she hissed through gritted teeth, pressing buttons at random to no effect. "Come on!" She slammed the stick shift forward and the engine sputtered. She pulled it all the way back and finally it roared to life. She was jolted back against her seat as the car leveled off just near the tops of the nearest buildings and started to shoot along, parallel to the ground instead of on a collision course with it.

Cassidy gripped the steering wheel and smirked, her cheeks flushed and red. She turned the car slightly right and headed for the shoreline she could just barely see in the distance, beyond the rise of the hills and over the tops of the buildings. "Now we're cooking with gas," she grinned.

There was a big bass noise, and the cruiser shook violently. A green light began to swirl to coincide with an alarm that reminded her of the one that went off whenever the Starship Enterprise was hit into Red Alert. She gritted her teeth and looked in the rearview mirror, which was shaped like an octagon to see below the car as well. Behind her, two other flying cruisers were in hot pursuit. One had an Officer leaning out the side window, aiming a large object at her. It flashed green for a moment, then a bright wave came at her and shook the car again.

She yelled, bracing herself. The car spun into a single barrel roll that made her stomach flip along with it, and her throat threatened to expel the sandwich she'd had earlier. She turned until she was above one of the main streets below, then slammed the stick shift forward and caused the engines to sputter.

She continued forward on momentum for a moment, then slowly the nose of the car tilted downward and she began to fall.

The two cruisers tried to follow her at first, then pulled up as she dove between the city streets. When she saw canopies in her windows she pulled the shift back down and blasted forward, slamming her back against the seat again. "Yes!" she screamed as she jolted forward. She heard screams beneath her and didn't want to know how close she'd gotten to the ground. The canopies fluttered in her wake, tearing from their bearings and catching in her back-draft like kites.

Cassidy exhaled through gritted teeth, her cheeks full of air and flushed red. She smiled and took a sharp corner in a way she hadn't in years then slammed on the gas and bolted forward, back towards the shore.

The bass noise sounded again and the car shook, the alarms and lights returning. She glanced furtively in her rearview mirror, but saw nothing behind or below her. The noise came again, then the shake. The alarms were louder now, and warnings in a language she couldn't read began to flash on the dash.

Cassidy grabbed the small control that jutted into the car from the mirror and tilted it up. The two other cruisers were keeping pace with her, hovering above the tops of the building and firing down.

The car rumbled again, and not in response to a shot.

"I appear to have ceded the high ground," she growled under her breath. She turned again, down another dark street, seeing the long line of buildings continue. In her mirror, the others cars turned in kind, able to make their corners more easily for not having to worry about hitting the side of the building.

They fired again, and the green warning light changed to blue. The flashing and the noise increased.

Before her was the market, all canopies and tables. Above the vinyl sheets were apartment buildings, each with their own small balcony that looked out over the crowd. Some stood out on them, steam forming from hot cups of tea in the cooling air of the evening, their heads cocked to look at the rogue police cruiser that was flying too low on their streets.

She pushed the gear shift as far forward as it could go, then scrambled to the passenger door and kicked it open. The car slowed and began to descend, and as it did she leapt from it, landing on a vacant balcony and rolling through the glass door behind it, crashing into a living room.

Behind her, that familiar bass tone leveled as her cruiser began to fall. This blast, when it struck, incinerated the vehicle. She felt the heat from it on her back as she brought herself to her feet and started to run.

A family at their kitchen table turned to look at her with surprise, the father's mouth hanging open. The air smelled fresh like vindaloo curry, steam billowing from a pot in the back.

"Sorry!" she yelled honestly as she ran past.

The Father's expression changed from fear to rage as he heard her accent.

She kicked open the door at the far end of the apartment and fell into the hallway. Her shoulder pulled itself loose as she hit the opposite wall and she grunted, pulling it up and into a usable position as she hobbled down the plush carpet. She could hear the throbbing whoosh of more police cruisers outside.

She turned to the first door on the side of the hall opposite the one she'd come through and tried to open it. It was locked. She kicked it open with one solid crack of her boot-heel, then finally hauled her left arm back into joint.

Inside the apartment a pair of teens jumped up from the couch. The young girl had her hands in the air and was rattling a series of vowels and hard R sounds with a high-pitched voice that Cassidy recognized as a long string of excuses, before she realized that it wasn't her father that had stormed in. The boy stammered and stumbled, unable to get out anything but a shocked series of K's: "Kay-Kay, kkkkkkk-kay. Kay."

Cassidy marched past them to the window on the far end of the apartment. She pried it open and stuck her head out. It opened to a fire escape, and there were no cruisers in sight in any direction. She pulled herself out as the boy behind her gathered himself and started to yell out in full sentences, but was already scaling down the grated stairs and making her way to street level.

She jumped from the last level to the alley below, not wanting anyone to hear the clang of the metal ladder descending to the street. She huffed, feeling the impact in her knees, and immediately began peeling off her coat again. She pulled the black elastic from her wrist and ran her hair through it, making it a high bun as she stepped out of the alley and seamlessly joined the flow of traffic.

There were hundreds of people on the street, just

as there had been before. Unlike before, a much greater number of them were police. They stood on the sidewalk but didn't walk, scanning and surveying the crowd. Some pointed, others stood with their hands on their hips, chewing gum as only police officers truly could.

There were three officers on the street twenty feet in front of her. They were stopping people as they passed and asking them for identification, which they then scanned with a gun that looked like the sort cashiers used on her world.

Cassidy huffed again, then turned into a corner store. She walked up to a display of sunglasses and tried a pair on as a fourth officer entered the store and walked up to the clerk. While she was pretending to admire one pair she slipped the other under her coat, then turned and stepped back out of the store and headed in the opposite direction of the men checking IDs. She slid the sunglasses on over her face, hauling the tag off quickly and discreetly.

People were flooding out of the apartment building she'd run through, being herded out in their pajamas (or less) by the police as they searched room to room. She tisked and turned, crossing the street to get away from the action.

"Slipstreamer!" came a frantic, haggard yell.

Cassidy stopped in her tracks and spun around to the source of the voice.

Standing at the edge of the sidewalk was the Red Nun. She was holding her boney finger out towards Cassidy, having dropped her collection plate and spilling the coins everywhere. *"Slipstreamer!"*

All the police turned and looked.

Cassidy cursed, then turned and broke into a run

again, her legs finding the new strength that came with the rush of adrenaline. She bolted between people who all pulled away from her, then ducked into the nearest alley and plunged herself down it towards the next street on the other side.

She was almost at its mouth when a uniformed officer stepped in front of it, raised his weapon, and yelled: "K-Freeze!" stammering and almost yelling the word in his own language.

Cassidy skidded to a halt, turned, and started back the way she'd come.

Two officers had filed into the alley behind her, and they both raised their weapons.

She skidded to a stop again, but only for an instant as the heavy gloved hand of the first officer landed on her shoulder and forced her to her knees. He kicked her shin and forced her onto her palms, and she felt the cold barrel of a gun against the arch of her spine.

Despite this, she laughed.

"Stay down!" the man bellowed, in that same tone the Swat leader had.

"I will," she said between laughs, nodding. "I will! I'm just catching my breath."

She could feel her heart, feel it pumping in her ears. She felt it in her fingers, the way it rushed with a tingling numbness. She smiled widely and honestly, bringing two of them up to her neck to take her pulse. After a moment she calculated it to be well over ninety beats per minute, and she laughed again, still feeling the blood pump in her ears even as her body started to wind down.

Cassidy felt the cold stock of a gun against the back of her head and went down smiling.

CHAPTER TWELVE

Cassidy woke in a holding cell with both her arms chained to the solid concrete wall at ninety degree angles. It was dark and she couldn't see the entire room, but she didn't need someone to tell her it was a holding cell to know it was one. She knew the smell of it, knew the taste of antiseptic in the back of her throat.

The room was large, clearly meant to hold many if it needed to. She was still wearing her clothes, but they were rumpled and dirty now. There were holes in her pants from where she'd been dragged, and scrapes on her knees beneath them. She could feel the soft trickle of blood that came from a gash on her forehead, and suddenly remembered the floor of the alley coming at her after she'd been struck.

There was no furniture or fixtures she could see, just bars along one side of the large cell and concrete walls on every other. It was private and yet as public as a panopticon, with anyone able to look into any corner of the cell at any time. There was a large hole with a grate over it in the center of the floor, and the entire room sloped slightly towards it. She tried not to think about that fact.

Her ears still throbbed with the beating of her heart, and her fingers still tingled with the numbness she'd spent the last two years searching to replicate. She smiled and leaned her head back on the concrete, smirking at the darkness above.

She pulled her arm and realized there was some give to the chains that bound her. She reached for the drive she'd stolen and found the pocket empty. "Dangit," she huffed, then reached for her zippered pocket and found the green pill bottle she'd placed there, still half full of Duplionyl. She produced it from the pocket and stared at it quizzically.

"Oh they wouldn't take that," came a voice from the dark at the other side of the room.

She startled, her head jolting up.

There was a shuffling in the dark, like bags of potatoes being moved around, and then all of a sudden she saw a figure emerge from the black. He had to lean forward to be seen -- he was chained to the far wall -- but his skin was sallow and cracked, reddened around the mouth and the eyes. His hair was messy and brown, and he was wearing a matching shirt and trousers the color of creamed coffee. He nodded towards the bottle again. "If they took that you might detox, and we can't have that."

She squinted at the man, remembering the woman on the street who'd had her shakes magically vanish as soon as she'd popped two Duplionyl into her system. She nodded, tucking the pills back into her pocket and zipping it tight. "You speak English?"

He smirked. He hadn't done it in a while, and the action cracked the skin of his cheek. "Right, yes. That is what you call it, isn't it? Here we just call it slipstreamer, Slip-streamer." He coughed, long and with a haggard throat, then chuckled.

"I won't detox from these because I've never had them," she said in response to his earlier statement, patting her pocket.

His eyes widened with humour. He looked like Gollum, the way she'd pictured Gollum when she'd read *The Lord of the Rings* as a child, before she'd seen the movies. She could see his dried scalp between his patches of hair. "You look good for someone who must be in the late stages of McMillon disease, then."

"I don't have McMillon disease."

He narrowed his eyes at her.

"Is that... is that what happened to you?"

He laughed, then brought up a chained hand and motioned to his cracked, dried skin. "This? No. No, this is what happens when you have McMillon disease and then you detox from the Dupe," he laughed, motioning again to the bottle bulge in her pocket. "It's a hell of a combo."

She winced, thinking back to her father shaking, and the way this man's hands shook. It was the way the woman on the street's hands had shaken. "How do you speak English?"

He smirked, shuffling closer to the bars so that he could be in the light and still lean back against the wall. "I was a cop," he said, looking past the bars and getting a faraway look in his eyes. "We all gotta know how to speak it, just in case one of you comes back through to our world. I never really considered why until I pulled guard duty a few times. Until I noticed that they weren't getting the green pills, they were getting blue ones."

Cassidy kept her eyes on him, but said nothing and asked nothing.

"It took a lot of digging -- a lot. In the end it was my own eyes that really proved it to me. These Streamers, they weren't getting the Dupe. But yet they weren't getting the shakes, the split-brain... none of it. So that meant they didn't have McMillon... until they'd been here for a while. Then: then they got McMillon."

Cassidy nodded.

"Do you get it? Do you see?" he asked, leaning forward. Spittle came from his mouth, he spoke with such force.

She nodded again. "They couldn't have people without McMillon around, even people in cages... so they were giving it to them, and then selling them an addictive cure."

He laughed. "See that's good, that's a lot. That's more than most get. But here's the kick," he grinned. "I think... I think Pharmakon made McMillon in a lab, too. I think they gave it to people and they pass it on to their kids and their kids' kids, but I think it starts *right here*." He reached into his pocket and pulled out a single blue pill.

Cassidy backed up a little without realizing it, as though he'd pulled a gun. "Pharmakon is the little red man with the cross on his belly?"

He nodded. "They left it for you in your food," the man said, poking the pill back into his breast pocket. He added shamefully: "I also ate your food."

"That's okay," Cassidy frowned, lolling her head to one side. "I won't be here long."

The man laughed. "You are good, Streamer. I'll give you that. But you're in Fredericks. *Nobody* escapes Fredericks."

She shrugged."Sad that I won't have bragging rights back on my own world then." She paused. "What's your name, Officer?"

He straightened at the use of his title. He hadn't been called it in years. "Scolders."

She nodded. "Officer Scolders, if I get you out of here, will you make a big enough stink that I can escape too?"

Scolders squinted, then smiled.

Cassidy reached and stretched her chains, plunging her fingers into her hair and producing a too-long bobby pin from it. It was longer on one side than the other, and had a series of calculated notches along that edge. She stuck her tongue into the side of her cheek and worked the tool up and into the locking mechanism of her chains.

CHAPTER THIRTEEN

The guard turned the corner and looked past the iron bars, immediately stopping short. Scolders was the only person in the cell, chained to the far wall, almost out of view. The guard's face went red and he reached for his key ring, producing it with a loud exclamation of scuttling K-sounds.

Scolders answered back calmly, but with the contemptuous tone that came with the use of more vowels than consonant. The guard cursed back, stepping into the room and over to Cassidy's vacant chains. He gestured wildly, picked them up as if to prove to himself that they were real, then turned back to Scolders with flushed cheeks. He was yelling, and he reached out and grabbed Scolders by the collar.

Scolders pushed back with hands that were suddenly free, forcing the guard off his feet. He fell back, landing hard against his tailbone and letting out a deep yelp. Just as he did, Cassidy stepped out of the shadows and picked up one of her chains, snapping it around his left wrist.

The man cursed, lunging at her, but she pulled away. He reached for his gun and she kicked it with malice, her heavy boot sending it spiraling into the dark. The guard reached for a lapel pin with three colored light on it, but Scolders quickly pressed forward and snatched it from his grip, placing it in his breast pocket.

Cassidy stepped around Scolders carefully, and when she found an opening she darted forward and latched the guard's second shackle, despite his protestations.

"That was harder than I thought it would be," she smirked, still feeling her blood pumping in her ears.

Scolders turned to her and couldn't help but smile. "Come on. There'll be more, soon."

They stepped out of the cell and he touched her shoulder, bringing her attention to him as he placed a finger firmly to his lips. She nodded silently, and they both crept down the hall. There was a large window at its apex, and they slunk past each and every door on their way to it, aware that there could be more guards behind any of them.

They reached the window and she opened it. There was a steel fence fifty feet below, and beyond that a row of flying police cruisers. She smiled, then turned back to Scolders.

"I want to thank you --"

Alarms sounded suddenly, and Scolders' eyes went wide. He gestured up to the devices that hung from the ceiling: "English detectors!" he chided.

She hissed. He turned and ran down the hall, calling out random words in English as he went. She watched him for a moment, considering whether she should stay and help or not.

Her Father held his hand out with the palm up and fingers

splayed, ready to receive.

She huffed, then made her way down the fire escape.

***

The police cruiser was a smoldering mess of fumes by the time she was over the Massachusetts shoreline. She assumed it was still called Massachusetts, in any event. It probably wasn't, she realized: not enough K or R sounds.

She spun the wheel hard and then pushed the stick drive as far forward as it would go. It paused for a moment then began to tip its nose down. She still had no idea how to land them, but had become an expert in crashing them. She opened up the driver's side door and stepped out, falling the ten feet to the rock below. The car kept going, until finally it hit the water's surface and started to sink.

Cassidy watched it for a moment, touched the bottle of pills in her pocket, then made her way up to the gap in the rocks she'd entered this world from.

"I told them you'd come," came a gruff, hard voice from behind her.

She turned quickly, her red hair whipping, catching her cheek sharply as she did.

Standing atop the bluff was the Swat commander, still wearing his uniform. He'd screamed so much that there were blood vessels broken in his cheeks.

She pursed her lips.

"They said there was no way you'd come back to the beach. You'd go back to Pharmakon, or hide out and wait for things to cool down. Or meet up with your new little friend, the inmate."

She paused a moment at that, knowing that Scolders had made it out.

"But I said no. She's a Slipstreamer. She'll want to get out, want to get home... she's dumb. It's in her nature. She'll go right back to that beach... and when she does, she'll lead us right to that portal. And then we can finally end this."

Her eyes went wide and she bolted forward, hitting her bad shoulder off the mouth of the cave as she tumbled into it. She heard the bass sound of his weapon and the rocks behind her exploded, sending shards of stone scattering across her back.

She screamed, and was about to hit the back of the tunnel when suddenly she was facing its mouth again. She stumbled forward, tripped on a round stone at its mouth, and fell past Dr. Herbert Gamgee onto the Massachusetts shoreline. She hit the water and felt it soak into her jacket: the tide was higher here.

"You're back!" Gamgee exclaimed, holding a steaming thermos.

"Blast it!" Cassidy yelled, turning back around and scrambling to her feet.

"What?"

"Blast the charge! They're *coming*!"

Gamgee turned around, seeing the early hints of shadows at play deep in the mouth of the cave. He dropped the thermos, hot coffee leaping from it and merging with the sea, then plunged his hand deep into his pocket, producing a small key fob. He aimed it at the mouth of the cave dramatically, and with one firm press, depressed the button.

The Swat Officer took his only breath of our world, then looked up to see several small, metal cylinders, all of them blinking red and screaming a loud, whining alarm. He stepped back, feeling the tug of his own world's gravity. No sooner was that done than the detonations exploded, caving in the stone of the shoreline all around the portal.

Gamgee sighed and tucked the key fob away, then turned back to Cassidy. "Are you all right?"

Cassidy laughed, even as the foam of the waves lapped at her bruised arm and shoulder. She smiled, feeling the steady beat of her heart in her ears, in her cheeks, and all the way down to her fingers. "I'm amazing," she said genuinely, holding out her hand for help up.

CHAPTER FOURTEEN

Cassidy hissed in air sharply as Gamgee applied gauze to her cut. There was a tenderness to his action that she wouldn't have thought his rough hands capable of. Behind him the projection of the map of the shoreline spun on its tilted axis, just as it had when he'd told her about the other world. It seemed like a lifetime ago now.

The red oval was still blinking in the middle of the rock face, despite the fact that she'd closed it behind her. She stared over his shoulder at it, her eyes glued to it. The rest of the map spun around it, the portal at its fulcrum, and her vision stayed fixated on it. Gamgee was speaking to her, but she almost didn't hear it: her heart was still in her ears, every fifth beat timed with the blinking of that glowing red light.

Her breathing was labored, but not painful, and she braced herself against the arm of the chair she was on.

"I can't believe you stormed Pharmakon," Gamgee said, shaking his head. He examined the gauze and tossed it into the waste bin with the others. He got a fresh pad and started applying it. "That was beyond stupid."

"It needed to be done," she said, not meeting his eyes

when she spoke to him, still looking past him.

He frowned, shaking his head again.

She let her gaze fall slightly, to the child-locked green bottle from another world that lay nondescriptly on Gamgee's lab table. "Did you know my father had had McMillon disease?" she asked, turning her head slightly to meet his eyes for the first time since he'd started to work on her.

He stopped short, his mouth hanging open. After a moment he closed it and shook his head. "Of course not. How could I have?" He followed her gaze back to the pill bottle. "I can synthesize the cure from that dosage, you know?"

She shot him a quizzical look, surprised.

Gamgee smiled warmly. "Do I look like I could have invaded Pharmakon? Really now?" He laughed, then leaned in and continued tending to her. "No, I can backwards engineer from that sample and get what we need. I may not be good enough to come up with it on my own, but even a physicist can do that much, I assure you."

Her expression did not seem alleviated.

He looked from her to the bottle once again, then tisked. "I will isolate and remove the addictive components before bringing my 'discovery' to the FDA... just as before."

Cassidy nodded and let out a long breath of air she hadn't been aware she'd been holding. She turned back to the bright red blinking light, and noticed that her pulse was no longer in synch with it, and no longer in her ears. She smiled. "This is going to sound bizarre but... it's almost a shame it got sealed. I haven't had my blood pumping like this in... years, really."

He leaned back from her slightly, making eye contact with her as he pulled away. He tossed the gauze into the trash can with the rest, then spun his chair around. Without a word he hit two buttons on his control panel.

The first zoomed the map out slowly: first the the tri-state area, then to the country, the continent, and finally the world.

The second made the bright red oval blink out for an instant... before a dozen more blinked to life, all around the country, blinking in unison. Then a dozen dozen, scattered throughout the globe. Everywhere, portals blinking into her awareness.

Gamgee smiled. "You were saying?"

Suddenly, she felt her pulse quicken to match the blink again. Felt it in her ears, and in the tips of her fingers.

THE ISLAND ARTIFACT

ALI HOUSE & JD RYOT

CHAPTER ONE

The wind whipped around Cassidy, blowing loose strands of her strawberry-blond hair across her face. As she neared the edge of the cliff, the wind grew stronger, almost threatening to blow her over the edge. Glancing back at the tiny town behind her, Cassidy couldn't believe where she was or what she was about to do. A month ago she would have never thought that travelling to different worlds was possible, but here she was, on the Northern coast of Newfoundland, Canada, about to locate a portal and travel through it to another world.

She still didn't quite understand how it all worked, but it wasn't her job to understand. It was her job to go to these strange lands and bring back anything that might prove useful or interesting. For many years she'd travelled all over the globe searching for long-lost relics, but nothing could compare to the thrill of experiencing a world that other people didn't know existed. Her last trip had been full of drama and danger, but she'd been in tough scrapes before, and this time she was a lot wiser.

To get to the portal, she'd flown into St. Anthony, rented a car, and driven from there to the small town of

Straitsview. The drive had taken about half an hour and through it all she'd kept a careful eye out for the many large moose that roamed the areas. The rental clerk had given her a warning to watch out for them because they could take a car down without blinking (her exact words), and when Cassidy saw her first one, broad and hulking and similar in density to a brick wall, she'd had to admit to herself that it'd be best to keep an eye out and stay a safe distance.

When she reached Straitsview, it was even smaller than she'd expected. The town was basically a handful of roads coming off a stretch of highway, all clustered around a small cove and cliff, wrapping around them like a hug. There wasn't much development up on the cliff, leaving lots of room for walking paths and forested area, which was convenient because it was the path she'd have to take. The area was peaceful and the scenery beautiful, but she wasn't here for that.

She was here for adventure.

First she double-checked the coordinates that Professor Gamgee had given her. He had no idea what was behind most of these portals, so for her second trip through they had decided to just throw a dart at the map and go wherever it landed. A strange thrill ran through her. What kind of world was waiting for her on the other side?

Approaching the cliff, she walked until the tips of her brown hiking boots came to the edge. Looking down, she saw a small landing about ten feet below, jutting out from the rocky cliff face. It was about two feet wide and almost ten feet long. The portal was supposed to be on that landing, which meant that she needed to get down there somehow. Gamgee had provided her with satellite images of the cliffside and the rocks had looked climbable. With the kind of weather this area experienced, anything not sturdy surely would have been blown away ages ago. Pushing her foot into the ground, she checked to see if it was sturdy enough to put in a pin and thread a safety line, but the grass was still damp from the morning dew and she suspected that the pin wouldn't hold. Better to climb down without a line rather than to risk having it break free at an inopportune time. The ledge looked wide enough to catch her if she fell, but there was the chance that she might tumble over the edge and down into the cold ocean waters below. And boy did that water look *cold*.

A large smile broke out over her freckled face, as she stared at the dangerous surf below. Her heart started beating faster, but her palms were completely dry. Cassidy smiled as she took some chalk out of her pocket and rubbed it on her hands. She carefully made her way over the edge and down the side of the cliff. Any other person would have to be crazy to go over an edge like this one, but she lived for this kind of danger. She loved rock climbing, and as soon as she mastered one wall, she immediately set out to find another, more difficult, wall to take on. She loved the feel of fighting against gravity, and the deliberate way that she had to make each move, choosing carefully where to put her hands and feet, making sure that the rocks were secure enough to handle her weight. A couple of times she felt rocks shifting under her weight, but she managed to keep her wits about her and made it to the landing without injury.

When both feet were safely on the ground, she let

out a sigh of satisfaction. It was time to head into the un-known.

Looking around, she tried to see the portal, but noth-ing was visible. Squinting her eyes, she searched for some kind of odd light or weird shimmer, but everything was perfectly normal. The surf pounded the cliff face below her and the wind whistled past. For a second she felt stu-pid, like she'd been set up as part of an elaborate prank. Any minute now Gamgee would pop out with a camera and laugh at how gullible she was. Shaking her head, she told herself that the portals had to be real. After all, she'd been to another world and had seen wondrous things, and the professor had no reason to lie to her or lead her on. The last portal had seemed invisible, so maybe they all were, which meant that even if she couldn't see it, it was there. Taking a deep breath she stepped forward, walking down the length of the landing.

At some point she expected everything to change, but nothing did. There was no flash or sudden alteration in the weather or an appearance of strange new scenery. The waves still crashed and the wind still whistled. The grass under her feet looked exactly the same. She wondered what the odds were that she'd travelled to a world exactly like her own. It had to be a small one — especially for a world with the exact same weather. Staring back along the ledge, Cassidy wondered if maybe Gamgee had been wrong about the location of the portal. She glanced over the edge of the landing, but there was nothing else, only a drop to the surf below. If the calculations were off and the portal was down there somewhere, there was no guaran-tee that she'd be able to reach it. Perhaps this location was a bust.

Sighing at the disappointment, she put some more chalk on her hands and started the climb up the cliff. Seeking out handholds and footholds, she tried to concentrate on her immediate task and not think about how she could be in Egypt exploring ruins or wandering through Mayan temples in Mexico. What if all of the locations were like this? What if she'd gotten her hopes up for nothing?

In a few minutes she'd reached the top of the cliff and was pulling herself onto the green grass. She lay back on the ground and stared up at the sky. Maybe this trip didn't have to be a bust – maybe she could drive to Lanse aux Meadows and look at the Viking ruins. It wasn't very far from here. Sure, everything there had already been discovered, but it'd be more interesting than hanging out in an airport, waiting for a flight back home.

Sighing, Cassidy pulled herself to her feet and started to head back to her rental car, but she'd barely taken two steps before the sight in front of her froze her in her tracks.

CHAPTER TWO

Her green eyes widened in shock. Before going over the cliff she'd been looking at a small town, but suddenly it was ten times that big. Where there was once a handful of dwellings, now multiple houses and streets stretched throughout the area, extending farther than she could see. The forest was still on her left, but part of the clearing she'd walked through to get to the cliff had been transformed into some kind of public park, opening into the streets.

It wasn't only the size of the town that had changed, it was the design as well. The previous buildings had consisted mostly of houses and shops, the majority of which were single-storied, but none higher than two stories. The colours had been muted, with faded blue and white siding and paint. Shingled roofs came in two colours, black or red, with the red mainly reserved for tourist shops and bed and breakfasts, which used red as an accent colour, probably to stand out from the local buildings. What the area lacked in population, it had made up for by spreading the buildings apart, leaving ample room for large yards and walking areas. But now the buildings were smaller and pushed up against each other, leaving little room for sprawling yards. Where one house might have sat, there were now four or five. Instead of muted colours, the buildings were bright and vibrant with natural wood accents. Some had grass roofs, others had clay, and the style looked less North American and more European — although she couldn't say for sure which country exactly. Most of the buildings had two or three stories, but she could see a four-story rising above the others, like some kind of clock tower.

Turning back to the cliff's edge, Cassidy wondered if she was seeing things. Perhaps her brain was trying to compensate for the disappointment she'd felt on the ledge by creating some kind of elaborate mirage. Maybe this time, when she turned around, she'd see spaceships or the Eiffel Tower.

Staring out at the cold, unchanged waters of the Atlantic Ocean, she told herself that it was okay the portal hadn't worked. There were supposed to be a bunch of portals all over the world, so it was okay that one of them hadn't worked. There was always next time. Taking a deep breath, she slowly turned around.

The larger town was still there. As she took a few steps forward there was no shimmer or change in the scene, so it had to be real. Cassidy held back a laugh. The portal must have worked after all. There was probably a one-in-one-billion chance that the landscape and weather would be the same on either side, and she'd lucked out. As soon as she got home she'd have to purchase a lottery ticket.

Pausing, she took a few minutes to observe her surroundings and get a lay of the land. There were colourful banners hanging from buildings, the kind you'd usually see during a fair or event. People strolled along the streets, enjoying the sunny day, in a normal human-like manner. They wore clothing similar to what she'd see back on her world — jeans, sweaters, jackets, and sneakers. The scene was odd, but strangely familiar.

She hadn't been expecting something so... normal. There were no flying cars or weird clothing or futuristic buildings. If she hadn't seen the smaller village before going over the cliff, she'd never believe that she was in another world. Was there some kind of catch? Were there lizard monsters roaming the city? Did everyone here have strange powers? Were the police outfitted with giant mech suits? Well, there was only one way to find out.

Taking in a deep breath, she headed towards the town. She didn't have a particular destination in mind, but if she followed the crowds, surely she'd find something interesting. Maybe she'd be able to find out what had happened to this town to make it change so much.

Walking through the park, she soon reached a wide cobblestone street that seemed to be pedestrian-only. Either side was filled with shops, all bearing signs in two strange languages that looked English-adjacent, albeit with strange characters. She wondered if these languages were spoken on her world or if they were strange hybrids? Most of the shops had bunting in the windows, making her wonder if today was some kind of holiday or festival. She recalled seeing a large field to the East while she was standing on the cliff. If there was a festival, maybe something would be happening there, like a sport or an event or a parade. If she couldn't find anything interesting, maybe that would be her next direction.

She continued to look at the shops as she passed, trying to figure out what each one was. Some were obvious — pastries in the window meant bakery, signs of food meant eating establishment, and racks of clothing meant clothing store. There were a few buildings she couldn't quite make out what they were — probably boring businesses or residential housing.

Groups of people passed her by, laughing and talking excitedly. Everyone seemed to be in high spirits, clapping each other on the backs and saying strange words that she didn't understand. The fashion around here seemed to be thick woollen sweaters, jeans, and boots, and with her hiking boots, jeans, and brown jacket she fit in rather well, and started to walk with a bit more confidence. Eventually she reached the end of the pedestrian street, which was a crossroads. It seemed like a good idea to head towards the field, but what if there was a museum or information centre down one of the other streets. She stared down each path, trying to see if anything of interest might be located down there.

As she turned to her left, she saw a tall blond man wearing a dark blue wool sweater with white accents standing near her. He smiled and spoke, but she couldn't understand a thing he'd said.

Her face twisted in confusion. "Sorry, what did you say?"

Suddenly she realized that she'd spoken. Memories of her first trip through a portal flooded her and she quickly shut her mouth, holding her breath as she waited for this person to react to her strange tongue. Luckily, her fears were for nothing.

The man laughed. "English, yes?" he said, in an accented voice.

She nodded cautiously, carefully watching him.

"Do not worry, most of us speak English. We have a lot of tourists here for the celebration."

"The celebration," she said, relief flooding her. "Sorry, it's my first time here and I forgot to get a map."

"That explains the confused look on your face. The information booth is near the game grounds over there," he pointed east, the same direction where the field should be. "They have maps and schedules and can answer any questions you might have."

She smiled. "Thank you."

"It is not a problem. Happy Landing Day!"

"Happy Landing Day," she echoed back as he walked away. When he was gone, she breathed a sigh of relief. Not only was she in a world that understood English, but some kind of festival was happening today — the kind where there would be lots of tourists. It was going to be even easier to blend in than she'd originally thought. Maybe she should buy two lottery tickets.

An information booth should give her some clue as to what was going on today, and maybe they'd be able to point her in the direction of a museum. Heading towards the field, she passed many jovial faces, and she had to conclude that this festival must be a good one. Judging from the amount of people out and about, most adults were probably excused from work and kids from school, which likely led to the abundance of mirth.

As she neared the field, the smell of pastries and warm spices filled the air. Although she'd eaten earlier in the day, her mouth started to water at the delicious scents, and she had to fight to stay on track. She passed by lines of white booths, all filled with different kinds of sandwiches and pastries and drinks. The signs were in three languages, one of which was English, but the other two were those odd characters. There were booths selling souvenirs and clothing, but she gave them little more than a cursory glance. Although she wasn't here to shop, perhaps she could find something interesting to bring back if nothing else caught her eye.

Finally she spotted the information booth. It was a red and white striped tent, and larger than any of the other booths. It also had a sign with the words 'Information Booth' written in English and about twelve other languages. As Cassidy approached she saw that there were bleachers on either side of the field, where people were sitting and watching. Inside the field were groups of kids playing games like tug-of-war and throwing stones. Her interest was piqued.

Walking into the booth, she saw two women stationed behind a table with lots of paraphernalia on it. One was fair-skinned with short blond hair and was wearing a red sweater with a white cross on it, and the other was brown-skinned with long dark hair, wearing a similar sweater.

"*Hej*," the blonde woman said.

"Hi," Cassidy responded cheerfully. "I'm looking for some information."

The blonde woman nodded. "Here is a schedule for today's activities," she said in an accented voice as she picked up a pamphlet. The cover had the words '*Landing Day Celebrations*' written on it and an image of two groups fighting a tug-of-war battle in the field while onlookers cheered. Cassidy noticed that there were many similar pamphlets on the table, each with different languages on it. She noticed that the one in her hand had a small British Flag in the corner and the words were all in English. Glancing at the others, she recognized a few flags: Denmark, France, and Sweden, but not all of them. Some of them looked like a strange mishmash of flags from her world, while others were completely foreign to her.

"If you're interested in learning more about Landing Day, you can visit the museum on Elmegade," the woman said helpfully, holding out a second pamphlet. "It's free all day today."

Cassidy took the offering. "Thank you."

"You're welcome."

Stepping away from the tent, Cassidy quickly read through the Landing Day pamphlet. It didn't say much about the history of the festival, instead talking about all of the wonderful things a person could experience — like their traditional food and drink, children's activities, adult activities, and evening entertainment. She glanced at her watch, which had been set to the Newfoundland time zone before going through the portal. What time was it here? She looked around for a clock, finding one on top of the tall building that towered over the rest of the town. She smiled as she noticed that it was the same as her watch, 12:10pm. This trip was easy as pie.

The children's games currently taking place would soon be over, and the adult tournament would take place at 1:30pm. She glanced through the tournament activities, sizing them up. There was a tug-of-war, a few strength competitions, and throwing competitions. It sounded interesting. A smile crossed her face as she noticed that anyone could sign up to compete. Originally she'd planned on watching the tournament, but now she was thinking of competing. The events sounded simple enough and she kept in good shape, so why not sign up for it? The pamphlet said that the winners would receive prizes, and while she didn't know what the prizes would be, maybe it would be something she could bring back to Gamgee. It wasn't like she'd be doing something crazy, since anybody could sign up, so why not go for it? Her smile widened as she thought about how exciting it would be to take part in a competition in a strange land. She could be a champion in multiple universes.

Checking the pamphlet again, she noticed that registration would take place between 1:00pm and 1:20pm, so she had plenty of time to kill before then. Her eyes went to the other pamphlet in her hand, the one about the museum. There was a small map on the back with instructions on how to find it, and a few review quotes saying how interesting and detailed the museum was. Shrugging to herself, Cassidy decided that she might as well head over there and try to figure out what exactly this world was all about.

CHAPTER THREE

The museum was smaller than she'd expected. It was on the same pedestrian street she'd entered the town through, but close to the crossroads. The building was a converted two-story house, painted white with red shutters and a red door. There was a quaint feeling about it, as if somewhere inside was a grandmother eager to invite you in for supper. A sign was hung over the door, but it was simply two words (both unknown to her), and other than some kind of 'hours of operation' sign, there was nothing else to give her a clue about the contents within. When Cassidy had first looked at it she'd imagined some kind of quaint tea shop or maybe a private club.

When she walked through the front door she found herself in a small entryway, probably the former front porch, with entryways to the left and right. There was a staircase in front of her, cordoned off with a rope barrier that likely led to the second floor. A desk was to her right and she was quickly greeted by the person sitting behind it, brown-skinned with short dark hair, wearing a white button-up shirt.

"Glædlig Landingsdag," they said cheerfully, smiling

widely.

Cassidy nodded and smiled. There was a word in there that sounded like 'landing,' and since she knew today was something called Landing Day she assumed that this was a greeting she'd hear a lot today.

"Hello," she said, before the person could say anything else, being careful to sound as Anglophone as possible. Cassidy could speak other languages, but these two were something she'd never come across before, and it was a relief that people seemed fluent in English here. She made a mental note to find some pamphlets with these languages to take home and see if they had any resemblance to anything back on her world.

The person at the desk nodded and switched to an accented English, giving Cassidy a brief introduction to the museum, telling her how it had been built hundreds of years ago to house the story of this town and to collect important artifacts back from the first landing in the 10th century. Normally they requested a small fee to view the history, in order to maintain the house, but on Landing Day entry was free and all were welcome. Once the spiel was over, the person also recommended that Cassidy start with the door on the right.

Cassidy thanked them for the information and walked past the desk, heading into the room to the right. It was a large room, probably a former living room or dining room. There was an introductory plaque with information in three languages, which she soon learned were Danish, Beothuk, and English. The first two were the official languages of the island, and the last was the most common tourist language. As Cassidy continued to read she learned that the town she was in was called Vandby, and that it was on the island of Vinland, which was a region of Denmark. The town had been built close to the original landing site of the Vikings, yet far enough away that they could preserve what remained of the site.

Pausing to recall what she could of Viking history back in her world, she figured that the splitting point for the timelines seemed to be when the Vikings first landed on this island. In this world it seemed that the Vikings and the indigenous peoples got along rather well and were able to co-exist in harmony with each other. As time passed, more Vikings settled here, building towns along the vast coastline, and eventually they began to intermingle with the indigenous peoples. Cassidy couldn't help smiling as she wondered what it must have been like for the British when they 'discovered' this island hundreds of years later, only to find out Vikings had already settled here.

Moving through the museum, she read about how this island was shaped and changed by this harmony between the two peoples, and how it eventually came to join the country of Denmark. Cassidy felt an itch to get her hands on a history book to see how the rest of the world had changed because of this. Were there countries that no longer existed? Had new countries been formed? What kind of ripple effects had this one change created? Or were there other changes from earlier that had led to this?

She paused to think about all the ways the world would be different if only 'B' had happened instead of 'A.' The possibilities were endless. Perhaps that was why there were so many portals — they all led to worlds where the paths had diverged and changed.

Focusing back on the world she was in, she looked over all the artifacts, which were mainly personal effects and tools. There were maps and drawings to help add a visual element to the history and timeline. Eventually she made it to the final room. There were more pictures along the walls, but in the middle of the room was a pillar holding a statue in a glass box. The pillar was encircled by a rope barrier, which she found strange, since nothing else had been barred off, other than the staircase. She immediately drew closer to the glass box, curious.

The statue inside consisted of two pieces of wood, one light brown and the other red, intertwined in an intricate way. It seemed to be made of four pieces of wood, two of each kind, that spiralled upward and around each other. The piece was about four inches in diameter at the bottom and eight inches high. About halfway up, one side started to slant inward while the other remained straight, and when it reached the top the spiral became thick and flat. The top then curved downward, creating a kind of loop, thinning out even more as it reached the bottom, where the small strands created a braid that encircled the base. The ends of the braid seemed to disappear into the base, creating the illusion that this was all one piece. Cassidy couldn't imagine anyone carving something so intricate and wondered if the wood had somehow been designed to grow that way.

Moving over to the display on the wall, she read about how this statue was hundreds of years old and was one of three that had been created to symbolize the understanding and respect that existed between the indigenous peoples and the Vikings. It was called Harmony, and the other two, Unity, and Peace, were in other cities on the island. It didn't say anything about how the artifact had been created, but mentioned that the light brown teak wood was from a tree popular in Denmark and the red wood was pine from this island which had been dyed with red ochre, an important pigment to the Beothuk. A few close up pictures showed that there were carvings in the wood — runes carved into the pine and geometric designs carved into the teak. The display gave a loose translation of what the carvings meant, which was some kind of retelling of the first landing from both perspectives.

Even though there were pictures, Cassidy felt the desire to leap over the rope barrier and remove the glass box so that she could get a closer look at the artifact. She'd never do such a thing, as it'd surely end with her being forcibly removed from the building, but her hands itched to get closer. Nothing like this existed on her world. And knowing that it had been created centuries ago made her want to examine it thoroughly.

A thought formed in her mind and she pressed her lips together, suppressing a smile. Perhaps there was a way that she could get a better look at the statue without involving the local authorities. Glancing around the room, she started taking note of the security measure around the museum. There were no cameras that she could see, and she couldn't find any sensors along the walls. The windows seemed to be reinforced and nailed shut, but not barred. If the rest of the museum had the same lax security measures then maybe she could wait until nightfall, sneak in, and get a good look at the artifact on her own terms.

Just the thought of sneaking in after dark and having the place all to herself started to get her heart pumping and she felt a familiar tingle in her fingertips. Perhaps it was the relative safety of this world, but she felt like she could do anything. It wasn't like she'd be around to deal with the consequences, after all.

It would be risky, but she liked risk. And there wasn't much else in this town to get her blood pumping. Sneaking into a museum after dark seemed like just the thing to make this trip more interesting.

CHAPTER FOUR

After finishing up her reconnaissance of the museum's security measures, Cassidy realized that the registration for the tournament had opened up, so she quickly made her way back to the field. It was a great day for an outdoor festival. The air was crisp with a cool breeze, the sun was high in the sky and there were only a few fluffy white clouds floating around. She noticed that a lot more people had gathered around the field, eating and drinking and talking excitedly. Perhaps it was the energy of the crowd or the beautiful weather, but she could feel her excitement rising.

Looking past the Information Booth, she spotted a tent that said 'Sign-Up' in numerous languages and made her way over to it. She wondered what Gamgee would say when he found out that she'd spent part of her time in this world playing games. Then again, he hadn't given her a specific item to find or task to do, so why shouldn't she get to enjoy herself? Considering where this town was located, there wasn't much that she could do. She could see the original landing site, but suspected that it wouldn't be much different from the one back on her world. And there was no point in renting a car and driving all the way to the other side of the island. Not only would it take almost half a day of driving just to get there, but there was no guarantee that she'd find anything more interesting over there than she could find here.

She also felt nervous about straying too far from the portal. If the weather changed it'd be too dangerous to climb down the cliff and she'd be stuck here for however long it took the weather to change back. If she wasn't on her world by midnight, the professor would think that she'd run into trouble, and if she didn't show up for a couple days then the professor would probably think she wasn't coming back. It was much safer to stick around this town and take it all in. If she came back here a second time she'd try exploring further.

Making her way into the the sign-up tent, she joined the line of people wanting to compete. As she waited, her mind drifted towards the museum adventure she'd be having later tonight, but she quickly shook those thoughts away. Now wasn't the time to think about that – now was the time to get into the tournament headspace and prepare for what she was about to do. Even though nobody knew who she was, she didn't want to make a complete fool of herself by failing horribly.

"*Velkommen*," the person manning the sign-ups greeted her as she arrived at the front. The woman had fair skin, black hair, dark brown eyes, and a wide smile on her face. Cassidy wondered how long the woman had been politely greeting people and if she was getting tired of it yet. Cassidy knew that she'd be exhausted and frowning after twenty minutes, but this woman seemed to have endless cheer. Perhaps that was why she'd been placed here.

"Hello," Cassidy said politely. "I'm here to sign up for the tournament."

"Ah, yes. British?"

Cassidy nodded, figuring that it was safer than taking a chance and mentioning a country that might not exist.

"Your name?"

"Cassidy Cane."

"Your preferred languages?

"English, please." She briefly considered mentioning her other languages, but stopped because of the same reason — they might not exist in this world.

"And is this your first time competing?"

"Yes, it is."

The woman smiled again and nodded. "Once we have all the competitors signed up, we will divide you into groups by size. There will be a light-weight, middle-weight, and heavy-weight division, and each will have a top three rank, who will win prizes. Each division will compete at the same time, but you will be in different areas of the field. If you would like to read about the contests, there's more information over there." She pointed to the side of the booth, where there was a table with small piles of paper on it.

"Thank you," Cassidy said, before wandering over to the table. A few people were milling around nearby, with almost twenty other people inside and around the tent. She briefly wondered which people would end up in her weight class before turning her thoughts back to the contests. After she figured out what each of the competitions involved, then she'd start sizing up the competition.

Picking up one of the papers, she saw that there were five competitions: axe throwing, stone throwing, archery, tug-of-war, and wrestling. They were all based on traditional island games that were played in the past. The descriptions weren't very in-depth, but from what she could make out they seemed similar to the kinds of activities she liked to take part in. As long as the games didn't involved turning into lobsters or using psychic powers, she should do quite well.

After a few more minutes, registration was closed and the volunteers were instructed to gather together. The organizers started calling out the names for each group, usually in a couple different languages. Cassidy had a feeling that she'd be put in with the light-weights since she was a trim 5'3, and sure enough, she was. Five others were sorted into her group, bringing the total to six, while eight people were put in the middle-weight, and eight in the heavy-weight. She exchanged looks with her other competitors, smiling politely but ready to get on with it. Sizing up her competition, she had a feeling that a couple of the others could give her a run for her money, but didn't feel dismayed. She didn't want this to be too easy.

Once the groups were sorted and appointed a volunteer as their leader, they were led through a partition in the back of the tent and onto the field. The smell of freshly cut grass and fairground foods wafted through the air. The groups clustered at the back of the field as the tournament announcer introduced the event in multiple languages while the large crowd gathered in the stands cheered.

Finally, it was time to compete. Cassidy felt a surge

of energy as she made her way over to the archery set-up with the rest of her group, led by Karla, their team leader. Karla's expression was much more serious than the volunteer who'd signed her up, but Cassidy assumed it was warranted, since they'd all be playing around with sharp things soon enough.

The archery rules were fairly simple. They'd be shooting arrows at the target and would get points depending on how close to the centre each arrow fell. They would get one practice arrow, which wouldn't be counted, and which Cassidy was thankful for. These bows were wooden and of a basic design, and the arrowheads looked to be made of carved stone, like they would have been back in Viking times. Neither would be as easy to control as the modern bows and arrows she was more familiar with.

There was no assigned order, so the first person to shoot was the one who volunteered the fastest. If the equipment had been more familiar, Cassidy would have jumped right in, but she held back. She watched how the others handled the bow and arrows, hoping to pick up on a few tips. The target they were shooting at was a large circle with a small red bullseye in the centre, a blue circle around that, then a green circle, then a yellow, and then a white background. The young man who'd volunteered to go first seemed unperturbed by the rudimentary items and confidently took aim, hitting the blue for his practice shot. His next two shots were also in the blue, with the third one getting so close to the red that they had to bring a judge in to confirm that it was actually in the blue. It was obvious that this wasn't his first time competing. Cassidy paid careful attention to the way he held the bow and pulled the string back, and how much tension was in his arms.

She decided to go fourth, figuring that after watching a few more people shoot she'd be as ready as possible. When the wooden bow was placed in her hands, she felt she had a pretty good idea of what to do. Knocking an arrow, she centered it on the bow and pointed it at the target. Pulling the string back, she took in a breath and carefully aimed, pretending that she was back in the temple in Yucatan, trying to set off traps from a safe distance. Her accuracy during that adventure had been perfect, but she'd been using her own equipment.

Her first shot landed in the green, but it was only her practice shot and it was close to the blue. She readjusted, landing the next shot in the blue, much to her delight. Her next shot went in the blue again and her final was in the red, which was extremely satisfying. Nobody else had landed in the red yet, so she had that as a bragging right, even if she messed up everything else.

After the final person in her group finished shooting, they all received a round of applause from the audience. While volunteers in blue shirts took away the arrows, Karla informed the group that they'd be staying here for the axe-throwing. A volunteer brought in a basket of small handaxes as Karla informed them that the rules for this contest would be the same as the last — one practice throw and then the next three would be scored.

Cassidy preferred archery, but she'd thrown a few weapons on occasion, including an axe. Hers had been larger than what they were currently provided with, but she'd also been using hers more to distract and discourage the people chasing her than to actually hit them.

As before, she used her time to watch the other competitors and their technique in holding and throwing the axes, using it to give her an idea of what to do. When her turn came, she did her best, but it took her a while to get used to the weight of the axe and she only managed to get in the green and blue. Luckily her score was on par or better than the others. And she was still the only person in both rounds to have hit the red.

After this contest, Karla led them across the field, where a pile of strange large stones had been gathered. The stones were smooth and oval in shape, with holes in the middle of them, making them look like squashed donuts. Karla picked up one of the stones and demonstrated to the group the correct way to throw it. Standing with her left foot in front of her right and the stone held with her right hand around the shorter end, she swung it down along the right side of her body before bringing it back up. She swung it three times, building up momentum, and on the third time she let go, arcing it across the field. Cassidy had no idea if this was considered a good distance for a throw, but the form was beautiful. While the stone was being retrieved, Karla demonstrated the left-handed throwing style, only without releasing the stone. She let the group know that if they threw the stone any other way, their score would not be counted and they would not get a re-throw. They had two chances to throw, and the field would be cleared after each person's second attempt.

Cassidy went over the throwing technique in her head as she watched the others take their turns. By the time it was her turn to throw, she realized that she hadn't been paying attention to where the stones had landed and had no clue what distance she was trying to beat. All she could do at this point was try her best. And if she was terrible at this round, at least she could think back on her awesome archery skills.

Wiping her hands on her jeans, she picked up a stone, planted her feet, and threw the stone as far as she could. After her second throw, she still had no idea how well she'd done, but at least she hadn't accidentally hit herself in the leg with it or let go of it while it was behind her. One of the throwers after her let go of the stone too soon, and cried out in annoyance as it flew only a few feet before thudding to the ground. Luckily he had a good humour about it, raising his arms in triumph as the crowd chuckled.

Soon the third contest was over and there were only two more to go.

As the group moved on to the next contest, Cassidy noticed that most of them were more focused on winning than being congenial; spending their time psyching themselves up for the task at hand. Two of the group were laughing and chatting with each other, not worried about winning or even scoring highly, but they seemed to be the outliers. Cassidy was just as determined as the former, but she made sure to occasionally smile politely to the other two, just to be nice.

Gathering around the wrestling circle, Karla explained that they wouldn't have to fight everyone else in the group. Instead they would each have two fights, with the people closest to their own apparent size and strength. Staying within the wrestling circle, they were to try and wrestle their opponent to the ground, getting both of their shoulders to touch the ground. If one of them was to step out of the circle twice then they'd both be eliminated, meaning that each of them would have to do their best to stay within the circle. As she looked at the circle, which had been sprayed onto the grass, Cassidy's competitive side quickly rose to the surface, and she had to stop a wide smile from breaking out across her face. Archery and throwing things was fun, but there was something about one-on-one competitions that made winning more satisfactory. Although she hated to lose, she had no problem being bested by someone who was genuinely better than her.

She was on the lower end of the weight class, and the way that the rounds worked out, she would be fighting first and second last. Normally she'd prefer to watch her opponent fight someone else, to get an idea of what their style was like, but she didn't have a choice in this matter.

Standing in the circle, she bent her knees and crouched down to lower her centre of gravity. Her opponent was a young man with roughly the same build as her, and one of the two men who still had a sense of humour about these games. When the whistle blew they both sprang into action, quickly ending up in a grapple. Cassidy turned and threw the man to the side, but there wasn't enough force to send him to the ground, only to break the grapple. She stayed low and waited for him to attack. He rushed forward, preparing to grapple again, but she side-stepped him and used his own momentum to throw him to the ground and quickly pin his shoulders down. After Karla declared her the winner, Cassidy held out a hand to her opponent to help him up, which he took.

"Good fight," he said once he was on his feet, smiling at her.

"Same," she replied, returning the smile.

Two new competitors stepped into the circle, one of which was Cassidy's next opponent. She watched carefully, hoping to glean some information about the woman's fighting style. The match lasted longer than Cassidy's had, but ended with her future opponent winning. The rest of the matches were about the same length, although one barely lasted ten seconds.

When it was time for Cassidy to get back in the circle, she stepped inside and immediately took a low stance. Her opponent was the kind of person who took these games seriously, so she knew that this match wouldn't be as easy as her first one — unless one of them slipped up. Her opponent was a woman who was marginally shorter but more built, and her starting stance was also a low one. When the fight started they rushed into a grapple, but neither seemed to be getting the upper hand. They were both too grounded for the other person to knock to the ground. The grapple broke and they backed up. Cassidy tried to think of a new plan of action, but didn't have much time before her opponent rushed at her. Cassidy tried the same move from before, but her opponent seemed to have been expecting it and tried to reverse it. Cassidy stumbled back, dropping to one knee, but didn't fall. Her opponent came for her, but Cassidy quickly rose, moving to the side and away from the attack.

The match was looking to be one of the longest in their group, with no clue yet as to who would be the winner. After a few more unsuccessful grapples, Cassidy knew that she needed to take a risk if she wanted to win this. The next time they met in a grapple, she dropped low to the ground, throwing her opponent over her. Landing on her side, Cassidy was careful not to accidentally touch both shoulders to the ground. She turned and lunged for her opponent, who had also landed on her side. Grabbing the woman's shoulders and pushing them the ground, Cassidy couldn't help feeling elated. A win was great, but a hard earned win somehow felt even better.

Her opponent looked displeased, but took the hand Cassidy offered and thanked her for the match. Cassidy kept her smile to an appropriately humble size, and thanked her opponent before falling back in line to watch the final match. It was hard for her to concentrate, though, as her mind was trying to tally up where she might be in the standings for her group. As far as she could tell, she was headed for a podium finish, provided on how she performed in the final round.

The last contest was tug-of-war, but it wasn't exactly like she'd ever played before. It would be person against person, with two matches each — against the same two people as the wrestling matches. But instead of standing up, they'd be sitting down, facing each other, with their feet pressed up against a short wooden board that had been topped with foam. The goal was to try and pull the flag that was on the middle of the rope towards yourself, and maybe your opponent as well.

"Let's have a good match, eh?" her first opponent, the man she'd pinned in wrestling, said.

Smiling, she nodded, glad that he would be her first match. It was daunting to go first in a game she'd never played, but her upper body strength was good and that's what she'd mostly be relying on. Sitting on the ground, she placed her feet against the board and grabbed the rope, readying herself.

When the match started, her opponent put up a good fight, apparently being better at tug of war than wrestling. However, he couldn't help losing small increments at a time until, eventually, the flag was over on Cassidy's side.

"Good match?" she asked him as they walked back to their group, breathing heavily.

"Quite good," he replied. "You gave a good fight."

His attitude reminded her of an old friend from university that she used to train with. No matter how often something went wrong, a smile always founds its way on his face. He looked at every failure as an opportunity to learn and refused to let a bad day stop him from achieving his goal. When he won, he was graceful and humble, thanking opponents for a good match, and if he lost, he was just as graceful. The training room always felt better when he was around.

Watching the other matches, Cassidy noticed that most of them were lost by the rope slipping through someone's fingers. Only one match, the one right before her second, was lost when one of the opponents was pulled over the board, landing on their side. It was at that moment Cassidy realized why the foam was on top, so it could help cushion the blow if someone happened to smack into it. Although the person seemed fine, she resolved to try not to let that happen to herself.

Her opponent had a determined look in her eyes as

they took their places, and Cassidy knew that this would be a tough fight. The worst part about competing with someone you'd just bested was that the previous defeat was still fresh in their mind, and they were ten times more determined to beat you. Planting her feet firmly, Cassidy gripped the rope tightly and waited for the inevitable starting whistle.

The first few seconds were a deadlock, the flag hovering over the centre, moving only the slightest either way. Cassidy could feel her muscles straining as she pulled, trying not to lose any ground. She thought of all those hours she'd spent working out and honing her skills so that she could climb cliffs and balance on thin rope bridges, cut her way through jungle vines and dodge traps. There was no way she was going to lose this. The only problem was that her opponent seemed equally as determined.

They both strained against the other's strength, sweat beading on their foreheads. If a person managed to gain a little ground, it wasn't long before the other gained it back. For a second, Cassidy wondered if this match would last forever and if she'd be trapped here in this eternal deadlock for all time. As they continued to pull, Cassidy could feel herself starting to lose ground and not winning it back. Her opponent was strong, and Cassidy could feel her arm and back muscles crying out in pain. If she stood any chance of winning, she'd have to bring something else to the fight. Allowing her knees to buckle slightly, she leaned back, lowering the angle of the rope, before trying to straighten out her legs. Her hope was that the sudden change in the rope's position, paired with the combination of her arm and leg muscles working together, would be enough to win, and it almost was. Her opponent lurched forward, losing precious inches of the rope, but stopping herself from going over the board. She was now trapped in a position where her shoulders were almost past her knees, but still wasn't ready to give up. Cassidy knew that she couldn't risk losing this momentum and she leaned further back, promising her body that once this was over she'd stay away from playing tug-of-war for a long, long time. After a few strained moments, her opponent toppled over, letting go of the rope and sending Cassidy to the ground. Cassidy's muscles cried out in pain and she knew that she'd have to take it easy for the next little while, but then the roar of the crowd filled her ears and she knew that it had been worth it.

Once all the contests were wrapped up, the competitors headed back to the sign-up tent, which had been transformed into a kind of waiting area, complete with water, juice, and pastries. They were told to wait while the judges tallied up the scores and prepared to announce the winners. As Cassidy took a bite of one of the fruit-filled pastries, she came to the conclusion that even if she'd come in dead last, it would be worth competing just for the food. Watching her first opponent take a large bite out of a chocolate concoction, she suddenly understood why he was so jovial despite not doing very well. He had this tournament all figured out.

When the scores were finalized, the competitors were brought out to the field again and greeted with a large cheer from the crowd. The announcer thanked all of the competitors and then announced the winners, starting with the light-weights. Third place went to the woman she'd fought so hard against, and after second went to a man who'd excelled at the last two contests, Cassidy couldn't help feeling her hopes rising. When they called out her name as the first place winner, she felt proud. Taking her place next to the other two, she bowed her head in thanks as she was given a medal and something that looked like a thin, sheathed knife. Looking out over the crowd, she was filled with a warm glow of accomplishment. Not too bad for someone who'd only appeared on this world a few hours ago.

CHAPTER FIVE

After all of the other winners had been declared, the tournament ended and people started wandering away from the field. People Cassidy didn't know congratulated her on her win, and she gave them all a polite smile as she made her way over to a quiet area outside the field where she could examine her prizes in detail. The medal was round and had a large '1' on it, with some words in the native language. Although she doubted that it was made of gold, it looked like it could be gold-plated. Or maybe it was made of some kind of strange material that only existed on this planet.

Moving on to the next prize, she carefully withdrew the knife from the sheath. It was one foot long and quite thin, only about an inch and a half at the thickest part, drawing to a point at the end. Carefully testing the edge, she realized that it was quite dull and was likely intended to be a decoration instead of an actual weapon. The blade wasn't perfect and seemed to be pounded into shape instead of mass-produced, but it had character to it. The sheath had two pieces of leather coming off the side with a loop at the end, one near the tip and one near the handle, and she supposed that it was intended to be worn with the knife parallel to the ground. The handle was wooden with a large, round metal cap on the end. Giving the metal cap a closer look she saw that some kind of strange rock had been set into it. The rock was the size of a quarter, but it had a quartz-like structure to it and was the kind of black that shone in brilliant colours whenever the light hit it. It was mesmerizing.

Holding the knife, she figured that this would be a sufficient enough relic to bring back. She didn't know what Gamgee would do with a dull blade or a strange rock, but he'd probably have some fun trying to figure out what everything was made of. She decided she should also pick up a book or two on the history of this world, so that they could learn more in case they ever wanted to come back. She had a feeling that Gamgee would appreciate something more than her second-hand knowledge from her visit to the museum.

A smile crossed her face — the museum. There was no way she'd leave this world without getting a closer look at the artifact. After all, she was an archeologist and it was her duty to find strange objects and learn whatever she could about them. She'd be doing her profession a disservice by walking away from something so intricate.

Tucking the knife and medal carefully into her backpack, she came up with a game plan. It was late afternoon now and the museum didn't close until 6pm. It would be best for her to wait until dark, when things quieted down in that area of the city, before going ahead with her plan, which left her lots of time to buy a book or two and maybe find a bit of supper. Of course, she'd need some money to pay for those things, and she didn't have any of the local currency on hand. Hopefully this town had a pawn shop close by.

She decided to head back to the information tent, as they'd already proven to be helpful. She didn't want to ask a random stranger, because there was a chance they'd watched her win the competition and she didn't want them to think that she was immediately trying to hock her prizes. She hoped that the people working the information booth had been too busy working to watch the tournament.

Although the games were over for the day, the information booth was still being maintained. Thinking back to the pamphlet she'd read earlier, Cassidy recalled that the day's events would be brought to an end with fireworks after darkness fell. Everyone was invited to gather at the field to watch together, and Cassidy wondered if the other booths would be open that late, selling food and souvenirs. A sudden thought hit her — the fireworks! That would be a great time to break into the museum, when everyone else's attention was towards the sky. She quickly filed that piece of information away for later.

The same person who'd helped her earlier took out a small paper map of the central part of the city and marked a pawn shop, a couple bookstores, and a few restaurants for her. Cassidy thanked her and headed off.

A few minutes later, she found a shop with a large window full of a variety of items. It was mostly giftware, a bit of furniture, and a few musical instruments; some of which looked similar to things on her world. Other items looked like they'd been made by an artist that had been half-awake and blindfolded as someone else described an object. Going through the shop door, she heard a small tinkling sound announce her arrival and was immediately greeted with a musty smell. The man working the counter looked up from what he was doing and nodded at her. She nodded back before moving into the shop, taking in all the strange objects inside. There were a few things that she had no idea what they'd been meant for, but most of the objects looked antique — aka expensive — or not as interesting as the knife she'd won.

Curiosity satisfied, she walked over to the counter. "Hello," she said cheerfully. "English?"

The shopkeeper nodded. He pushed aside something that looked like a word puzzle, with half of the answers filled in. "How may I help you?" he asked, his accent thicker than any other she'd heard today.

"I'm looking to trade." She reached into one of the pockets of her backpack and took out a couple of gold coins that Gamgee had given her. "Do you take gold?" As she put the coins on the counter she hoped that gold existed in this world and that it was still worth a lot of money. If this world had an abundance of it, the value would be terrible. Should she have gone with silver instead?

The shopkeeper picked up one of the coins and examined it. "Well, I cannot give you much," he said. "Although I can tell that these are mostly gold," he squinted and brought the coin closer to his eyes, "seems to be some copper in there. I cannot tell where they come from or if they are of much value, so although I cannot place the country of origin, they look like something a trader might be interested in. Where did they come from?"

Cassidy shrugged. "Sorry, they were a gift from a friend overseas. Well, former friend," she added, hoping that would stop him from asking more questions.

"I can give you this," he counted out some bills and placed them on the table. Cassidy picked them up and counted them, still unsure what the currency was like over here. But it seemed like a good amount, and the shopkeeper seemed honest enough, and she thought it should at least get her some supper.

"Seems fair," she said, and they made the exchange. "Oh, could I ask you a question?" she added.

He frowned but then nodded, so she took that as a yes.

She reached into her backpack again. "I'm not looking to sell this, but could you tell me something about the rock in the handle?" She took out the knife, still in its sheath, and held it towards him.

A slight smile crossed his face. "Ah, an ornamental Viking Seax..." He leaned in closer to look at the handle. "That is a piece of a space rock. Every few years or so a couple fall from the sky. Scientists have studied them a lot, so the rest get used for ornamentation or decoration. Mostly jewelry. It's not worth a lot."

Her mind started racing a million miles an hour. Meteorites fell from the sky every few years? And in such supply that they were no longer something amazing but instead were almost as common as ordinary rocks? What kind of crazy world was this? Did they feel like dinosaurs with all the space rocks falling down? Did dinosaurs exist on this planet millions of years ago? She had so many questions she wanted to ask, but didn't want to push her luck with the shopkeeper's patience.

"That's what I thought," she bluffed, returning the knife to her backpack. "Thank you. Happy Landing Day."

He grunted a goodbye before turning back to his puzzle, and she quickly walked back onto the street.

***

An hour later she was in a pub, planning the museum break-in while she waited for her meal. She'd chosen a pub for dinner because she knew the food would be affordable, but also because it was likely to be loud and crowded enough that nobody would pay her much attention. A few people had recognized her from the tournament and congratulated her as she walked in, but after that she'd mostly been left alone. The pub was styled like an old cottage, with large wooden beams and a few fireplaces. It had a cozy feel to it, with low lighting and well-worn furniture, but it was boisterous enough to keep her on her toes.

After finding a seat near the back and placing her order, she'd set about rummaging through her backpack, looking for items that could be of use during the break-in. There wasn't a lot of room left in there, as she'd ended up purchasing three books instead of the one she'd been planning on buying. After looking at the prices of the books, she realized that the gold coins had fetched her enough to buy more than she'd anticipated. Figuring that it'd be better to be safe than sorry, she purchased an English-language history book and two more books, one in each of the regional languages. Setting the books aside for the moment, she continued taking stock of her supplies.

She quickly found a lockpick, penlight, and camera, and placed them in pockets where they'd be easily accessible.

The server arrived with her meal, interrupting her thoughts, and Cassidy quickly put everything back in her backpack and set it aside. For a second she couldn't remember what she'd ordered, but then saw that it was some kind of cold chicken sandwich with pickled vegetables on a strange kind of bread with a side of fries. She wasn't too sure about it, but it had a star next to it on the menu, signifying that it was one of their most popular dishes.

Eyeing the sandwich thoughtfully, she picked out one of the vegetables and tested it. It was crisp and slightly pickled but also sweet. The flavour reminded her of a banh mi, so she picked up the sandwich and took a bite. It was quite delicious. The spice mix was unfamiliar, but it worked with the cold ingredients.

Finishing the sandwich, she took her time munching on the fries and going over the steps of her plan in her head. During her examination of the museum she'd noticed a back door, which would be the best way to sneak in as there'd be fewer passersby, and she could take her time unlocking the door. The penlight would provide a concentrated beam of light and wouldn't be as obvious as a flashlight, but she'd still have to be careful about where she shone it and would have to use it sparingly. Once she reached the artifact, it'd be best to take it to a different room, where her examination wouldn't be noticed by anyone walking by.

A voice in the back of her head said that if sneaking into the museum was going to be so easy, then it should be just as easy to take the artifact and bring it back to her world. They had two others on the island, after all, so would they really miss this one?

Giving herself a mental shake, she tried to bring her thoughts back to the plan. Normally her modus operandi was to recover lost items, not to steal them. But it wasn't like she could stay here and pretend to be a historian who needed to study the artifact. Maybe if she 'borrowed' it and brought it home to study it more in-depth, she could bring it back a few days later. Sneak it back during the dead of night, maybe with a little 'sorry' sticker on it. That wouldn't be so bad. Would it?

By the time her meal was finished, she still had a couple of hours before the fireworks, so when the server came by to take her empty plate, Cassidy ordered a cup of coffee. Her day was going to be a late one, so it wouldn't hurt to have more caffeine in her system.

CHAPTER SIX

The sky had grown dark, but the city was still alive with celebration. After Cassidy finished her second cup of coffee, she left the pub, which was now almost full of patrons. She wandered around the town for a little while, admiring the architecture while getting an idea of how crowded the streets would be this time of night. Most of the people she saw were heading towards the field, and as she made her way towards the museum, she saw fewer and fewer people around.

Turning onto the pedestrian street where the museum was located, she was pleased to see that there was only one other person in view. They were moving at a quick pace towards the other end of the street, and Cassidy wondered what they could be hurrying towards. There was only the park, forest, and cliffside at that end. Perhaps the fireworks were visible from the cliffside, and the person was hurrying to get a good seat? Whatever it was, at least they'd soon be out of sight and the street empty except for her.

As she walked past the museum, she double-checked that the lights were out and that nobody was inside. That was something she hadn't considered before now, that there might be a security guard on duty, but luckily there was nobody around. She wondered what the crime rates for this area must have been like, for there to be such lax security. Did nobody ever steal anything in this world?

Most of the buildings on the street were pressed up against each other, but because of the museum's older design it had a small alleyway beside it. After making sure that nobody was around to see her, Cassidy slipped into the alley and made her way to the back of the museum. There was a large fence separating this area from the other houses, and when she looked around there were no lights on in any of the windows that she could see. Everyone was probably at the field by now.

Making her way over to the door, she heard the first sounds of fireworks exploding in the air and knew that it was time to get moving. There were two locks on the back door, one on the door handle and one that was a deadbolt. The deadbolt would be more difficult to pick, but it wouldn't be impossible. Luckily, working with Gamgee meant that she could get the best supplies and not have to resort to hairpins.

She quickly opened the lock on the handle, all the while keeping an ear out for anyone who might be close by. There wasn't much light back here, other than the moonlight and occasional glow from the fireworks, but if someone was to stumble through and find her back here, she'd have a heck of a lot of explaining to do. Moving up to the deadbolt, she noticed that it was already unlocked. The employees must have forgotten to lock it, which was lucky for her. This town really was a thief's paradise.

Slowly opening the door, Cassidy tried to stop it from creaking as she slipped into the museum. Closing the door behind her, she noticed that there was also a chain lock hanging lazily next to the door. Shaking her head, she wondered if she should leave a note for the employees to be better about locking up at night. Not that a chain lock would have stopped her, but it would have taken her much longer to break in if she'd had to tangle with a deadbolt and a chain, and too many deterrents could make a person think that something wouldn't be worth the trouble.

With the door closed, there wasn't much light, so she paused to let her eyes adjust to the darkness. She wasn't yet in the museum proper — it was more like an enclosed porch with stairs to her right that led down, and another door on her left.

She cautiously walked forward, stepping lightly on the floor, and tried the handle for the door. The handle turned easily and she almost laughed out loud. Other than the artifact, there wasn't much in this museum worth stealing, but she still thought it'd be harder than this. Maybe they had figured that since there were two more copies of the artifact, they didn't have to put that much effort into protecting this one. And if that were the case, maybe nobody would mind if she happened to borrow it for a few days...

Keeping her mind on the task, she carefully stepped into the museum, waiting to hear if there were any alarms that might alert someone to her presence. During her earlier visit she hadn't seen any motion sensors, alarms, or other security systems, but it was possible that they might be hidden and would set off if anyone came nearby. Luckily, it was silent except for her breathing and the occasional muffled firework. Moving quietly and carefully, she headed straight for the artifact, not paying attention to anything else in the museum. The room with the artifact had two windows facing the street, both tall and rectangular. She paused to look out, but from this distance she could only see an empty street. Some light came in through the windows, but it didn't fall far inside the room, and the centre area where the pedestal was located was far enough away from the light to not be touched by it.

Cassidy crept up to the pedestal, being careful not to get too close because of the rope barrier. When she figured she was near enough, she stood with her back to the window and used her penlight to locate the rope and cautiously step over it. Then she used the concentrated beam of light to look at the bottom of the glass box on the pedestal, shaking her head as she noticed that there was nothing holding it in place. There were no screws or grips, or anything else that might make this job even the slightest bit harder. Maybe they wanted her to get a close up view of this statue. Pocketing the penlight, she put her hands on opposite corners of the glass, being careful not to leave handprints, and lifted it up and over. She placed the glass carefully on the floor and turned back to the artifact.

There was nothing there.

Her body froze, her hands half-way to where the statue had been sitting just hours ago. Taking out her penlight she flashed it over the area where the artifact should have been, but there was nothing but empty space. She wondered if perhaps the statue was some kind of illusion that was only visible inside the box, but that seemed like a lot of effort for a simple museum. Earlier it had looked like a real object, not some kind of trick of the mind, so where was it? Did they lock it up at the end of the day? Was that why the security was such a joke?

Her mind raced. What should she do now? The best action would be to put the glass back on and get the heck out of here. Obviously she'd been outsmarted by the employees, and although she could probably wander through this building to her heart's delight, it would be best to cut her losses and head back through the portal. It was growing late, after all, and the fireworks had died down a few minutes ago.

She bent down to pick up the glass box, but before she could grab hold of it a loud noise startled her. Doors slammed open and light flooded the room, almost blinding her. Cassidy instantly stood up straight as people in dark uniforms raced into the room, surrounding her.

CHAPTER SEVEN

"Stop what you're doing!"

"Put your hands up!"

"Stay where you are!"

The orders came from everywhere as eight people in dark uniforms surrounded her, pointing weapons at her. Cassidy obediently put her hands in the air, her eyes sweeping the bright room as her mind calculated if there was a way out of this. The people surrounding her were all wearing uniforms with badges on them. Had she missed a silent alarm?

"I'm sorry," she said, her eyes still adjusting to the light. "I'll leave right away. I promise."

"You aren't going anywhere," one of them said, in almost perfect English. "You're under arrest for the theft of the Artifact of Harmony."

Cassidy frowned. "Wait. What?"

"You are under arrest for the theft of the Artifact of Harmony," the woman repeated, her voice tinged with impatience. "Please co-operate or we will be forced to—"

"Hold on!" Cassidy interrupted, still holding her hands in the air. "I didn't steal the statue. It was gone when I came in."

The other officers looked confused, but the woman who'd spoken continued her steely gaze. She was older, with grey streaks in her short brown hair, but her body looked broad and strong. Judging by the number of stripes on her uniform, she was a higher rank than the other officers, maybe even the captain.

"It's gone because you stole it," the captain replied, her voice filled with conviction.

"If I stole it, where is it?" Cassidy countered.

"In your backpack."

"Check it."

The captain looked uncertain, but then she turned to a young officer standing next to her and nodded at him. He put his weapon away and walked over to Cassidy, taking hold of her backpack. It was a strange and awkward dance as Cassidy tried to slip out of the backpack while keeping her hands in the air and in plain sight. She hoped that she could put her arms down once she was proven innocent. Television shows always underplayed how exhausting it was to hold your hands in the air for a long period of time.

The officer rummaged through her backpack, and although she couldn't see him, she could hear him making a few curious noises, probably trying to make sense of everything she'd stuffed in there.

While she waited, Cassidy wondered what her next move should be. At first she'd wanted to run out of here, but that was before she'd been accused of a crime she hadn't committed. Sure, stealing the artifact had crossed her mind more than once today, but it had been missing before she'd arrived, and she'd be darned if she was going to be accused of a crime she hadn't committed.

The officer walked over to the captain, holding out the backpack. He sighed and shook his head. "It's not in here, Captain."

"Then she hid it somewhere," the captain replied.

"And then I went back to replace the glass?" Cassidy shook her head. "It'd make more sense to replace it right after taking the statue from the pedestal or to leave it on the floor and get out quickly."

Her words made the captain frown, and she hoped it was because they made sense.

"You talk like a thief," the captain said.

"But on this occasion I'm not. I only wanted a closer look, honest. I wanted to study it. I'm an archeologist."

"You could have applied to the museum for a permit," the man holding her backpack replied.

Cassidy nodded. "I'll be sure to remember that next time."

"No matter what," the captain said, her voice filled with authority. "You have been caught breaking into the museum and an artifact has been discovered missing. You will have to accompany us to the police station for processing."

Cassidy's mind raced as she felt panic creeping up inside of her. She couldn't get arrested. If they put her behind bars, how could she prove that she was innocent? And, more importantly, how long would it take before they figured out that she wasn't from here?

"Look," she said firmly, "I didn't steal the artifact, but I can help you find it. Just give me the chance to clear my name and I'll see to it that you get your artifact back."

"We don't even know your name," the young officer said.

"Cassidy Cane," she replied. "It's a great name, and one I'd hate to see tarnished by false accusations."

The captain shook her head. "Even if I allowed that, there's still the breaking and entering."

"Fair enough. Honestly, I have no qualms about being accused of a crime I committed, but I didn't steal anything. And the longer you fight with me, the more time the actual thief has to get away with your artifact."

The captain paused to think. After a while, the officer on the other side of her whispered, "Are you seriously considering this, Captain?"

"She doesn't have the artifact on her," the captain answered in a low voice. "If she'd stolen it, where is it? Why is she here and not the artifact?"

The other officer tried to think of a reply, but wasn't able to say anything.

"All of you can leave," the captain said. "Jensen, you stay."

The other officers looked confused and surprised, but everyone obeyed the order. Six of the eight officers filed out of the museum, leaving Cassidy, the captain, and the man holding her backpack —whose name was apparently Jensen — behind.

The captain put her weapon away, but she left the holster open so that she could reach it quickly if needed.

"You can put your arms down," the captain said to Cassidy, "but don't try anything funny. We don't like to use weapons, but if I have to take you down, I will."

Cassidy nodded and lowered her arms. Something in the captain's voice told her that the woman wasn't kidding, so she stayed where she was. If she could gain these people's trust, it would be a big step towards clearing her name and getting out of here without going to jail.

Now that the immediate threat of being arrested or shot was gone, Cassidy could focus on the more important subject — where was the artifact and who took it?

"If I might ask a question," Cassidy started carefully, not wanting to step on any toes, "was the artifact definitely on this podium when the museum closed up for the night? Or was it stored in a vault or in another room?"

The captain paused. "I'll have someone contact the employees who closed and check on that."

"Oh, and could you ask them if they'd locked the back entrance?" Cassidy added. "The deadbolt and chain lock were open when I arrived."

The captain gave her a strange look, but then she took out a radio and called her orders back to the station.

Cassidy glanced around the room, trying to see if there were any clues that might prove she wasn't the thief. She didn't see any visible footprints or dirt tracked around the floor, but even if there had been any, the police raid would have made it impossible to tell which tracks belonged to who. Turning to the pedestal, she looked for anything that might have been accidentally dropped on the floor, but all she noticed was some smudging on the glass box. When she'd lifted it she'd only touched the edges, but there was one smudge right in the centre of the glass on the side, and another on the opposite side. Those definitely hadn't been there when she'd visited the museum earlier, and surely one of the employees would have cleaned it off if they'd noticed it after closing. It looked like someone with sweaty palms had lifted the glass. Not exactly a masterstroke of thievery.

While the captain continued talking to the station, Cassidy turned her attention to the young man. He had light brown skin, with brown hair cut regulation short, and his dark eyes regarded her curiously. He had the air of someone who hadn't been in the job for a long time, but definitely wasn't new to it.

"How did you know that I was in here?" Cassidy asked him. "Did I trip some kind of alarm?"

He shook his head. "We had a concerned citizen call us. They said that they'd noticed someone in the museum after hours and wanted the police to take a look."

Cassidy frowned. She'd glanced through one of the windows on her way to the alley and hadn't been able to see much more than shadows inside. She supposed that there was a possibility that someone could have noticed her moving around, but they'd have to have looked in at the right moment or have been watching for a while. Her luck must have been used up during the tournament. Unless...

"Did the concerned citizen who called you stick around? Did you meet up with them when you got here?"

Jensen shook his head. "There was nobody in the area when we got here, but that's not strange. Most people who call in tips leave before the police arrive."

He had a point, but she was starting to wonder if maybe the call hadn't been from a concerned citizen, but instead from someone hoping to pin a crime they'd committed on someone else. It was a fact that someone had been in the museum before her, and that this person would have a very good reason for calling the police and splitting before they got here. It was far-fetched, but it made more sense than a passerby getting lucky. If the thief noticed her coming in here, then they might have decided to stick around and call the cops once she was inside, framing her for the theft. And if that was the case, then the real thief might not be far away.

"The museum closed at six," she said, mostly speaking to herself. "It started to get dark around nine, and I came in at ten. It'd be risky for someone to break in during daylight, because anyone could see inside and call the cops, so they'd likely waited until after dark..." She paused. "So they may be close by after all..."

The captain finished with her radio, and informed them that the artifact had been left on the pedestal at the end of the day. They'd need to make a couple more calls to confirm about the locks, but that wasn't a priority, as they already knew that someone else had been in here. Cassidy quickly pointed out the marks on the glass, and explained that the real thief might still be close.

"We have to hurry," Cassidy said. "Every second we delay is more time for the thief to get away!"

She could see that the captain wanted to move but was also wrestling with the fact that she'd have to trust a stranger who'd already proven themselves to be untrustworthy.

"How do I know that you won't run away and leave us with nothing? In fact, how do I know that you weren't working with them?"

Cassidy knew she needed to be smart about her answers, and fast. "I'm not working with the thief because you caught me and not them. And if I *had* been working with them, I'd be extremely angry right now because they left me here to take the fall, so I'd want to find them out of pure spite. I have nothing but my word right not, but I know not to run away because you'll hunt me down and you kind of scare me."

For a second it looked like the captain was going to smile, but she quickly masked it. "Jensen, keep an eye on her and don't let her out of your sight for a second. If she somehow manages to find the artifact, call me immediately. You two do your thing, I'll conduct my own search, and hopefully the two will run together at the end."

When Cassidy looked over at Jensen she saw a surprised look on his face, but then his expression neutralized.

"Yes, Captain."

The captain nodded at him. Then she walked over to Cassidy and gave her a stern look, the kind that would turn most people into a quivering mess of fearfulness, before moving towards the pedestal. As she examined the glass box, she noticed that neither Cassidy nor Jensen had moved and turned to them.

"Well, get going already," she said. "I thought time was of the essence."

The two of them quickly obliged and hurried toward the exit.

CHAPTER EIGHT

"Well, where should we go first?" Jensen asked as the two of them stepped outside into the cool night air. He handed over her backpack. "Know of any secret thief hangouts in Vandby? Some kind of illicit black market?"

Cassidy shook her head. "Unfortunately not." She looked around the streets, trying to figure out where the thief might have gone after stealing the artifact. There weren't many people around, but she knew that the next street had some bars along it, and that it was sure to have people around, even with the fireworks. However, at the other end was the park and the forest.

She thought back to the smudged handprints on the glass. The thief been nervous about something, and nervous people usually tried to avoid crowds. If someone noticed that they were sweating or nervous, and asked if they were okay, and then there was a risk that the whole thing would fall apart. The woods were much safer.

Her eyes widened as she remembered the person hurrying towards the park just as she turned onto the street. She'd thought that the person had been running to see the fireworks, but what if it was because they'd just stolen something and were making a quick getaway? Maybe they'd looked back and saw her sneak behind the museum and decided to use that opportunity to call the police. Now that she thought about it, the forest would be a good place to hide out for a few hours or to hide the artifact in. Then the thief could wait until the heat died down and safely take the artifact somewhere else.

"I think we should go to the forest," she said to Jensen. "The city's full of people celebrating Landing Day, but there's probably not a lot of people in the forest."

"Sometimes kids hang out in the woods, but I guess most people would be near the field tonight," Jensen said, uncertainty tinging his voice. She worried that he might disagree, but then he motioned for her to start walking.

They walked in silence, being careful to check every alley they passed, just in case. It gave Cassidy time to wonder just how good of a cop Jensen was. He must be a good one, if the captain decided to let him watch her. Perhaps he was secretly as ruthless as the captain was.

"So, do you get a lot of people trying to steal the artifact?" she asked, in an attempt to make small talk.

He shook his head. "Most people understand that the artifact is very important, not just to this town, but to all the people who live on Vinland. That's why we spoke in English when we burst in, because we knew someone who lived here would never try to steal it."

"But aren't there two other artifacts in different towns? Why make such a fuss about this one?"

"There are, and those have never been stolen either." He gave her a pointed look. "If you'd studied the history of the artifact, you'd know that while it's a very beautiful piece, its importance is symbolic. When the Vikings first landed here, they never would have survived if it hadn't been for the help of the indigenous peoples. Could you imagine what would have happened if they'd decided to treat each other as hostile? How many needless lives would have been lost? These artifacts show that we are stronger together, and are a reminder that it's better to be peaceful and respectful."

"Is there a monetary value to the artifact?"

He shook his head again. "The woods that it's made of could easily be found elsewhere, and there are skilled carvers and artists all over the island that could make something similar, although it'd be a lot newer. Replicas can be bought as souvenirs in all shapes and sizes. In fact, I've got one." Reaching into his pocket, he pulled out a set of keys. After some shuffling, he held up a keychain that was the shape of the artifact but only an inch and a half high.

"Neat," Cassidy said, admiring the replica, but inside she was kicking herself for not looking closer at the souvenir stores. If she'd been smart and purchased a replica then she could have avoided this whole misunderstanding. ...Well... That wasn't entirely true. Most replicas weren't as detailed, so she'd probably still have found herself itching to get a look at the real thing. Perhaps getting caught by the police was an inevitability.

"So the artifact is really important to this town, huh?" she said as they walked.

"To some, yes," he replied. "There are a few superstitions around it, actually. Some say that if an artifact were to ever disappear then a terrible calamity would befall this island and it would be destroyed, sinking below the waves, never to be seen again."

"Wow. If that's the case, you should definitely get better security for it."

He frowned and turned to her, but when he noticed she was trying to make a joke, he relaxed a bit. "I'm sure that we'd be able to remain civilized even if it wasn't here. But I'm sure we'd all rather not test that theory."

Cassidy wanted to say that superstitions usually started somewhere, but figured it'd be better to keep silent.

"So what does a tournament champion want with our artifact anyway?" Jensen said, turning the conversation around to her.

"How did you...?"

"I watched the tournament before my shift started," he explained. "Plus I saw the knife and medal in your backpack when I was searching through it. So, what was your plan? Come here, win the tournament, steal the artifact, and hightail it out of here?"

"I wasn't going to steal it," Cassidy protested. "I wanted a closer look and I didn't know about appealing to the museum, so I made a stupid decision."

"Stupid is right."

"Or," she countered, "was it a great decision, because if I hadn't been there to take the fall, you never would have known about the theft until tomorrow morning, and the thief would probably be in another country by then."

He looked like he wanted to argue with her, but didn't end up saying anything, which she took as a win.

"So, did you always want to be a cop?" she asked.

"Mostly. Did you always want to be a thief — I mean, an archeologist?"

"Are you making fun of me?" she said, pretending to be aghast.

He smirked. "I can't arrest you yet, so I figured I'd mock you."

"Fair enough." His words reminded her that even if she helped find the artifact, they'd still want to bring her in for breaking into the museum. As soon as the real thief was discovered, she'd have to hightail it out of here.

They stepped out into the park, and after seeing that nobody was in the area, they headed for the forest. Cassidy wondered if the thief would risk taking one of the trails or if they'd be paranoid enough to blaze their own. Probably the latter.

"Look for any newly formed paths," she instructed Jensen. If they ended up not finding anything then they could go down a regular path.

It only took a few minutes before she spied an area with broken branches a few feet from the main trail entrance. Looking at one of the branches she saw that it was a new break. A wide smile broke out on her face. A nervous and paranoid thief was much easier to follow than a sly and logical one.

"This way," she instructed Jensen, and he obediently followed her. It occurred to her that she wasn't explaining her thought process, and that he wasn't asking her to explain. Was he able to pick up on her reasoning or was he simply following her blindly until finally, he'd had enough and felt like arresting her? Maybe if she didn't find the artifact in an hour, he'd knock her over the head and take her to the station. The captain hadn't given them a time limit, but Cassidy had a feeling that they wouldn't want to spend hours or days on this. Hopefully she was on the right path.

Jensen offered her a flashlight to light the way, which

she took as a good sign. He might arrest her after all this was over, but at least he was helping her now. Cassidy kept the flashlight focused on the ground, not wanting it to shine through the forest and give anyone notice that they were coming. Unfortunately, she couldn't do much about the branches and leaves that crunched under their feet. Her only comfort was that the thief had left an easy path to follow. As they walked, she continued to spy more broken branches and footsteps, letting those lead her way.

After ten minutes of walking, Cassidy and Jensen passed close to a group of six kids sitting around a lantern in an open area, passing around a bottle. They had been talking and laughing, so hadn't heard their incoming footfalls.

"Hey, you guys seen anyone come through here in the past while?" Cassidy said loudly.

The group startled, looking at her guiltily. Then one of them noticed Jensen.

"Cops! It's the cops!" he yelled, panicking.

"No, it's not," Cassidy said, but the group had already risen to their feet, ready to bolt. The one holding the bottle looked confused, like they were unsure whether to throw it into the woods or run away with it and finish it later.

"Sit back down," Jensen said in a very official-sounding voice, and the kids obeyed, nervously taking their places around the lantern. "Now, if you answer our questions, I'll do my best to forget what you've been doing out here. Okay?"

Cassidy was impressed. Jensen could have a real authority about him when he wanted to. She turned to the kids. "So, have you seen anyone come through here in the past hour?"

The kids stayed silent, but then one of them raised his hand and spoke. "I don't know how long, but a while ago someone came crashing by. They saw us and quickly hurried off. That's it."

"Did they look like they were holding something or had a large bag?"

"Don't know," the same kid said. "It was really dark and they were fast."

Cassidy tried to think of anything else to say, but it was all variations on the same questions. "Well, thanks for that."

"Thank you," Jensen said.

The kids stayed silent and wide-eyed as the two of them made their way back on the trail, watching as they walked away.

"Nice job," Cassidy whispered to Jensen once they were out of ear-shot. "Those kids were terrified. You sure you're not going to report them?"

He shook his head. "Hanging out in the woods is a rite of passage for some kids, and they don't seem to be out of control or doing anything stupid. After this scare, they'll likely call it quits for the night, in case I change my mind."

She turned back to the trail, carefully guiding them further into the woods. She wondered how far the woods went and if they'd have to travel all the way through, eventually ending up on the opposite side of the town. Or would they wind around, back to where they started? It could be easy enough to lose direction without a compass.

Eventually they came to a clearing with a rocky hill on one side. Cassidy looked around for a sign of the trail continuing but there were no more broken branches. There was a well-worn path nearby and she wondered if the thief had gained enough of their nerves back to take it out instead of continuing to plow through the trees.

"Where to now?" Jensen asked.

"Not sure." She paused and looked around the clearing again. The trail had been pretty easy so far, and she'd been hoping the rest of it would be the same. How great would it be to find the thief cowering in fear at the end of the trail, the artifact sitting next to them? But things were never that easy in real life. All she needed to do was figure out which path the thief took and they'd be back in business.

Going up to the trees, she searched for recently broken branches. The clearing wasn't very big, so as soon as she'd ruled out everything else, they could go down the path and continue following the thief. Behind her, Jensen was looking around the clearing, staring at the ground. She was about to ask him to search the trees, but figured that maybe he'd find some footprints that would help them, and let him continue doing his own thing.

As she searched, she thought back to what the kid had said, about how the person had come through the woods a while ago. It had to be their suspect, but how much time had passed since the cops found her in the museum? It wasn't that long, maybe thirty minutes, tops. Was that long enough to count as 'a while?'

She paused. Perhaps the thief hadn't called the cops on her, perhaps it had been a concerned citizen after all.

A startled sound behind her broke her from her thoughts, and when she spun around she saw someone jump from the shadows and lunge for Jensen.

CHAPTER NINE

The stranger crashed into Jensen and the two of them fell to the ground, wrestling with each other.

"Stop it!" Cassidy said, pointing her flashlight at the person, and raising her left arm and holding her fingers like a gun. She hoped that in the darkness he would think she had a weapon and stop, and sure enough, it worked.

"Please don't hurt me!" a low voice said, sitting back and raising his arms in the air.

Jensen pulled himself to his feet and quick pulled his own weapon, training it on the stranger.

"I'm sorry!" the man continued. "I didn't mean to do any of this! I swear!"

"What are you doing here?" Cassidy asked, keeping the light of the flashlight focused on his face. He was blinking and turning his head in an effort to stay out of the bright glow, but she didn't move the light. She didn't understand why he was still here. He should have had plenty of time to hide the statue and get out, but instead he'd chosen to hide.

"I'm waiting for someone," he responded, fear creeping into his voice.

Something in his tone unsettled her and Cassidy quickly glanced behind, searching for a shape in the shadows. She couldn't see anything in the darkness, but moved away from the trees anyway, stepping closer to the stranger while holstering her imaginary weapon.

"Did you steal the Artifact of Harmony?" Jensen asked, getting straight to the point. The man didn't say anything. "We tracked you here, so it'd be best for you to tell us the truth."

The man was breathing heavily and shaking, and Cassidy wondered if Jensen should ask the question again.

"*He* made me do it," the man said, his voice a strangled whisper.

The words sent an unexplained shiver down her back and Cassidy looked at the trees again, shining the flashlight around. She saw nothing, but still felt unnerved. She brought the flashlight back to the stranger, but instead of shining it in his eyes, she held the light in a way that she could see him without blinding him. He had short blond hair and pale skin, and was wearing a black hooded sweater and black pants.

"Who is *He*?" Jensen asked.

"I don't know. He found me on the street earlier today and said he needed to talk to me. Then he started saying all of this stuff about my family and my home and how they'd all be in danger if I didn't do what he asked..."

Cassidy exchanged a look with Jensen, both of them caught off guard by the strange admission.

"Noah?" Jensen said, taking a closer look at the man. "Is that you?"

The stranger paused and looked hard at the two people interrogating him. "Jensen? And who's that?"

"Her name's Cassidy and she's been helping me," Jensen replied. "So you're saying that someone threatened you and made you steal the Artifact of Harmony?"

Noah nodded emphatically. "I didn't want to do it, but he knew my address, and my wallet and keys were missing, so I knew he'd be able to find where I lived. I was supposed to meet him a while ago to give him the statue, but he never showed up. Do you think it's all an elaborate prank or do you think he's on his way to my house?"

It now made sense to Cassidy why it had been so easy to find the thief, because he wasn't a thief — he was some unfortunate local who'd been roped into this.

Jensen put his weapon away and took out his radio, calling the station and asking them to check in on Noah's apartment and family ASAP. "Now, what does this person look like?" Jensen asked.

"I don't know. He was fair skinned and wore a hat, so I couldn't see his eyes. I think his hair might have been auburn, short, mostly hidden under the hat."

"Okay," Jensen said, keeping his voice calm and soothing. "I'm going to take you back to the station so you can tell us everything. Okay?"

Noah nodded.

"But first, where is the artifact?"

Noah took in a deep breath and reluctantly pointed to the large stone he'd been hiding behind. Cassidy kept an eye on him as Jensen walked around the stone and retrieved a black sports bag from the darkness.

"I'm so sorry," Noah said, his voice filled with regret.

"It's okay," Jensen reassured him. He opened up the bag and took out a bulky object wrapped in a thick fabric. Unwrapping it, he saw that it was the artifact. Nodding to himself, he carefully re-wrapped the artifact and put it back in the bag. Then he took out his radio again and called the captain, letting her know that they had found the culprit in the forest and were on their way back to the station with the artifact, and that he'd radio as soon as they were out of the woods.

"Let's get back to town," he said.

Noah's eyes grew wide and he looked at the dark trees surrounding them. "But... What if *He's* out there?"

"We could take the trail," Cassidy said. "It would be harder for someone to sneak up on us." She didn't know if it was the power of suggestion, but knowing that the person who'd threatened Noah was still out there made her feel uneasy. He could be in the woods, watching them, right now. Taking the trail would be safer than trying to go back through the path that had led them here. Although it wasn't very wide, it left more space around them and would give them a clear path to run down if they heard anyone approaching.

"I agree," Jensen nodded. "I'll take the lead, Noah will follow, and you bring up the end. Keep an eye out, and if we hear or see anything suspicious we stop and group up."

They began walking along the trail, taking a quick pace. Jensen held his flashlight and the bag with the artifact. Cassidy had offered to hold the bag for him, but he'd quickly declined. She didn't take it personally, considering how she'd been caught breaking into the museum. She obediently took up the rear, sandwiching Noah in between them, in the safest place. She'd dug into her backpack to find her own flashlight — the penlight wouldn't be much help out here — and was using it to shine around the forest, looking for anyone who might be following them. She didn't see anything, and for a moment she wondered if Noah's paranoia had transferred to her, but it was better to be safe than sorry. She tried to keep an ear out for any strange noises, but it was difficult to hear anything over the sound of their own footfalls. Despite their path being a well-worn trail, it was still covered with broken branches and dried leaves. At least they didn't have to dodge tree branches and large roots.

Noah seemed to grow more and more nervous the further they walked. His head darted to the sides, as if on a swivel. Cassidy thought he'd get calmer the closer they got to town, but that wasn't the case. This mysterious man had really done a number on him.

"Shouldn't be long now," Jensen said quietly, and Cassidy wondered if he was saying this to try and calm Noah. She had no idea where they were or how close they were to town, but she hoped that Jensen's words were correct. The sooner Noah got put into police custody, the better.

It occurred to her that she'd also get put into police custody once they made it out of the forest. Her original plan had been to sneak away once the artifact had been found, but now that there was a possible supervillain stalking them through the woods she didn't feel like doing that. Maybe she didn't have to run away. Maybe they'd take it easy on her since she'd successfully discovered the artifact. Noah's story concluded that she hadn't been involved in the plan, so maybe they'd give her a slap on the wrist and let her go. After all, without her help the artifact would probably have been half-way to Russia by now. If Russia even existed in this world...

A loud noise broke her concentration and drew her attention to her right, where it sounded as if someone had stepped on and broken a large branch.

Noah let out a shriek. "He's here! He's coming for me!" He pushed past Jensen, shoving him to the side, and raced down the dark trail. Sensing that this was her moment to flee, Cassidy started to run after him, but then she noticed that Jensen wasn't getting up. She shone her flashlight around the woods, but there was no movement or any more noises, other than Noah's footsteps quickly fading away. She told herself that she was being paranoid, and quickly moved over to Jensen.

He was breathing, but unconscious. She figured that he must have hit his head when Noah had shoved him. Cassidy sized up the situation she was in. She really wanted to get out of the forest, but that would involve carrying Jensen, the artifact, and a flashlight. If anyone was watching them, she'd be a very easy target. But she couldn't stay here, and every time she thought about leaving Jensen behind she felt terrible.

Sighing, she shouldered the bag with the artifact, being careful not to knock it against her backpack, and lifted Jensen to his feet, placing his arm across her shoulders. Her muscles still ached from her earlier activities in the competition, but luckily Jensen wasn't much bigger than she was, and she managed to keep him upright. Holding him by the waist with her left arm, she held the flashlight in her other hand and shone it along the path.

"I hope you were right about us almost being out," she whispered to his unconscious form. She could almost feel unseen eyes watching her, following her through the forest, and had to resist shuddering. Taking in a deep breath, she told herself that there was nothing to be afraid of.

Her progress was slow, and she stopped often to make sure that there were no sounds of someone following her. She was glad she'd had a rest after the tournament, as dragging another human was not the easiest activity. Jensen didn't wake up, but every so often he'd let out a groan, and she was thankful that his injury didn't seem to be too terrible.

Finally she saw a light and realized that the path was coming to an end. Breathing a sigh of relief, she sped up, hurrying towards the park.

Once she was out in the open, all of her fears went away. She wondered if she'd overreacted. She was old enough not to get scared by tales of boogeymen, but there was something about Noah's tale and being in a dark, unfamiliar forest that had brought out long-forgotten fears. Whatever it was, she didn't want to go back in that forest any time soon.

It was late and there was nobody else in sight, not even Noah, so she dragged Jensen's body over to the nearest bench and sat him down. Opening up the bag, she carefully unwrapped the artifact, telling herself that she was doing it to make sure it hadn't been damaged in the fall. It was so beautiful and complex, and again she felt the call to take it with her. It would so easy to grab it and run to the cliffside, escaping back into her own world. Jensen was knocked out, but he knew that she was innocent. And he'd never know if she had taken it or if it had been lost in the woods during his fall. It would be so easy.

But as she stared at the artifact she couldn't help remembering all of Jensen's words about what the artifact represented. If she took this statue through the portal would she bring about a curse and sink this island?

Why would the universe present her with this kind of opportunity if it didn't want her to take the artifact?

Sighing, she looked from the statue to Jensen, very aware that time was ticking away.

CHAPTER TEN

When Jensen awoke, his head was pounding and someone was calling his name. Opening his eyes, he saw Captain Andersen standing in front of him. It was still dark outside, but there was enough light around to see the concerned look on her face.

"Where is she?" she asked.

It took a few seconds for him to realize who she was talking about. He looked around, noticing that he was in the park outside the forest. There were a couple officers standing further away and a few onlookers, but Cassidy was nowhere in sight. His eyes widened and he searched more frantically before his gaze fell on the black bag at his side. Opening it up, he lifted out the bundle and quickly unwrapped it, revealing the artifact.

Sighing, he leaned back on the bench. "I guess she's gone," he replied.

Andersen looked at the artifact. "At least she got it back for us before clearing off. I half-expected that she'd run off with it when I got here and saw only you."

"But why are you here? I thought you were waiting for us at the station?"

"Got a call from her on your radio. Said to come here because you'd been injured in the woods."

Recalling the last memory he had before waking up, Jensen looked around again. "We need to find Noah Leth. He got scared and ran away. He's been mixed up in this whole thing and we need to keep him safe."

Andersen gave a half-smile. "He's already at the station. Raced in, looking like he'd run a marathon, apologizing all over the place. When I left, Ostergard was still trying to calm him down."

"Then I guess this case is over..." Jensen said, but he couldn't help looking around the clearing again. It seemed fitting that Cassidy had disappeared like a ghost in the night, but he would have at least liked to say goodbye. As well as thank you. If it hadn't been for her, they might never have gotten the artifact back.

"Don't look so lost," Andersen said. "At least she saved me the trouble of having to figure out whether to arrest her or let her go."

Jensen laughed. That she had.

"Now, let's get you to the hospital to get checked out."

***

From where she was watching, Cassidy saw the whole interaction between the captain and Jensen. She couldn't hear anything, but neither of them looked furious or upset, so she considered herself to be safe. After calling the station to have someone check on Jensen, she'd thought about going back to her world, but she didn't want to risk someone stealing the artifact while Jensen was still unconscious. As much as she didn't like the idea, she knew that it'd be best to hide in the forest, so she'd concealed herself in the trees, hoping that there were no supervillains hiding nearby.

It was past midnight when the park was finally empty of onlookers and police. Freeing herself from the forest, she used the moonlight to guide her to the cliff. As she reached the edge, she looked back at the town and wondered if she'd ever be back here. Maybe it'd be best if she stayed away for a while. Maybe the police would spend the rest of their lives talking about the mysterious stranger who'd helped find a stolen artifact. Or maybe she'd be forgotten after a few months.

She thought about the knife she'd won in the competition, and was glad that she was leaving with some kind of artifact to bring back to the professor. A smile broke out over her face and she reached into her pocket, taking out the keychain she'd 'borrowed' from Jensen. The tiny replica wasn't as magnificent as the original, but it would do. Hopefully Jensen would forgive her taking it, considering how she'd left him the real one.

Laughing to herself, Cassidy put some chalk on her hands and started the climb down the cliff, towards home.

BOULDERS OVER THE BERMUDA TRIANGLE

PETER J FOOTE & JD RYOT

CHAPTER ONE

"Rescue ship to Cassidy Cane, come in Cassidy," the voice crackled over the speaker that bounced like a Hawaiian doll on the dash of the experimental plane.

Jamming the steering yoke between her knees, Cassidy risked taking one hand off the vibrating yoke to flick the radio on.

"Cane here, kinda busy at the moment, you want something in particular?" Cassidy said as she tucked the loose strands of her hair behind her ear, before taking the yoke again.

The speaker crackled once again before emitting a blast of static that was strong enough to drown out the struggling engines of the aircraft. The static faded in intensity and Cassidy could make out the words coming from the ship far below.

"We're having a hard time keeping you in our sights, Cassidy. The storm is growing and the cloud cover is getting thicker. Please report your status."

"My status?" Cassidy muttered under her breath as she looked out the windscreen of the plane. Wipers beat a rapid tempo to push away the drawing rain, but did little except add to the overwhelming din within the cockpit. The altimeter read 27,000 feet and climbing, while the fuel gauge was at less than half and falling fast as the engines struggled against the storm. An instrument panel with more lights, readouts, and gauges than she knew what to do with or even what they did had Cassidy shaking her head.

"How did I let Gamgee talk me into this...?"

***

"Just think of the possibilities, Cassidy!" Dr. Gamgee exclaimed as he brandished his hands in the air and paced from one end of his cluttered lab to the other. Without knocking over any of the precariously placed pieces of equipment that threaten to avalanche at any second, he spoke again. "If we could make a practical radio that provides contact between dimensions, we could expand the frontiers of human knowledge to limits never dreamed of," Gamgee said as he removed a handkerchief from his vest pocket, using it to clean his glasses while staring along his nose.

Cassidy, perched on the bare corner of a cluttered table, stared back. Twisting her long braid between her fingers, Cassidy did her best not to disturb anything in the workshop. Health and Safety had never been a priority for Gamgee or his inventions. "So before you get yourself too sidetracked, let's start at the beginning. Rocks are dropping out of the sky...." she lead Gamgee.

"Ah yes, the meteors," Gamgee muttered, replacing his glasses. "The Bermuda Triangle has been the home of the strange and unbelievable since the Spanish first sailed that part of the Atlantic."

"Sorry to interrupt again, Doctor, but that's inaccurate. The 'myth' of the Bermuda Triangle is just that, a myth, perpetuated by authors to manufacture an enigma when logic will produce the answer." Cassidy proceeded when Gamgee beckoned her with his handkerchief. "It's basic environmental science. Any decent researcher will tell you that areas frequented by tropic cyclones and unseaworthy vessels have a high probability of disappearances."

His cheeks turning red, Gamgee gave a pointed nod and replied: "Perhaps you're right, but that doesn't explain this," he said, and with a melodramatic flourish, whipped off a sheet from a crowded table.

Her interest piqued, Cassidy wandered over to the table and peered at the lump of rock that had been underneath. Pulling a magnifying glass from her shoulder bag, Cassidy leaned in to examine the medicine ball-sized rock as Gamgee continued his account.

"Setting aside the history of the Bermuda Triangle, I can tell you some facts," Gamgee began, his tone taking on the smooth cadence of one used to speaking to crowds. "Meteors entering the earth's atmosphere aren't anything unusual; it happens countless times a day. Though few meteors are the size of this one. Until now no one has suggested that they entered from anyplace but our own solar system."

Cassidy's attention piqued, she interrupted her study of the meteor. "You're suggesting that this rock came from another dimension?"

"Yes, for three reasons," Gamgee said, and started ticking off his fingers. "One, there isn't any sign that this rock suffered atmospheric reentry, no melting or heat stress. Two, metallurgical analysis reveals this rock is unlike anything ever found on earth before, and three, a cruise ship sailing in the area witnessed the rock falling through a portal."

"You realize you could have lead with that," Cassidy muttered. "Okay, I believe you. It sounds probable this rock came from another dimension. How is it worthy of exploration? What makes this one so extraordinary that it jumps to the front of the line?"

"That's an excellent question, my young friend," Gamgee replied. "When the divers returned from the crash zone, they brought back several fragments, but this piece had something unique within it. A green crystal embedded into the rock, which displayed some fascinating properties." Gamgee was becoming excited, once again pulling out his handkerchief but this time using it to mop his brow, and allowing Cassidy to notice fresh scrapes on his arm. "I damaged the crystal in a lab accident and it splintered into two fragments. While investigating afterward, I discovered that some power still linked the pieces in a way I don't understand. I observed light and sound aimed at one segment manifest in the other, like a reflection."

Playing with her braid, Cassidy puzzled out this discovery. "That's delving into quantum mechanics, isn't it? Connections between things even when the cause isn't apparent?"

Gamgee's eyes widened, and he gave a reluctant nod.

"Hey, my focus might be archeology, but I'm well read," she replied.

"I'll remember that. As I was saying, these crystals have the potential to remain connected after we cleave them. I've postulated that we could create old-fashioned crystal radios that provide instantaneous communication between vast distances and even dimensions. But to have a working prototype I require more of the crystals to experiment with, and that's where you come in Ms. Cane."

CHAPTER TWO

"Repeat, Cassidy, we can hardly understand you."

Jarred from the memories of her briefing, Cassidy realized the storm that had been on the horizon now surrounded her. Remembering that the rescue ship was awaiting her response, she yelled over the buffeting wind, creaking plane, and crashing thunder.

"I said," Cassidy looked into the sky and watched the swirling portal in the storm's centre. "I said," she reiterated, "maybe Gamgee was correct about a portal in the skies above the Bermuda Triangle."

Both hands white-knuckled the plane's yoke, and Cassidy watched as the compass mounted to the dash of the plane spun one way then another, as if it were tipsy and staggering its way home from the bars.

"Great... what else could go wrong?" Cassidy muttered as she banked the plane against the hurricane-force winds. Perhaps in answer to her query, a bolt of lightning flashed, leaving spots in her eyes and half the plane's electronic panels dark, including the radio.

"Just wonderful... me and my fat mouth," Cassidy cursed as her brief glance out the window confirmed what she felt in her heart. Billowing clouds filled the sky, with no trace of the rescue boat nor the roaring waves of the Atlantic Ocean. The dying glow of the fuel gauge, that showed less than half full, highlighted her. "Nothing to do but get on with the mission then." The grin on her face might have been considered mad, considering her desperate circumstances.

Trusting that the plane's homing beacon was more heavily shielded than the other electronics on board, Cassidy slapped the huge red button and exhaled through clenched teeth as it pulsed a steady red, matched by the homing device on her wrist.

Leaning forward, Cassidy could pinpoint the portal now. She and Gamgee had speculated that the Bermuda Triangle portal would be parallel to the ocean, and it turned out they were correct. Cassidy doubted she'd ever know whether the storm or the portal were here first. What she realized was that the portal to the dimension where the crystals had originated was another 10,000 feet above her.

Once again, Cassidy used her knees to hold the bucking yoke to control the plane from becoming captured in a murderous crosswind and spinning out of control. Tightening her seatbelt until it dug deep, she tugged the harnesses on the parachute strapped to her back to reassure herself that it was there. Next she picked up the oxygen mask Gamgee had insisted that she pack and turned on the flow.

As prepared as she could be, Cassidy used her wiry arms to yank back on the steering yoke, forcing the nose of the experimental plane to point in the general direction of the portal. She engaged the booster rockets strapped to the frame of the airplane. The punch was immediate and unpleasant as it thrust Cassidy deep into her chair, her arms striving to keep the plane in line with her target.

"Why does this blasted thing have to be so tough to get to?" she yelled through gritted teeth.

Thirty seconds of acceleration later, loose articles in the plane bounced around like socks in the dryer. Cassidy watched as gauges spun, their numbers meaningless at this stage, and as the swirling portal loomed larger.

Every rivet on the airplane seemed to rattle loose, but Cassidy's face was alight with pleasure. A surge of adrenaline coursed through her veins and she screamed out in delight as the nose of the plane pierced the portal.

The howling storm over the Atlantic Ocean disappeared into silence, and Cassidy saw stars.

***

The void of the vacuum of outer space rushed into the cockpit of the airplane. The only thing that saved Cassidy from a sudden death was the oxygen mask over her face.

Sadly, it couldn't help her from the cold, which sought to strip her body of its warmth and vitality. In seconds the sensation was leaving the tips of her fingers and toes as she grappled to think and not allow panic to set it.

With the frosting of her face mask making vision difficult, Cassidy turned her head side to side to see the mess Gamgee had dumped her into this time. The faint flashing pulse of the red homing beacon on the dash and her wrist provided a slight comfort, though how that would help in outer space she didn't know. The remaining controls within the airplane were dead, only the emergency batteries were available, and Cassidy didn't know how long they would last in outer space.

Hitting the emergency clasp on her seatbelt released the pressure against her. Doing so disorientated her; the absence of gravity carried her forward until it forced her face up against the front cockpit window.

The black of the void was stifling. Emergency lights along the wings of the airplane did little to penetrate it, but shifting shadows resolved themselves into tumbling asteroids and it explained the question of the alien rocks.

"Just marvelous. Gamgee said nothing about outer space," Cassidy said. Ice crystals crackling on her face mask and her supply of oxygen hissing in her ears were the only noises she heard in the soundless void.

Cassidy struggled with frozen hands to unlock the canopy's release mechanism. On her third try, she got her fingers around the lever and tugged. Tiny explosions vibrated through the plane and it blew the canopy clear of the fuselage, leaving Cassidy exposed to the vacuum of space. Her breathing ragged, vision blurring, Cassidy struggled to think straight and not give in to the appealing call that she just close her eyes and go to sleep.

"Lights... I'm sure, light," she whispered, as her sluggish mind forced itself to accept what her eyes were showing. A broad grouping of lights twinkled and shone through the dancing asteroids. Spending the last of her waning strength, Cassidy Cane pushed away from the airplane, into the unknown.

CHAPTER THREE

"Now Agnoix, I want you to promise to listen to your brother. If he tells you not to enter a section of the station, you don't go in. I don't care what the other youngsters are doing, if they're seeking to get a glimpse at alien visitors, you are to remain within the Xik'en zone. Do you understand? And Axaik, I appreciate this is your last time to enjoy Sastreni before you enter the ranks of adulthood. I'm only letting you go if you agree to watch your sister and keep her safe," Orlol said from the kitchen as she used her prehensile tail to hold a giant mollusk. With long experience she extracted the struggling creature, plopping it into the steaming stew pot.

Axaik stuck his forked tongue out between needle-sharp teeth at his sister, but retracted it when Orlol walked into the living room, cleaning her hands on a cloth.

"I asked a question; did you hear me?" Orlol asked her offspring, her reptilian eyes narrowing until the two siblings settled and intoned "Yes, mother," in unison.

"Good. I realize you two have your father wrapped around your talons, but while he's outside the star system trading, and buying you," Orlol pointed a talon tipped finger at Axaik, "an apprenticeship with the trade guild, I'm in charge and I won't have my children being the gossip of this space station."

Orlol's posture relaxed as she made herself understood to her children. "Okay, let me have a look at your costumes. Agnoix, who are you supposed to be again?"

Straightening her homemade mask, Agnoix replied: "I'm Brauxel, the Warden of the Two Divines. The Saint who championed the destitute, as well as the rich and powerful. Our rulers executed her for non-traditional Xik'en beliefs."

"Ah yes, and your father approved this choice didn't he? I'm uncertain this is a true role-model for you. A proper Xik'en should lift themselves up, not rely on others," Orlol said, holding up her taloned hand in resignation as Agnoix opened her mouth to argue. "I appreciate you have different points of view and wish things were different, but this is reality. You'll be an adult soon, required to be a functional part of Xik'en society, not a careless dreamer like most of the aliens that frequent this mining station. Please, just think about who you wish to be for the rest of your life."

Turning her attention away from her daughter before they got into one of their frequent and repetitive arguments, Orlol addressed her oldest child. "And you're honoring Tox'eix once again, correct? The architect of the Xik'en Interstellar Empire?"

Rolling his shoulders in a gesture of bravado, Axaik flicked his tail and bowed to his mother. "Who better to celebrate tonight than the reptile who founded our Empire thousands of years ago?" He adjusted the sweeping white robes decorated with golden stars and talons, a handmade copy of the one worn by Tox'eix. Axaik curled his lip, exposing needle-sharp teeth at his sister when she turned to open the airlock of their residence.

With the airlock door open, Orlol bid her children farewell.

"Remain together. Honor our ancestors with your games and puzzles, eat nothing not given to you by fellow Xik'ens, and be home before the next shift change in the refinery. I'll have mollusk stew in the food saver for you. I'll be straight home after my shift in ore processing."

As her children fled the residence, Orlol allowed the airlock to seal, then hastened back to the kitchen where the mollusk was trying to escape her steaming pot.

"I swear, those kids will be the death of me," she complained.

***

"What are we doing here, Axaik? You promised Mom that you'd escort me through the residence sections to show off my costume for Sastreni and get candied treats."

"You don't want to do any of the stupid kid stuff do you? This is my last year to enjoy Sastreni and I will not waste it knocking on doors for a slice of fruit leather. Me and my friends will have a proper party, and if you want to fit in you'll come along," Axaik said as he watched to make certain they were alone before rapping a series of taps on the maintenance hatch. The hatch lock squeaked, swung open, and a gaggle of near adult Xik'ens tumbled out.

Even in their inaccurate costumes, Agnoix recognized them as her brother's classmates. Other Xik'ens on the verge of maturity, many of whom would waste their lives counting shipping crates or repairing mining pods and feeling they had life by the tail.

Skipping backward as the landslide of hyper Xik'en youth tried to wedge themselves back into the maintenance tunnel, Agnoix pleaded with her brother. "Come on, Axaik, you promised and I even said I'd give you my treats from Sastreni tonight. What will Mom say?"

Agnoix realized that she had crossed the line when her brother stomped up to her and gripped the front of her costume, his sharp talons ripping the cheap fabric.

"Now listen here, alien lover. If you don't want me to tell Mom how you're missing classes to slink into the forbidden mammal section, you'll say nothing about this," Axaik hissed, his hot breath right in her snout. "Do we understand each other?"

Agnoix could do nothing but nod, her mask slipping on her face. His point made, Axaik released his sister, tearing more of her costume.

Baring his pointed teeth, he swung back to his companions and said: "Get yourselves together. We have a party to make happen and we don't need any alien lover to hamper our style. Let's move!"

With a generous measure of pushing, the group of young Xik'ens charged down the narrow maintenance corridor packed with pipes, wires and metal catwalks. Axaik flicked his tongue along his razor-sharp teeth and closed the maintenance hatch with a loud bang, leaving Agnoix alone in the hallway.

CHAPTER FOUR

Abandoned by her brother, and stung by his words, Agnoix fled without heed to her destination. Tears streamed down her scaled face, making her vision issues worse as Agnoix raced through the halls, past others out enjoying Sastreni. There were squeals of laughter as parents with small Xik'en children and older kids garbed in colourful costumes offered deference to the role-models of Xik'en society with treats and games. Blinded by tears, Agnoix brushed past a small group only to stumble, then stop in a maze of limbs and tails.

Her mask slipped off and Agnoix found herself snout to snout with a crying child and an irate parent.

"I should have known. You're that Agnoix, aren't you? Orlol's daughter? Always making trouble, upsetting your poor mother, wait until I see her..."

Agnoix didn't listen to any more of the woman's ranting. With the angry parents' shouts ringing in her ears, she scooped her mask up off the floor and rushed away.

The energy provided by embarrassment and shame soon failed her. Agnoix collapsed against the cool glass of one of the mining station's many exterior windows. Heaving lungs struggled to bring in fresh air and ease the sobbing that had overtaken her. After a pause, she regained her composure and took in her surroundings.

Her mad rush through the halls of the sprawling mining station had brought Agnoix to a quiet, seldom-used space. Unlike the grand viewing galleries, where the trade ships, space yachts, and other vessels arrived and departed the space station, Agnoix was in a smaller gallery. Her view showed where the mining pods and tractors towed in the various ore rich stones from the asteroid belt into the mining complex.

Standing, Agnoix looked past her reflection in the thick glass. Past the shamble of the costume she'd spent weeks bartering materials to produce, and stared into the graveyard of rocks that brought her species here.

It was taught to every school-aged student that this massive asteroid belt that the great Xik'en Empire laid claim to centuries ago was within the Vao 63I system. The asteroid belt was once two planets that collided millions of years ago. There were other planets within the star system. The Xik'en ignored them because they were without atmosphere or material significance. 'Vao' referred to the asteroid belt and mining station within it.

Every minute of every day, mining pods piloted by Xik'ens jetted through the crowded belt and assessed the remnants of those two planets, tagging them based on their mineral property. Then, depending on demand and market conditions, her people carved up those asteroids in space and hauled the chunks to the ore processing part of the station. Agnoix's mother worked in the processing side of the operation, helping smelt base metals in zero gravity furnaces, while her father worked in sales to other races.

Sighing, Agnoix came face to face with the reality that her life would fit into the machinery that is Vao Station, no matter her ideals and interests.

"Maybe I should just listen to Mom and yield to proper Xik'en tradition, be a cog in the machine. It was here before me and will be here long after I'm gone," Agnoix said, her voice forlorn and without hope, just as Cassidy Cane's fingers dragged across the outside of the glass window.

***

For a moment time stood still for Agnoix, until what she was seeing registered in her reptilian brain. Then a lifetime of existence on a fragile mining complex amid a hazardous asteroid belt kicked in.

"Help, I need help!" Agnoix yelled, her cry reverberating down the narrow hall as she rushed towards the nearest life station, her costume flapping in her haste.

Built into the outer walls of the mining complex, life stations resembled round blisters that jutted out from its metal surface, like moles on the body of the space station. They allowed an individual to see along the exterior walls of the complex better, to aid in rescue of distressed ships and people working in the void of space. Dashing into the life station, Agnoix smashed the huge yellow button set into the facade, releasing the pistol grips of the bubble gun. Ignoring the flashing lights and siren that hitting the button had activated, Agnoix gripped the dual pistol grips of the bubble gun and a screen flashed to life. Cross-hairs bobbed and weaved as they mirrored her movements of the grips.

Shaking with adrenaline, Agnoix struggled to bring the cross-hairs on the screen to overlap with the shrinking form she saw through the window. With the sensors unable to detect a warm body to lock onto, Agnoix made her best guess and fired. Her sharp talons depressed the buttons on top of the pistol grips, firing the bubble gun.

From some place beneath her, a flashing disk shot out towards the body and sailed past without making contact, missing it by several meters.

"Come on, you can do this, every child has shot a bubble gun," Agnoix said to herself as she pushed her mask off her face. Adjusting her aim, she enhanced the view screen to maximum and discharged the bubble gun again. The flashing disk shot out and, this time, the viewscreen strobed yellow, saying that it had struck something and was returning to the life station.

Jumping in excitement, Agnoix almost didn't hear the computerized voice instructing her to exit the life station since a rescue was ongoing. Her tail striking the wall as she skipped out of the life station, Agnoix hurried to comply. When the sensors read that it was empty, the entire thing rotated outward. The interior of the tiny life station Agnoix was standing in moments ago, was now out in the void of space. And the protruding window was poking into the gallery corridor, oblivious to the strobing lights, sirens, and computerized voice of the life station.

It stated that she should remain on the scene of the rescue in progress, and that emergency staff had been dispatched. Agnoix watched as the 'bubble' and its occupant grew closer.

Seconds that felt like hours passed. The 'bubble,' a portable life-saving sphere used when there wasn't time to don a spacesuit, glided into the life station. The flashing disk, the 'cap' of the life-saving air bubble, connected with the interior of the window where Agnoix had stood, aiming her cross-hairs, minutes ago.

Agnoix couldn't get an unobstructed view of the being within the 'bubble.' The warm air being generated by the flashing disk had formed a thick layer of vapor within it, creating a sealed environment. As the life station received the rescue bubble, Agnoix felt the vibration through the metal floor. As the life station rotated back to its regular configuration, with the 'bubble' now inside the safety of the mining complex, Agnoix rushed towards it.

It's task completed, the flashing disk shut down and burst the life-saving bubble. Hot, moist air, with the faintest scent of disinfectant, flowed towards the young Xik'en. She saw the shadow of a body roll towards her out of the fog, its scale-less hand coming to rest on her foot.

Looking down at Cassidy, Agnoix, her voice on the edge of panic, yelled: "By all the ancestors, it's a mammal!"

CHAPTER FIVE

Scared and also intrigued by the alien *creature*, Agnoix leaned closer to the mammal. Tales of such Bogeyman were used to scare Xik'en children when they didn't eat all their supper or finish their homework. Agnoix knew that sentient mammals frequented the mining complex to trade for the metals produced here. Mammals were isolated and quarantined from all common areas, so that the ordinary work force and citizens of the complex never met them, nor risked being tainted.

Agnoix reached out a shaky talon and nudged the mammal. Feeling the chill radiating off of its skin, a small moan told the young Xik'en that the mammal was still alive.

"Great, you're alive... whatever you are," Agnoix said as she struggled to understand the strange clothes, hair -- *by all the ancestors, hair is ugly* -- and body shape of the warm-blood, and that's when she decided: *I can't leave you here. There are so many questions I want to ask about you, your world, your life.*

Looking around at the flashing lights and sirens, Agnoix realized what she'd done, activating the life station.

Her actions had no doubt caused several control boards in the mining complex base of operations to light up as if there was a magnetic storm. Agnoix knew she couldn't allow this mammal to fall into the talons of the stations security. She wanted to learn more about the mysterious alien: where it came from, and how it got into space without a suit. Something clicked within the young Xik'en, and she knelt beside Cassidy.

"Likely, they would throw you into a cage and charge you with trespassing, sabotage, or worse. I can't let that happen, at least not until you can speak on your own behalf, but that means we have to hide and quick."

This brilliant piece of reasoning only got Agnoix another moan from the warm-blood. Cassidy's eyes fluttered, her cheeks pulling in as she struggled to breathe through the face mask, no longer receiving oxygen from an empty tank.

"You can't die now, I just rescued you," Agnoix said, wishing that she was doing the proper thing as she pulled aside the oxygen mask, allowing Cassidy to inhale the foreign air. There were gasps that turned into great gulps of breathing, and Agnoix watched as colour appeared on the mammal's skin, her blood warming and oxygenating. Convinced that she did the correct thing, she searched for a place to hide them both, knowing that emergency personnel would be there at any moment.

With the central hallways away from the gallery likely to have Xik'ens rushing down them, Agnoix spied a tucked away maintenance area. Little better than a custodian's closet, but Agnoix decided it was for the best. Grabbing the tiny emergency kit from the life station and gripping it with her prehensile tail, Agnoix hesitated a second, looking at the alien at her feet. Staring at the warm-blood, her mind swirled with fear and excitement. The young Xik'en hooked her talons under the armpits of the strange mammal and pulled. Trying not to think that she was touching a horror of her culture, Agnoix dragged Cassidy towards the room, even as she heard steps running over the sirens.

Heedless of any suffering she might cause to Cassidy, Agnoix tugged her to the door of the custodian's closet. With little grace, she rolled Cassidy inside and stumbled after her, dragging the door closed just as she saw station personnel turn into the corridor.

The door to the janitor's closet jammed a talons width from closing. Agnoix looked down to see that the mammal's foot covering -- *why cover your feet?* -- was jamming the door. Leaning over the warm-blood, her nostrils drawing in the foreign scent, she reached to tug it clear. As she did so, she saw a running pair of Xik'en security guards with stun sticks in hand stop in front of the life station.

Frozen in place, squatting in the pitch black closet, Agnoix felt the soft breathing of the alien against her scales. Agnoix watched as the security guards holstered their stun sticks and rebooted the life station. It surprised Agnoix how intensely her heart was beating. She wondered if the guards would have been able to hear it, when the piercing siren of the alarm was shut off.

Leaning her head as close to the door gap as possible, Agnoix could hear the two guards outside.

"Control, this is Krolzan. No visual emergency at life station 42, don't bother sending medical aid. Unit reset, we're investigating," a mature female voice reported.

A communicator hissed. "Acknowledged. Awaiting a final report."

Another voice uttered, young to Agnoix's ears: "Do you... do you think it was a spirit called here on Sastreni? My Father's elder used to tell me tales of souls who visited on tonight; some appeared to help, some to harm."

Agnoix could pick out the agitation in Krolzan's tone, so similar to that of her own mother. "Tuds, if you wish to go on working security, learn and think for yourself. What is tonight, Tuds?"

"Ah... Sastreni, Sergeant Krolzan."

"That's right, and what did you do on your last Sastreni?"

"Attended a remembrance service to pay tribute to our ancestors," Tuds replied.

"Of course you did. Okay, let me ask it another way. What did your peers do that night while you were at the service?"

"Oh, you mean the cool kids. They partied, played practical jokes on people and caused mischief with security... I follow you now Sergeant, you think young Xik'ens activated the life station as a prank?"

"There's no dullness to your scales tonight is there, Tuds," Krolzan said in a deadpan tone, as she switched on her communicator.

"Krolzan to Control. Confirmed no emergency at this life station, likely just kids out causing trouble on Sastreni. Do you wish us to continue our investigation?"

The communicator crackled and an annoyed voice answered. "Negative Krolzan. Haul tail to the food court in section seven. A group of young Xik'ens, their leader dressed as Tox'eix, are creating a disturbance, more petty vandalism and lewd behaviour."

Thank you, Axaik, for once you did me a favour, Agnoix thought, as the pair of security officers hurried off, their stun sticks grasped in their strong talons.

Able to breathe a sigh of relief, Agnoix pulled the foot of the mammal out of the door, closed it, and turned on the light in the custodian's closet.

Climbing off the odd smelling mammal, Agnoix got her first clear view of Cassidy.

"Ugly aren't you?" Agnoix said as she struggled to make the unconscious woman comfortable. Realizing that Cassidy's extremities were as cold as ice and that the slight pulsing of her neck was becoming feeble, Agnoix felt her own stomach go cold.

"Please don't die!" Agnoix exclaimed, then tore open the emergency kit, flinging the contents throughout the cramped closet -- sanitation supplies falling from racks. While yet a youngster in the minds of Xik'en society, Agnoix and all like her that grew up on the space station were educated in basic first aid and emergency procedures. "Yeah, but the broadcasts on the transit tubes never mentioned what to do with frozen mammals," Agnoix muttered to herself as she grasped the injector for 'cold space'.

Bending down until her snout was almost touching Cassidy's ear, Agnoix whispered: "I'm giving you an injection, okay? I don't know what it will do for a warmblood like you. They created it for Xik'ens when there is a rupture in the mining complex. Sorry if this hurts." And with a moment's reluctance, Agnoix placed the tip of the injector against Cassidy's neck. The soft hiss of the injector let her know that she had administered the medicine.

The result was instantaneous. Cassidy thrashed, drumming her heels against the floor of the closet. One of Cassidy's arms lashed out, knocking over a cleaning wand, and the other slapped Agnoix in the skull, making her tumble backward. Shaking her head to clear her vision, Agnoix climbed atop Cassidy and held her down. The talons of the Xik'en youth ripped the fabric of Cassidy's clothes, scratching the skin and drawing blood.

Cassidy made several cries, and her eyes rolled up into her sockets until only the whites showed. However, over minutes, Cassidy's struggles lessened and an intense glow radiated through her skin that Agnoix hoped meant good news.

As the alien creature's struggles lessened, Agnoix climbed off, confirming in her own mind that the 'cold space' had reversed the effects of being exposed to the vacuum of space. With the immediate danger behind them, Agnoix's curiosity took over, and she slid herself closer to the alien for a decent look.

"You're fragile, aren't you?" Agnoix said as she examined Cassidy. "Delicate skin, no scales to protect you, so you wear many layers of clothes. I bet your sense of smell is terrible with a snout so ugly and stunted as that, and why are your teeth blunt? Do you grind your food between your jaws? A very inefficient design. How your species attained space is beyond me, or are you a stowaway? I just wish I had my sketchbook to capture this!"

Maybe it was Agnoix's excited tone of voice, or that

the stimulant had worked, but Cassidy's eyes opened wide at the creature leaning over of her.

***

Mother was right, mammals are dangerous! Look at the fury in its ugly face, how it grabbed for a weapon, Agnoix thought to herself as she struggled to grasp the handle of the custodian's closet, her flee to safety monopolizing her thoughts.

"Stop it you twit, do you expect you'd be in any better condition if you were just recovered from the void and woke up in a strange place?" Agnoix chastised herself. "You're letting your racial bias show; don't judge without evidence."

With deliberate effort, Agnoix released the door handle and turned towards the alien mammal.

I've never seen this species of warm-blood before, just images on a screen. It's probably as terrified of me as I am of it, Agnoix thought as she regarded Cassidy. She lifted her taloned hand. "My name is Agnoix, are you feeling okay?"

She repeated herself several times and attempted the gentlest voice she could. It worked because she watched as the mammal lowered the window cleaner wand, picked up as a weapon, and leaned it against the wall, still within easy reach.

Straightening to its full stature, less than Agnoix's own, the mammal tapped its chest with a blunt and ugly finger and answered: "Cassidy."

"Well, at least it can communicate. That's something at least," Agnoix said, and the mammal turned its head sideways as if struggling to understand.

"I appreciate you can't understand me, warm-blood, but I have something that I hope will work," Agnoix said as she reached her hand into the pleats of her costume, causing the mammal to reach for its weapon.

"Please don't. I'm getting something to help us communicate, okay?" Agnoix whispered, and the mammal stopped reaching for the window cleaner. Pulling her Branch of Languages from her robe -- the golden nanotech wires cradling slivers of green Vao stones -- Agnoix didn't see any shock of recognition from the alien mammal. Placing the branch against the right side of her scaled jaw, Agnoix showed Cassidy how the intelligent device weaved itself along her jawline, around her ear, and stopped at the crest of her head.

Things were about to get interesting.

CHAPTER SIX

Cassidy's eyes widened in confusion as she watched the dinosaur creature reach into its clothing and draw forth a piece of the very crystal Gamgee sent her to find.

Her shock continued as the alien laid the jeweled necklace against its scaled face, and it coiled itself around the skull as if it were alive.

The final straw was when the alien dinosaur held out the necklace to Cassidy. What was worse was that the device itself appeared to reach out to her. Trauma of the past several minutes took its toll. Her knees weakened, she slumped down the wall, and passed out.

Reality returned to Cassidy much sharper than it appeared the first time, but it was no less disconcerting.

The alien had stretched out her legs to make Cassidy as comfortable as she could, and had even put her makeshift weapon beside her hand.

The desire to take up the weapon was powerful, but Cassidy pushed it from her thoughts. Instead, she focused her mind on the alien sitting on its haunches, watching her, its scaled tail flicking like a cat's.

Think Cassidy, apply your training instead of acting out of fear. You've been in strange and perilous places before -- even though this must be near the top of the list.

Okay, I'm lying in a tiny room with an intelligent reptile. Focus on that.

Cassidy took several deep breaths as she slipped back into her training as an anthropologist and cataloged what she saw in front of her.

She did her best to remain objective in her analysis, and wished she dared risk digging out her notebook.

Bipedal with a prehensile tail since its operating it as a third hand to carry an empty box, the contents strewn throughout this room. More of a closet, maybe? Doesn't feel like a home or a hospital.

Focus! Concentrate on the alien, Cassidy.

It's tough to know, since I'm prone and the alien is squatting, but I'd estimate it's at least my height when standing, maybe taller. It has the typical number of limbs and fingers and toes, though what I consider normal in this situation I don't know.

Protruding snout, broad nasal opening, a mouth full of tiny sharp teeth and a tongue that flicks out every few moments. It reminds me of how a snake samples the air, drawing a sample into its mouth and its vomeronasal system.

Large round eyes with lavender pupils, exquisite eyes to be honest. They rest on the front of the face rather than the side, which denotes a predator verses prey ancestry, analogous to humans.

Its scales are like tarnished bronze, like the jewelry I helped excavate from that Roman-Britain dig a couple seasons back. Its outfit is baffling, it's a series of robes striped in yellow and blue, though the colours appear to be painted on -- and not skillful, if

I'm being fair. Strapped over that is armour, but it's homemade or ceremonial and not for combat. I can say the same for its weapon, a fork on one end, and a hook on the other, either a prop or a toy. My best guess is that the attire is for ceremonial rather than everyday use.

Years in the field, exposed to various cultures, had allowed Cassidy to catalogue people and items as second nature, and she did so again in moments.

Relying on her abilities and feelings, Cassidy sensed that while this alien looked fearsome, it didn't mean her immediate harm.

Pleased that her hand had stopped shaking, Cassidy reached out for the necklace.

Alien talons brushed against Cassidy's palm, but she didn't allow herself to jerk away.

Holding her breath, Cassidy lifted the piece of alien jewelry up to her face, and she felt it become alive.

Moving like a snake, it slipped along Cassidy's jawline, and its "head" disappeared into the hair above her right ear. The living wire followed her jawline on one end, while the other weaved its way into her braided hair.

A comfortable warmth replaced the tingle, and a thought occurred to Cassidy. The pauses and word groups of the alien language reminded her of the Khoisan languages of southern Africa with their clicks. *I wonder if any member of these aliens has ever been to Earth in the past? I must attempt to research this. The results could open up a new branch of linguistics.*

Cassidy tested her theory. Taking a deep breath with lungs that minutes before were about to breathe nothing but the cold of space, she said: "Is this thing working?"

A warm tingling raced along her scalp. "This is amazing," Cassidy said, only to see disappointment on the female reptile's face.

I don't understand it... I know it's alien technology, but I'm sure it should work, she thought, as she allowed her fingers to glide along the golden wire cradling the right side of her head.

Fool, you should head back to school when this is all over, Cassidy chided herself, as she beckoned Agnoix to remove the device. Once it was free, Cassidy patted the left side of her face, and while the young Xik'en shook her head and said something in her own language, she did as Cassidy requested and repeated the ritual on the left side of Cassidy's face.

Once she felt the warm tingling along her scalp again, Cassidy said: "How about now?" and Agnoix clapped her taloned hands happily in response.

"I can understand you!" Agnoix said.

No, that isn't right. If I focus, I can still hear Agnoix's alien speech patterns, but what she says is an echo in my mind. This alien device must be in direct contact with my brain.

The mere thought of what this piece of alien technology might do to her brain nearly caused a panic attack, so Cassidy hurried to distract herself.

"In humans, the language portion of our brain is on the left side," she said, tapping the left side of her head. "That's why it didn't work the first time, I bet."

***

Relieved that the mammal seemed unhurt and relaxed after donning the Branch of Languages, Agnoix forced her heart to slow down and her conflicting instincts to flee, with Agnoix standing firm.

Tapping her breast once again with her talon, Agnoix said: "My name is Agnoix, what is your name?"

Agnoix smiled as she watched Cassidy shudder, remembering the tingling sensations as the Branch of Languages attached to its users speech centre.

The warm-blood's tone of voice was deeper than most intelligent species. Its tiny mouth mispronounced some words, but Agnoix learned that the mammal called itself Cassidy Cane and came from a place or planet called Earth.

While many of the terms the mammal used were unfamiliar to Agnoix, making her blink in confusion more than once, she was able to gather that this mammal -- correction, 'human' -- was here on a voyage of exploration in general, and after ARC crystals in specific. The ARC crystals, Cassidy Cane explained, look like larger versions of the stones in her Branch of Languages, and Agnoix could understand why.

The Vao stones were one of the major exports from this mining station. While the base and precious metals, mined and refined from the asteroid belt, made up the shear bulk of the material that went through this mining complex, the Vao stones were the most expensive.

Xik'en scientists had a complicated means of describing their ability, but all that Agnoix knew was that they allowed the Xik'en Interstellar Empire instantaneous communication across space. That communication was the primary reason that their reach and control was so vast.

Pieces of the Vao stones used with base level intelligent nanotechnology could create the Branches of Languages. These personal translation devices were a staple on the mining stations and other places where many races coexisted under one roof.

Agnoix was grateful for the one her parents had gifted her on her last hatching day. Her mother hadn't want to give Agnoix such a tool, fearing that it would encourage her willful daughter to mingle with more outside their own species.

"Mother! I'd forgotten, it must be way past the time I promised to be home. I don't know what to do."

CHAPTER SEVEN

Much of what the alien -- *make that Xik'en*, Cassidy corrected herself -- said was confusing.

The alien language was high-pitched, like a parrot trained to speak, but the alien device connected to her skull translated the words for Cassidy.

The speech patterns were like a nervous teenager on a first date, speaking without thinking. *Well, from what this Agnoix says, I gather she is like a teenager.*

Reviewing what she'd learned, Cassidy found herself at a loss for words.

She was on a mining station that doubled as a trade port for a vast reptilian empire, inhabited by the Xik'ens.

Cassidy found out she was lucky that Agnoix had saved her, because her culture saw warm-bloods -- mammals -- as bogeymen, a barbaric sub-intelligent species prone to violence and cannibalism.

Doing her best to force the visuals of that out of her mind, Cassidy tried to straighten out the rest of the knowledge that Agnoix had supplied her with.

Tonight was Sastreni, which appeared to be a cross between Halloween and Founder's Day in Xik'en culture. The youth dressed up as the founders of their culture, though Cassidy wasn't clear on if they were mythical characters or actual people. Agnoix was dressed up as 'Brauxel', which -- as far as Cassidy could determine -- was a Joan of Arc type personality, and not very mainstream.

When Agnoix got to the part of the narrative about how her brother, Axaik, had abandoned her to attend a party with his buddies, Cassidy spoke up.

"I have siblings, sisters of my own, and I understand what you mean. Many times my sisters ditched me to hang out in the mall or go for a ride with their friends when they had promised to do something with me." Realizing that some of her language and terms were confusing the younger Xik'en, she clarified: "Sorry, I just mean I understand where you're coming from. Can we start fresh?" She stuck out her hand. "I'm Cassidy, thank you for saving my life, and I'd like to be your friend."

***

Much of what the mammal -- no. Correct that, her name is Cassidy, Agnoix thought to herself. Much of what Cassidy is saying makes little sense, but I don't think she means me or the mining complex any harm.

Doing her best to explain herself without sounding like a child, Cassidy startled Agnoix when she reached out an open palm in friendship.

Stretching towards Cassidy, Agnoix reached out her own hand and placed it palm to palm against the human's, and did her best not to jump when Cassidy wrapped her fingers around her hand and shook it. Puzzled by the odd ritual, Agnoix gripped Cassidy's hand and, likewise, shook it.

"So what now, you can't stay here?"

***

Doing her best not to grimace as Agnoix's taloned hand almost crushed hers, Cassidy responded to the young Xik'en. "I think my priority is to figure out a way home, but I'd also love to pick up a sample of these Vao stones for Doctor Gamgee back home. This is your home, do you have any suggestions?"

Touched that this adult, even if it was a mammal, was seeking her guidance, Agnoix considered. *I don't think Cassidy is conscious how much danger she is in. An unlisted mammal on a Xik'en space station and inside the alien free zone. If she's lucky, she'll get roughed by security, but if the wrong people find her it's the airlock for sure, and this time without a breathing mask.*

Counting on the differences in their societies to conceal any doubt, Agnoix thought, and the hint of a solution began to take hold.

"I think I might have an idea that fits both your goals, but it will involve some risk. I have one condition though: you must take me as far as this portal in the asteroid belt. I want to see it." Even while being translated through the Branch of Languages, Agnoix's excitement came through. "Are you agreeable?" Agnoix asked.

"Agreeable? Heck yes. Risk is my middle name," Cassidy said. Observing the bewildered expression on Agnoix's face, Cassidy tried to explain. "Ah, it's an expression where I'm from, it means that is acceptable."

I wonder if all humans are this strange, Agnoix thought to herself.

CHAPTER EIGHT

Agnoix couldn't believe her luck when Cassidy agreed to take her as far as the portal. Unknown to Cassidy, Agnoix planned on following Cassidy through, to explore this strange new world called Earth.

"But work comes first, as my mother would say," Agnoix began as she stepped backward to look upon the human. "And we have some work to do if we don't want you looking like a... a... warm-blood. Sorry."

Cassidy's blunt-toothed grin startled Agnoix -- *their teeth are so ugly* -- but she proceeded.

"We need to get you into a disguise..." Agnoix muttered, and started rooting around the custodian's closet to discover what she had available, as Cassidy watched her and grinned.

I'm certain she could snap me in two with no effort, and by her own admission she's not yet matured. I realize I've only known her for minutes, and maybe it's the lack of oxygen to my brain or that strange drug she injected me with, but I like the kid, Cassidy thought to herself. She then asked Agnoix: "So this Sastreni of yours sounds like our Halloween back home. We'd dress up as superheroes or witches or goblins and go door to door in the neighbourhood saying 'Trick or Treat'. We always got treats."

The young Xik'en rummaged through the custodian's closet, putting material into a heap. The heap contained the contents of the emergency kit, a disposable sanitation bio-suit, and other items that might be useful in disguising the human.

"So you dressed up as well? And did this Treat-tricking?" Agnoix asked.

"It's called 'Trick or Treating'. But yeah, I would do it with my sisters, though more than once they ditched me to go off with their friends, not unlike what your brother did. I'm sorry, it sucks, I know."

Agnoix could figure out the essentials of what Cassidy said, and suspected that 'sucking' is something bad. "So what was your costume?" Agnoix asked as she realized that all her hard work needed major repairs after its ordeal tonight.

"I mostly went with classic monsters, even though my Mom always wanted to dress me as a princess. I enjoyed dressing up as the Mummy, a witch, and even one year as the headless horseman," Cassidy said, and at Agnoix's puzzled expression elaborated: "Ah... I'll explain it another time. Wait, I have an idea. What about a ghost?"

"The ghost of whom?" asked Agnoix.

"Does it matter? Can't it be a generic ghost? Does it have to be a specific individual?"

"Well, in Xik'en society, we honour our notable founders with our Sastreni costumes, but your idea should work!" Agnoix said, starting to pick out different pieces from her pile.

"Here," Agnoix said, thrusting the bio-suit at Cassidy. "Put this on. It will cover your... un-Xik'enness." The complete absurdity of the situation struck the two of them, and they both laughed. Struggling to control herself, Agnoix said: "We must be quiet in case anyone passes the hall."

Still chuckling, the pair did their best to get Cassidy into the bio-suit, but the void where a Xik'en would stick out their tail stumped them for a moment. "I have it," hissed Agnoix, as she attempted to contain her laughter. "Here, stick the window cleaner in the belt of your pants and it should fill in the tail section." Picking up the tool that Cassidy had meant to use as a weapon minutes before, Agnoix helped Cassidy fit it as she had proposed. She shook her head. "I do not understand how you walk around without a tail. I'd think you would fall on your face, being unable to balance."

This started the laughter between them anew but, with a force of will, the two stopped and finished Cassidy's costume.

They sealed her up in the janitor's disposable bio-suit, fake tail and all. Agnoix took the emergency heating blanket from the first aid kit, which she kicked herself for forgetting about when she could have used it, and passed it to the human. Cassidy used her pocket knife to cut two neat eye-holes in the blanket. They draped the blanket over her and -- using orange flapping tape from her field kit to secure it around her neck and arms -- she presented herself for inspection.

"Well..." Agnoix said as she looked Cassidy up and down. "It is a unique costume. No one will wonder what species you are in this: rather they'll question your mental abilities." Seeing her new friend slump, she hastened to add, "But what do they know? I think this ghost costume could take off. Now we just need to make sure no one talks to you. Your odd voice will make people curious," Agnoix said, then slapped her tail against the floor in agitation. "I'm such a mammal sometimes," she cursed. She stopped and looked at Cassidy, her eyes wide. "Sorry, it's just a figure of speech. I just forgot something. We need to get this blanket off you for a minute. You don't have a proper snout."

Agnoix grabbed Cassidy's depleted breathing mask. Disconnecting the mask from the hose and tank, Agnoix helped Cassidy drape the mask around the Branch of Languages. Within the blanket, Cassidy would have the shape of a Xik'en face as long as no one looked too close.

"I've never heard of another race of beings such as you. I'm not allowed to study alien biology as much as I would like; they forbid many of those records to Xik'ens outside of scholarship."

"Well, you're my first alien friend, so that makes us even," Cassidy replied, and could see that her vow of friendship had touched the youthful girl.

Grinning in pleasure, Agnoix tried to maintain her cool and turned her attention back to the matter at hand.

"I'm glad it works... friend Cassidy, but we should get you covered again and start moving to the mining bay before shift change."

Together, the two got Cassidy under the blanket again and got Agnoix's costume back into a semblance of order. A liberal amount of wound glue from the emergency kit and flagging tape from Cassidy's pack got the job done.

Their faces concealed, the two nodded at each other and turned to the door of the custodian's closet.

Agnoix reached out and slid the door open a fraction, and realized that the light within the room could easily highlight the pair to anybody in the hallway.

"The light -- turn it off Cassidy," Agnoix hissed.

Cassidy couldn't help but notice how the Xik'en's tongue curled as she spoke and was disappointed the translation device didn't add extra "sss" sounds like it would in a B-Movie.

"The Light!" Agnoix said again, and Cassidy shook the errant thought from her mind and did as she was asked. Figuring out the switch wasn't unduly hard. She just needed to place her finger within a socket and turn it, until the only light within the closet was that coming in from the outside.

After several minutes of watching, with her entire view of the mining complex a narrow slice of empty hall seen over Agnoix's shoulder, Cassidy was about to ask if there was a problem. Before she could, Agnoix slid the door open and stepped into the hallway, waving for her new friend to follow her.

***

With a tentative step, Cassidy walked into the gallery hallway of the mining complex and took in the spectacular view of being inside an alien space station.

Ignoring Agnoix's pleas to follow her, Cassidy walked, spellbound, to the window, her fake tail swinging behind her as if it had a mind of its own.

Standing in front of the immense window, her heavy breathing ruffling the sheet over her face, Cassidy watched the asteroid belt of the Vao system before her.

Like a bag of glass marbles tossed in a gravel driveway, the glistening rocks tumbled around the sky of the mining complex, highlighted by an exquisite shine.

"It's breathtaking," Cassidy said, as she placed her palms against the window. It was as if she were yearning to seize one of the asteroids.

Coming up behind her friend, Agnoix looked upon the asteroid belt that had been her home for her whole life through the eyes of the human, and saw it anew.

"You're right, it is, isn't it?" Agnoix said. "The glow is the super fine dust that is being highlighted by the rays of the sun. During solar storms it lights up like fireworks."

Touching her friend's arm, Agnoix said: "Cassidy, we need to move." With a slight tug, she drew the woman along with her, away from the mesmerizing view.

While drawing her attention away from the spectacular view outside the mining complex window, Cassidy couldn't help but wonder aloud: "Why don't the asteroids hit the station?"

"Magnets," Agnoix answered.

"Magnets? You can't be serious," Cassidy said. She pushed herself to keep up with the Xik'en youth and take in as much of the detail of the space station as she could through her costume's eye holes.

"The mining complex is enveloped by a field of magnetized orbs, which operate as a security blanket around the complex, and it cushions against any strike. Any asteroids too massive or without sufficient iron content are steered away by the mining pods," Agnoix said to ease any fears. *She is only a mammal,* Agnoix thought to herself, and then was ashamed that her racial bias came so easily to her. She hastened to explain: "There hasn't been a strike on the complex since my Father's Father's time, and that was during a terrible solar storm before they upgraded the magnetic shield. You're safe here, Cassidy."

Agnoix saw the shadow of a smile reflected in the eyes peering at her through the holes of the costume.

"I know I am Agnoix, but like you said, we should go."

Cassidy turned away from one wonder to take in another.

From Cassidy's point of view, the Xik'en mining complex was too bright for her eyes. The pounding headache behind her eyes attested to that, though Cassidy did her best to catalogue the home of Agnoix's people.

The light level is probably the same on their native world; what their eyes have evolved to accept. That must go for the atmosphere, too. Whether it's the alien drug Agnoix injected me with causing me to feel light-headed or not, but I'd say the oxygen content is higher than what I'm used to. That goes double for the mugginess, Cassidy thought to herself, as she tried to scratch her back where the thin trickle of sweat was forming.

But even that discomfort couldn't distract Cassidy from her experience.

The mining station feels very organic to me. The tunnels are rounded and they raise, dip and curl as if formed by water over thousands of years. Along the walls are shelves, I guess, and each has various plants and mosses growing within them, whether it's for oxygen production, simple decoration, or both I don't know. I must ask Agnoix.

You're so busy gawking around that you neglected your primary source. Who knows how much time we have together? I need to make the most of it.

"Agnoix," Cassidy began, and watched as her friend peeked around the curving tunnel to determine if anyone else was close.

The coast clear, the young Xik'en hurried back to her new friend. "Yes, is there a problem? Do you smell someone behind us?"

"No, nothing like that. I just wanted you to tell me a little about yourself and your people while we have the time," Cassidy replied.

And while Agnoix understood the peril better than Cassidy, the adolescent Xik'en girl also wanted to hear something of the world from which Cassidy was from.

"Okay, Cassidy, but let's go back and forth. I'm curious about your world too," Agnoix said, motioning for Cassidy to follow her. They continued slinking down the tunnel.

"It's hard to know where to start," Agnoix began. "The Xik'en are an ancient and prideful race; our reach is vast, though most of us don't like to travel far unless it's necessary. Though I've always wanted to stand beneath a true sky."

Looking behind her to make certain there wasn't anybody near them, Cassidy turned back to Agnoix. "You mean you've never been outside before? Isn't there a Xik'en home planet?"

"Oh there is, it's called 'Xik'en', very original isn't it?"

Agnoix puffed her cheeks in amusement. "I might go there someday. It's a pilgrimage every Xik'en is supposed to do once in their life, but I'd rather travel to an alien planet like yours. What's 'Human' like, Cassidy?"

Through the sheet over her face, Cassidy could conceal her grin. "Earth is the name of my home world, and we're nowhere near your level of technology. My people haven't traveled farther than our moon."

Hearing movement and seeing shadows flicker in the tunnel up ahead, Agnoix pushed Cassidy back a step so they could wait and see if they needed to hide. While waiting, Agnoix continued in a soft tone: "I don't understand. Then how did you end up outside? Were you a stowaway onboard a ship? Are you a lawbreaker on the run from the authorities?" The young Xik'en's lavender eyes grew wide.

"Ha ha, nothing like that, Agnoix, I promise. A portal brought me here. I work with a scientist named Gamgee, and I am exploring these portals for him. Each one leads me to a unique dimension: some are like my world's history, and others are alien like here. I flew my airplane -- that's an atmospheric craft -- through a portal and found myself amid your asteroid belt. If you hadn't rescued me when you did, your miners would have discovered my frozen body someday. I didn't expect to end up in space."

With a tale that outlandish, I'm inclined to believe her, Agnoix thought to herself. *I mean there are a hundred other stories that would almost make sense. She jumped ship, tossed out an airlock in the quarantine zone. Or even pirates trying to steal asteroids, but portals and alternative dimensions?*

"Scale rot," Agnoix cursed. "I believe you, Cassidy,

though if anybody else were to hear that story, especially from a mammal... I mean 'human', they would detain you in a flash."

"Then I guess we had better not get caught," Cassidy said, and put a hand on the Xik'en's shoulder just as a new voice asked: "What do we have here, my fellow Sastreni celebrants!"

CHAPTER NINE

Oh please, don't let it be him... Agnoix prayed, even as she looked past Cassidy and saw her brother Axaik and a crowd of his peers -- all dressed in their Sastreni costumes -- walking towards them.

"Spread out, my fellow revelers; don't let them slide down some hole like the mammal loving scum they are," Axaik hissed, and before either Agnoix or Cassidy could act, the group of nine nearly-mature Xik'ens fanned out in a half circle to block the two friends from fleeing.

Axaik handed off his beverage container, which smelled like rubbing alcohol to Cassidy's nose, to a fellow costumed Xik'en and walked towards his sister, who had placed herself in front of Cassidy.

"I'm right aren't I?" Axaik reached out a taloned finger and poked Cassidy in the chest, hard, causing her to inhale sharply. "Only a stinking mammal lover would hang around with my sister. The sister that everyone says is so smart and could do grand things if she just applied herself like a proper Xik'en."

"That's right, my friends," Axaik said over his shoulder, wobbling on his feet. "The disappointment in the family gets all the attention while I work hard, do all I'm asked. Apprenticed to the Trading Guild in some backwater station away from you fine reptiles."

"Axaik, you're drunk. How did you get Grove juice? That's forbidden outside of official celebrations," Agnoix said, shoving her brother's hand aside and directing his attention away from Cassidy.

"Forbidden!" Axaik roared, and his friends echoed the laughter.

They raised their own containers of the alcoholic beverage, several of them staggering on their feet. One even fell over, and needed help to stand again.

"Nothing is forbidden on Sastreni to those who have connections. You're not the only one interested in the aliens that come through this station. For the right amount of credits, a smart Xik'en can get anything he wants."

"And what will mother say when she finds out that you have been drinking Grove juice?" Agnoix threatened her older brother, then realized that might have been a mistake, as his eyes narrowed and his lips retracted, showing pointed teeth.

Tilting his head to the side, Agnoix lashed out with lightening speed and grabbed each of the women, his talons ripping into their costumes. "My mother will not find out about this, will she gang? Not if these two mammal lovers spend some time locked in a storage cage." His alcohol laced breath assaulted them. "Spend a night away from home and Mom won't believe anything you say. Especially after I tell her how you slipped away from your older and caring brother, and myself and my hard-working Xik'en friends sacrificed our last Sastreni to look for you."

"Don't do this Axaik, I know we're not close but..."

Axaik interrupted by shaking them, the sound of ripping fabric getting louder. The front of the reserve parachute strapped to Cassidy's chest poked out.

Releasing his hold, Axaik pushed his sister aside. His friends grabbed her when she struggled to escape.

"You haven't said a word. Do I know you?" Axaik asked as he flicked a tattered piece of Cassidy's makeshift costume. "And what are you supposed to be, anyway? That's not like any Sastreni costume I've seen before."

"You leave her alone, Axaik, she's just a friend, someone new to the station, you just haven't met her yet."

"I'm sure if you had gotten a friend I would have heard about it," Axaik said, focusing all his attention on the costumed Cassidy. "You're outnumbered, and if you don't want to spend a night in a cold dark storage cage with my little sister then you better tell us who you are."

The Branch of Languages allowed her to speak and understand the Xik'en language, and Cassidy knew what was happening and decided that she didn't like Axaik.

Knocking his talon-tipped hand aside, Cassidy stood as straight as she could. And while she only reached Axaik's chin, her physical presence caused the drunken youth to take a step back, his weak laugh a poor mask for his hesitation.

"You want to know who and what I am? Then let me show you!" Cassidy exclaimed, the genderless voice produced by the Branch of Languages making her words menacing. Cassidy gripped the bottom of the sheet and ripped it over her head.

Ignoring the cry of "Stop" from Agnoix, Cassidy flung the costume aside. With her braided hair swinging, wide eyes, and sweat-covered face, Cassidy yelled: "I am Cassidy Cane, Explorer from the planet Earth: a warm-blooded mammal that wants nothing more than to grab as many Xik'ens as I can and eat them!" She then mock-lunged at Axaik.

Brain clouded with drink, stuck in a situation that wasn't going the way he'd planned, and faced with the bogeyman his race had feared since they left their home world, Axaik did the only thing he could. He screamed in terror, then turned to flee.

Like a stampede, the other scared and confused youths reacted on their most primal levels and followed suit. Stumbling over each other while yelling and screaming in fear, they clawed their way down the hallway, heedless of the harm done to their fellows.

Dusting her hands off, a wide smile on her face, Cassidy leaned down, picked up one of the dropped containers, and smelled the alcoholic contents. She scrunched up her nose. "What is this stuff? Smells like something my father used to clean paint brushes."

Not getting an answer, Cassidy turned and saw Agnoix staring dumbstruck at her.

"Agnoix? Are you okay?" Cassidy said, taking a step towards her friend, and the young Xik'en jumped backward.

They're told their entire lives that warm-bloods are the devils of their culture and you used that against your friend. Likely the only person on this entire mining station that would have saved me and I do this. Why do I leap before I think? Cassidy thought to herself, sobering her mood. "I'm sorry, Agnoix, I wasn't serious about eating your brother or anyone. I was just trying to get them to leave us alone, and I wasn't thinking how it would turn out. I really am sorry, Agnoix. Can you forgive me?"

For several seconds a wide-eyed Agnoix just stared at Cassidy, as if fighting a war within herself. Should she do what her instincts were telling her, to run in fear just as her brother had, or should she stay with her strange new friend, the only friend she'd ever had?

A slight shiver went through Agnoix, and then the youthful Xik'en smiled. "I'm okay, Cassidy. I'm not ashamed to say that you nearly scared the scales off me. All I could think of was the monsters they threatened me with as a child, the ones I KNEW lived in my closet and came out at night." Looking at the uncovered human, Agnoix stepped forward. "We need to get you covered again. The yelling will bring trouble, no matter how late it is."

And as if called, the two women heard the sounds of clawed feet and loud voices racing towards them.

They did their best to get Cassidy's costume in order as a pair of Xik'en security guards rounded the corner. They saw the two costumed figures and hurried towards them, stun batons in their taloned fists.

With the focus being getting Cassidy back into her costume, Agnoix's own looks were in disarray. Her yellow and blue striped mask was on the ground. Realizing that she looked like a victim, Agnoix played into that, and waved at the security guards to hurry faster.

That simple gesture likely changed the whole outcome of the rest of the night.

Skidding to a stop in front of them, Agnoix found that it was the same two security guards who had responded to the life station when she had rescued Cassidy from outer space.

Focusing her attention on the older of the two, some tiny part of her brain remembered that her name was Krolzan. "Please, could you help two young Xik'en tormented and set upon by a group of older kids?" Agnoix said, hoping her innocent act came across as more believable than it sounded to her ears.

The older Xik'en looked a little ragged around the scales, but her eyes scanned the two youths in a professional matter before answering Agnoix. "What's going on here? It's getting a little late for you to still be out for Sastreni, isn't it?"

Forcing her eyes wide, Agnoix stuck her tongue out until it was just past her teeth, just as she'd seen the older girls do when looking for sympathy. She willed her tail to stop twitching in nervousness. "Myself and my friend..." She paused a second. "...*Caskad*, were out enjoying Sastreni when this group of older kids started teasing us and trying to destroy our costumes." Agnoix held her arms out wide to show her much abused costume as proof. "I won't want to get anyone in trouble, Officer, but a good Xik'en must do their duty and tell the truth, correct?"

"That's right, young miss," the young Xik'en named Tuds replied, even as he looked Agnoix up and down in an appreciative manner. "You and your friend should tell us everything." Tuds looked at Cassidy with fresh eyes.

Fearing discovery, Agnoix stepped towards Tuds and looked up at him. "I so want to be a dutiful citizen, so I'll tell you. I fear this group was drinking Grove juice. You could smell it on them, and look." Agnoix pointed to a container that Axaik and his friends had dropped in their rush to get away from Cassidy. "One of them dropped the smelly stuff when you scared them away." A flash of inspiration struck Agnoix, and she finished by saying: "They also were bragging about messing around and discharging an emergency life station earlier in the night, if that means anything."

"So that's who was responsible!" Krolzan growled, grabbing Tuds by the sleeve of his security uniform. "Come on, Tuds. I will have these trouble makers if it takes all night. This will be a Sastreni they won't forget." Krolzan turned to chase after Axaik and his friends, then stopped to looked at Agnoix and Cassidy. "You two are all right, aren't you? Do you need medical attention or an escort home? I could send for someone."

"We're fine," Agnoix blurted. "We're both okay. My friend and I are going right home like dutiful citizens, aren't we Caskad?"

Why did you do that?! They'll recognize the Branch of Languages and they'll discover Cassidy, Agnoix thought to herself.

Relief flooded through her when Cassidy didn't say a word, only nodded in agreement.

"See that you do. Come on, Tuds, we have work to do," Krolzan said, dragging a reluctant Tuds after her.

Once the sound of the security guards running faded out of earshot, Cassidy laughed. "Boys are the same no matter the dimension!"

Agnoix began shaking as she realized how close to

discovery they had been and how she had lied to the security guards. The young woman she had been this morning wouldn't recognize herself now.

"That scared me, Cassidy. I don't think you realize how close that was or what might have happened if they had caught you."

Walking over to her friend, Cassidy placed her hand on her shoulder. "Maybe I don't understand everything, but I know that you risked yourself to save me because you thought it was the right thing to do. Maybe lying isn't the best way to go about it, but at least this way your brother will get what's coming to him. I always sailed close to the wind when my friends were in danger."

Agnoix's mind raced as she visualized the problems that were awaiting her brother if the station's security personal found him and his friends. She found that it didn't bother her as much as she would have thought it would and chuckled, her tongue curling in joy.

"Okay, maybe you're right, Cassidy, but let's not do anymore of this 'wind sailing', I don't know how much more I can take." Agnoix picked up her fallen mask. "We still have the most dangerous part ahead of us. We need to sneak you into the mining area of the station and get you into a pod so we can get you home."

Cassidy stood up straight. "The ghosts of all Xik'ens are with us. Let's go."

Tugging on her mask, Agnoix smiled and led her friend deeper into the station.

CHAPTER TEN

Even Cassidy could tell that the station was changing. The beautiful flowing walls and tunnels of what she thought of as the residential area made way for plain square tunnels, with motorized carts of people whipping past.

The first couple of times the pair saw traffic or people moving around, Agnoix and Cassidy had tried to hide until they went past. That had soon proved impossible, and Cassidy had suggested something that was, for her, a tried-and-true course of action. "Act like you know what you're doing. Look straight ahead and walk with purpose, and most people will assume that you belong even if their instincts tell them otherwise. I can't tell you how many times that simple bluff has saved me grief."

Their bluff had worked; most of the Xik'ens did nothing but glance at them. But the increase in traffic made it hard for Cassidy to ask questions, fearing that someone would recognize the artificial voice of the Branch of Languages. Struggling with her words, Cassidy asked about the change in light levels.

The work and working life within this section of the

mining station didn't respect the clock. The lights shifted from a bright yellow to a bright orange, which Agnoix said signified the second of three stages of light on her home planet. Xik'en was a world that never went dark.

"The home world of my species, Xik'en, has one large primary star and two enormous gas giants. They're so close to the planet that they provide light upon its surface at all hours," Agnoix explained in a tone like someone repeating something from a class lecture. "The light of the primary is white, the gas giant Ilmone is orange, and Alnosie provides red. They reflect the three phases of a Xik'en's life, service and death."

She leaned towards Cassidy as a group of Xik'en, smelling of mineral dust, passed in the opposite direction. Agnoix whispered: "I wish we had more time to just get to know each other. Maybe you can tell me more of your human world while we hunt for your portal, Cassidy?"

I don't want to lie to Agnoix -- she's a friendly kid, nearly a grown woman herself. But I can't allow her to risk herself outside with me. I never really think of the risks I take, but allowing her to come into open space is just something I can't allow. I wonder if parenthood feels like this?

As the mineral processing workers passed, the dust following in their wake tickled Cassidy's nose, threatening to send her into a sneezing fit.

That brought the errant thought: "Do the Xik'en sneeze?", before she realized that she was avoiding answering Agnoix's question. "If there is time, my friend, I'll tell you whatever you want to know, I promise," Cassidy said, and the words soured her stomach. Upon the thought of her stomach, it grumbled.

"Are you hungry?" Agnoix asked. "I have some fruit leather that those who liked my Sastreni costume gave me."

"I'd try it, Agnoix. It must be better than those terrible molasses candies I got Trick or Treating as a kid. But until we get to a place where I can take off this costume, my stomach will just have to stay hungry," Cassidy said as she pointed to the large opening in the tunnel ahead of them. "Are we close?"

"Yes. We better not risk you talking anymore, just let me get us through the gates and then we can go from there."

I wish I was half as sure as I sounded. But Cassidy is relying on me to help get her home and I must do what I can if I want a chance to explore her world, Agnoix thought as she steered Cassidy away from the heavy traffic leading into the mining hub and towards the walkway that led to the checkpoint.

Agnoix watched as a series of automated work carts with equipment, supplies and personal each pulled up to the barrier, thumping her tail as she did.

Vehicles, customs trackers, buying agents, and miners all passed through the mazes of bridges and walkways of the hub. Thumping her tail again, Agnoix waved away Cassidy's questioning look.

If I'd been thinking, we might have been able to sneak onto a work cart and slip into the hub unnoticed. Too late for that now, she thought as they walked up to the inspection station. Two members of Xik'en security watched them, with their pointy teeth bared in agitation.

"Not more Sastreni revelers... haven't we had our

share tonight?" a female Xik'en said to the other, a smaller male.

"At least we haven't had the night Krozlan has. Those kids and their wild stories of murderous mammals has gotten too many spooked tonight," the smaller male said to his partner.

"You're right there Qhoxen." The female turned to Agnoix and Cassidy. "Now what are you kids doing here at the hub? You know you're not supposed to be down here without an escort."

"Nuzon, it's me, Agnoix," Agnoix said as she slid her abused Sastreni mask onto her head, exposing her face.

The puzzlement on the security guard's face turned to recognition. "Agnoix? Orlol's daughter, right? The one who wants to be an explorer instead of a dutiful Xik'en citizen." Her words were more playful than hurtful.

"That's right. I promised my Mom that we would come visit her and show her our Sastreni costumes. Oh, Nuzon. This is Caskad, a friend and newcomer to the station, so we're spending Sastreni together."

"Agnoix, you know the rules. We allow no unescorted youths in the mining hub, there's too much traffic and machinery in use, you could get hurt," Nuzon said, planting her taloned hands on her wide hips and blocking the way.

"Please, Nuzon!" Agnoix whined. "She knows we're coming and will meet us in the break room in the processing area. This is her only chance to see our costumes. She's working extra hours and my father is away. You know me, we'll be in and out quick, no one but us will know."

"Well," Nuzon said. She looked at her partner.

"They didn't sneak past, or pull any Sastreni pranks," Qhoxen said, his interest more focused on what was going on inside the hub than outside it. "I say let them go. You're only a kid once."

"Hmmm..." Nuzon replied. Eventually she nodded. "Okay, just this once, because it's Sastreni. There, wear these visitors' badges," Nuzon stuck two blue tags on the front of Agnoix's and Cassidy's costumes. "And stay on the blue path until you get to processing. You know the way, right? Agnoix, you won't stray? I'm putting my trust in you two."

"I know where we're going, Nuzon," Agnoix said. "Thank you for this, it... it means a lot."

As Agnoix and Cassidy passed by the security station, following the blue line on the floor, Nuzon shook her head. "Kids these days."

"I know what you mean," replied Qhoxen. "And what was up with their costumes? I didn't recognize either of them. In my day we dressed up as Tox'eix or another of the founders of our Empire like a good Xik'en. They waste youth on the young."

CHAPTER ELEVEN

The floor was a maze of colours as Agnoix and Cassidy followed the blue line through the open walkways of the processing hub. Fresh colours got added as routes branched, and they left behind some colours as the two walked along.

I hope Agnoix is paying better attention to where we're going than I am. I just can't believe how massive this place is, Cassidy thought to herself as she struggled to peer through the jaggedly cut eye holes of her costume at her surroundings.

As far as Cassidy could tell, she and Agnoix were in the middle of a vast cylinder that was criss-crossed with walkways, equipment elevators, and twisting cart ramps. A quick glance over a low railing showed that she and Agnoix were coming into the cylinder some place in its middle, since neither a floor nor ceiling were in view.

When no one was close to the pair, Cassidy leaned close to Agnoix and said: "How big is this station? It seems to go on forever."

Agnoix stopped at the junction point as a cart filled with Xik'ens dressed in harnesses and sporting purple badges passed by. She thought before she replied. "I don't know how to explain it in terms you would understand. Only that this mining complex began inside the largest asteroid in the belt and has grown through the generations, with other asteroids connected like a spoked wheel. This hub is the void left by the original asteroid."

Once the cart with harnessed Xik'ens passed, Agnoix looked around and stepped off the blue line they had been following and onto the purple.

"We need to hurry, Cassidy. We won't be able to talk our way out of the miner's area if we're caught; we will have to rely on your human luck."

"My dear Agnoix," Cassidy replied, her smile unseen by her friend. "Luck is how I live every day."

With the cart carrying the harnessed Xik'ens ahead of them, Agnoix and Cassidy crouched down and hurried to keep them in sight. As the cart left the open air hub and entered a tunnel opening with a purple display written above the hole, the women hurried after it.

Reminds me of Assyrian. I would love a direct word to word translation, Cassidy thought to herself.

They went as quietly as they could, though any noise they made was drowned by the echoing thunder that was being created in the hub.

Agnoix stopped and stared up at the purple display. "That means a group of miners are getting ready to fly out into the asteroid belt. They were the ones in the cart wearing harnesses." Pausing, Agnoix looked back at Cassidy and the spiraling walkways and bridges with people and equipment moving, and found herself rooted in place.

"Agnoix, what's wrong? I thought you said that this was the only way you could think of to get back outside."

"It is Cassidy, but... but I've never been in there, nor know what to expect. We've come to the end of my knowledge and I fear it won't be enough," Agnoix said. The distress in her voice was clear even through the Branch of Languages.

You should be ashamed, Cassidy. You should have guessed what kind of strain you were putting on the poor kid. You were always so focused that you failed to see the plain and simple, Cassidy chided herself.

Cassidy placed her hand on the younger woman's shoulder. "I can take it from here, Agnoix, you have done way more than I could have ever expected. You saved my life at least twice and we've only known each other for less than a day. You head back home. With a bit of luck, your brother will be in enough trouble that they will ignore anything he says about me. I'm sorry that I have gotten you into trouble and didn't source any of the ARC crystals for the doctor, but just getting home will be challenge enough." She held out her hand. "We part ways here, friend Agnoix. I owe you more than I could say and I wish we could spend more time together. There is so much I could learn about your people, and share my world with you, but we must each go back to our own worlds and lives."

When Agnoix didn't take Cassidy's hand, Cassidy pushed forward and gave the young Xik'en woman a fierce hug, before dashing back into the tunnel towards her way home.

***

Turning away from Agnoix, who hadn't moved an

inch nor said a word, Cassidy pushed aside the emotions turning in her and got to work.

Okay, smarty pants: you left your guide behind and you're on your own. What are you going to do? Cassidy asked herself as she jogged down the winding tunnel, the fake tail in her costume banging against the wall as she moved.

"That's a good question," Cassidy muttered to herself, then froze in place as she came across the cart which had been transporting the Xik'ens that Agnoix identified as miners.

Cassidy leaned in and checked it out.

Other than the Xik'en equivalent of a fire extinguisher, a forgotten lunchbox, and the weirdly designed seats that took into account the Xik'en tail, Cassidy saw nothing of interest.

As she continued down the tunnel, Xik'en voices, too faint for the Branch of Languages to translate, issued from a narrow opening that branched off from the main tunnel.

Let's hope that two plus two makes four in this situation and those are my missing miners. Let's hope that is the tunnel to the flight deck or whatever they call it here.

Making sure that no one was nearby, Cassidy stepped into the tunnel, then stopped and looked back at the cart.

She cursed, then hurried back to the cart and picked up what she hoped was a fire extinguisher, holding it in both her hands. "I hope I don't have to injure anyone, but it doesn't hurt to be prepared." As she held her makeshift weapon at the ready, she once again followed the voices.

Whether it was the removing of the fire extinguisher from the cart or some other automated signal, the cart started to hum, and it drove on its own back the way it came.

"Probably pre-programmed. At least I hope so," Cassidy said, as the cart disappeared from view.

The tunnel wound around to a large open pit with a ramp leading down. Edging closer, Cassidy saw that the Xik'en miners were in a locker room and were suiting up in the same spacesuits and harnesses she had seen them with before.

Retreating from the edge of the pit, on the chance that one of them might look up, Cassidy retreated to the gallery window. Overlooking the locker pit, she got her first view of the mining bay.

"Holy scale rot," she said, her mouth open with shock.

CHAPTER TWELVE

"Goodbye Cassidy," Agnoix whispered to herself; the human woman having left her alone.

Goodbye to the first genuine friend you've ever had. Goodbye to your one and only chance to break the mold your family and culture are forcing you to fit within. Are you going to stand here and let it happen?

Scared and frustrated, Agnoix slammed her taloned fist against her thigh, the dull throbbing pain allowing a moment of clarity.

You've always idolized Brauxel, Warden of the Two Divines. Defender to all, whether they were outcast and refugee, and if Cassidy doesn't fit that then who would? So why did you wimp out? You're no hatchling that needs an adult to hold her hand. You're almost of age yourself, a grown Xik'en woman able to make her own decisions, so what do you decide? Are you going to let your friend walk into danger on her own, or are you going to defend her?

Slamming her fist against her thigh again, this time cracking her much abused homemade armour, Agnoix exclaimed: "I will defend my friend!"

She hurried after Cassidy, hoping to catch her before

anything bad happened.

The tunnel, with its purple lines on the floor, led off into several branches. But a quick look at the narrow script at the top of each door told her that what she wanted was further on, if for no other reason than the transport cart couldn't have travelled into those smaller corridors.

Maybe thinking about the cart isn't such a wonderful idea, she thought, for as soon as she did she heard the hum of its motor. It was getting closer -- FAST!

"Scale rot," Agnoix cursed, dashing into the nearest branching tunnel without time to see where it went.

Hurrying down the tunnel, Agnoix found herself in some kind of leisure room. Stools lined the walls, along with dust-covered work clothes and safety gear, and the sharp smell of fungal tea filled the air.

Emergency protocols pinned to the walls were covered in hand-written scribbles, along with a calendar featuring pictures of mining tools supplied by a well-known contractor. Then it dawned on her.

She was in the break room for those who did the rough job of sorting the asteroids before going into processing, those called 'Breakers'.

Agnoix knew little of these kinds of workers. The biggest and dumbest members of her society did this rough and dangerous work. At least, that was what her mother had always said, and had forbidden her to associate with the children of the Breakers. But as she had no friends regardless of social status, it hadn't mattered much to her.

Seeing an opportunity to find herself not in her colourful Sastreni costume, Agnoix acted.

Finding a pair of the thick, rough coveralls in her size

was her first problem, and where to change into them was her second. Shaking her head at the time she was wasting, Agnoix stripped off her costume. Heedless of the damage she was doing, the tortured and repaired fabric gave up the fight and she destroyed the costume of Brauxel without a second thought.

In place of the yellow and blue striped armour that signified the dual nature of Brauxel's commitment as a defender, was a new hero. Now stood young Agnoix in a patched and dust-covered pair of coveralls, with a helmet and face shield.

I should blend right in, Agnoix thought. As voices came up from behind her from the lavatory, her confidence evaporated and she made for the hatch at the other end of the break room.

Just as the shadows on the walls resolved into adult Xik'en, Agnoix passed through the hatch and into chaos.

***

"It's massive," Cassidy whispered as she looked down into the mining bay. She wasn't sure what she had been expecting. Asteroid mining wasn't really something she'd even given a second's thought about, but if she had, she doubted it would have looked like this.

It was shaped like a tiered valley, not unlike the Sacred Terraces in Peru, Cassidy reflected. Metal mining pods that resembled giant spiders filled the mining bay.

They were hauling chunks of sliced asteroid and dropping them into the centre of the valley, and the churning teeth within.

"It's massive," Cassidy repeated, as she tried to get

some sense of the scale. Her best guess would have been that it was several times larger than the largest airport she had even been in. "I was wrong, there's more than just that large grinder, each level has its own. I wonder if it's for processing different metals."

The voices in the locker pit below her changed in tone and Cassidy's musing cut itself off. Feet stomped, buckles snapped, and she heard a hatch open. With it, the smell of mineral dust flowed into the locker pit and up into the exhaust grill above Cassidy's head, threatening to make her sneeze.

In seconds, she saw the miners striding out to the top tier of the asteroid processing bay. They were walking to a group of eight mining spiders that had crew fueling and working on them, if her experience on Earth was any guide.

Must be shift change, as Agnoix said, Cassidy thought and felt a sense of shame. *I used that poor kid for my own ends and likely have gotten her into trouble, and I don't see any way to make it better than to leave. Gamgee will just have to do without his precious ARC crystals. It will be a miracle if I even get home.*

Breathing deeply, Cassidy looked down at the mining pods that were being made ready for flight, and she acted. Trusting that no one was below, she ran down the ramp, into the changing area and looked around. Several tunnels branched off. If she guessed by the smells, at least one was a bathroom, though she wasn't keen on putting her theory to the test. Along the walls were recessed lockers, with tags above each, which common sense would suggest were names. Clothes filled several of the lockers, while others were empty, and three contained spacesuits. The suits were of the same design that the miners who just left had been wearing.

Luckily enough, the first one she grabbed was close enough to her size that it didn't matter, though at this point she couldn't have afforded to be picky. Ripping off the costume that Agnoix had made for her, Cassidy was once again clothed as she had been when she'd abandoned her plane after coming through the portal.

"I need a long shower when I get home," she muttered as she got a whiff of herself, her nose crinkling.

Taking off the parachute and the homing device strapped to her left wrist, Cassidy felt a weight slide off her shoulders. The faint red flashing light confirmed that the beacon on board her plane was still active.

"That means I can find the way home, with a little luck. Okay, maybe more than a little."

Climbing into the Xik'en spacesuit wasn't the easiest thing to do on one's own, Cassidy found as she put one leg into the tail hole. But after some struggling she sealed it up, refastened the parachute over the suit, and strapped the homing device over the suit's wrist.

"It isn't fashionable, but it should do," Cassidy said as she looked at herself in a mirror.

Trusting that she had gotten the suit sealed, Cassidy picked up the awkward helmet and connected it to the neck ring. There was a hiss as the hot, muggy air filled her nostrils, telling her she had a good seal, even as the smell reminded her of a compost pile.

The view through the helmet was awkward for some-one without the snout of a Xik'en. Cassidy managed well enough to walk over to the hatch, the sad empty tail portion of her suit dragging along the floor.

With gloves that felt more akin to oven mitts, she hit the yellow button beside the hatch, opening it. The vibration of its opening travelled up her body.

Feeling only a fraction of the confidence that she hoped her bearing was showing the world, Cassidy walked into the Xik'en filled mining bay.

CHAPTER THIRTEEN

Agnoix found herself in a press of bodies also suited like her, all bumping and jostling each other. Like a twig caught by a raging river, the young Xik'en found herself caught up in it.

Her panic was building the more the press of bodies tossed her around. There was the overwhelming smell of rock dust that even the best air filters couldn't extract. A tiny part of her mind remembered the words Cassidy had said: *Act like you own the world and people won't question you.*

Clenching her taloned fists, her lip curling until it exposed her needle-sharp teeth, Agnoix stopped fighting against the flow and hurried to run with it. Her yells of "Let me through; out of my way!" mingled with the other shouts and yells from her fellow Xik'en as they neared their destination.

Unseen hands thrust an air tank into her hands as she moved along. Agnoix watched the woman beside her clip it to her belt and connect it to her face shield, creating an airtight seal. The other Xik'en turned her head to regard Agnoix, her expression confused. Agnoix slid between bodies and out of the woman's view. Watching the others, she connected her own air tank and saw a tiny yellow bar light up on the side of the tank, showing it to be full.

The push of bodies formed a bottleneck at a hatch just ahead. Two blue suited Xik'en checked each miner in a procedure they had done countless times before, letting them into the mining bay.

Agnoix stopped breathing as one of the two blue suited Xik'en ran his talons over her suit, checking the air tank and helmet connection. "Nod if you can hear me," crackled over her helmet's speakers and, without thinking, Agnoix nodded. "Good, pass through." And in such an unceremonious manner, they thrust Agnoix into the massive mining bay that had given her race all the advantages it had.

Two steps into the mining bay, Agnoix stopped walking just to stop and stare. While she had lived here her whole life, like most people she had never been in the mining bay that had brought her society the wealth and privilege that it enjoyed. Sure, she had been in some processing departments, such as the ones where her mother worked, but that was cleaner, more civilized work, using a low gravity furnace to smelt base metal from stone into wire or ingots. Agnoix remembered a school trip in which they had refined the radioactive minerals and bars of gold, the products of each made faster than she could track them, but this was something else. Her people looked like ants as hundreds of them worked at different tiers. They supervised the crude crushing of the raw asteroids into their base parts and ejected the stone waste back out into space.

It was one of the most dangerous jobs on board the station, except for the actual mining and transport of the asteroids. Only the toughest -- or the most desperate -- took a job in primary processing, at a risk of life and limb just too great for most Xik'en.

Bumped from behind, Agnoix stopped her musings as the press of bodies heading to their assigned tier nearly ran her over. Shift results determined how much the workers earned, so more than a few eyes fell on the unmoving Agnoix.

Remember why you're here. Cassidy is likely close by, and while I've only known her a brief time, I'm sure she has everything well in hand.

Agnoix fell into step with a smaller group of suited Xik'en, who made their way up the winding ramps to the top of the grinding tiers. She couldn't help but wonder if the stone she saw, being moved in skids driven by suited Xik'en, would end up in her mother's processing area tonight. *I know so little of what happens here; I was eager to explore and see unknown worlds. Maybe looking at ourselves should be part of my exploration too.* Agnoix struggled up the winding ramp. The long night, with no food and the extra weight of suit and tank, began to sap her energy. She reached the top tier before she collapsed, her legs wobbling from exhaustion.

People, mining pods, and hoists crowded the flight deck, moving the fresh rocks into the many tiers below them. So very far below, Agnoix realized, as the extreme height made her dizzy and forced her to refocus on her level.

Unlike the other grinding tiers devoted to metals and

minerals, Agnoix had come to where the Vao stones went through their pre-processing.

The group of nine suited Xik'en took up their stations on a conveyor belt and, with hand-held lasers, began cutting the hunks of the rare crystal from the surrounding stone.

Agnoix watched as one large male Xik'en gripped a hunk of grey asteroid half as big as Agnoix. Standing it on its end and balancing it one-handed, he used a hand-held laser to slice out three pieces of green Vao stone. They were each as big as her hand, and he dropped them onto the conveyor that led into the wall for more refining. The major pieces of the valuable stone harvested, the worker pushed the rest of the rock into the grinder. They would harvest any smaller pieces and use them in smaller pieces of technology, like Agnoix's Branch of Languages that Cassidy was wearing.

His task done, the large Xik'en stretched and was about to reach for another hunk of asteroid when he spied Agnoix. She was standing at the end of his workstation, staring at the nine workers, her tail twitching in nervousness.

Without thinking, Agnoix waved. "Continue on, just on my inspection tour," she said, picking up a handful of the rare Vao stones and turning them, pretending to examine them. She left the male Xik'en confused.

She jumped when alarms sounded, and panic spread through the flight deck above.

And here I was concerned that I wouldn't be able to find Cassidy, Agnoix though, making a dash for the last ramp leading to the flight deck, Vao stones in hand.

***

The inside of the mining bay was a maze of activity, with people and equipment going in every direction. Mechanical arms grabbed the massive hunks of asteroid when the mining pods dropped them after they came 'inside.' Slowing her steps to get a better look, what Cassidy took as random movements by the pods, rocks, and arms was in fact choreographed. It made her think of dancers in a massive stage production. The flying dust and constant rumbling of the grinders that sent vibrations were special effects. The entire atmosphere put her in the mind of a Shakespearean tragedy, and she half expected to see three hags materialize off to one side.

Realizing that the distance between herself and the Xik'en pilots she was following was getting larger, Cassidy picked up speed. She fought the urge to grab the empty tail of the spacesuit to make walking easier, and focused on what was in front of her.

From what Cassidy could tell, there was an invisible barrier at least four times the size of an Olympic swimming pool in front of her. Each mining pod passed through the barrier to reach the pressurized -- though dusty -- primary mining bay. The weight of open space and her recent brush with death at its hand gripped her chest with a fist of ice. Cassidy forced herself to continue walking toward the void of space as her instincts screamed at her to flee.

To distract herself from the approaching barrier between her and the void of space, Cassidy tried to follow the several conversations that were being broadcast through her spacesuit.

As far as she could tell, she was tuned into a passive channel. It seemed to only pick up those conversations happening within a five metre radius, but she didn't want to test that theory by speaking.

The first of the Xik'en mining pilots got to their craft and began an inspection of the space pod. Cassidy watched as best she could for any tips that would make this hare-brained idea of hers have a better chance of success than its current percent: zero. Once he was done, he watched as the rest of the crew did the same before waving them over to an empty spot in front of the line of mining pods.

Her radio crackled again, and this time it seemed that it was the first pilot speaking.

The Branch of Languages once again translated the Xik'en language, and Cassidy realized suddenly that she had no way to return it to the adolescent Xik'en girl.

Pushing her regret aside for a minute, Cassidy tried to focus on what the lead mining pilot was saying.

"... and you and Zausk take the targets in sector 42 Alpha. We have tagged those rocks for that order of copper wire on that fresh colony world we're putting a trading hub on. That leaves Sist and myself to cut and grab that rich vein of Vao stones the surveyors found last week. There should be three trips each if we can cut the raw rock small enough for easy transport. Sound good?"

As the other eight members of the Xik'en mining crew made various noises of agreement, Cassidy worked her way behind them. Heading for the lead ship, with its bubble hatch open and inviting, Cassidy started to get her hopes up.

Within metres of the ship, her radio crackled again.

"Hey you, what do you think you're doing at my pod?"

Fearing capture when freedom of a sort was within reach, Cassidy ran towards the mining pod, when disaster struck. With a swinging tail section and boots more akin to clown shoes than human-sized boots, Cassidy made it only three strides before the toe of her boot caught. She stumbled and could not recover. She went down in a heap, her helmet bouncing off the deck.

Shaken and holding an elbow numb with pain, Cassidy didn't pay any attention to the voices coming through her helmet speakers until she felt a heavy hand on her shoulder.

"Are you okay, citizen? Are you supposed to be here? That's my pod and..." The Xik'en miner broke off in mid-sentence as he rolled the injured human over and got a look at the face within the helmet.

For several moments the Xik'en pilot just stared, his reptilian face trying to puzzle out what he was seeing. As the reality of the situation dawned upon him, he let go of Cassidy. The Xik'en miner stood above her, looking at the space-suited mammal with a pack strapped to its chest and a red blinking light attached to its left wrist.

"Everyone get back! Flee!" he shouted over the radio, so loud that it threatened to deafen Cassidy. "It's a murderous mammal, and it's carrying a bomb! Terrorist! Flee!"

Taking his own advice, the Xik'en pilot pushed past his confused comrades. He knocked down the first one, which had the ripple effect of a piece of meat thrown into a pool of piranhas, as chaos broke loose.

Frantic and garbled radio transmissions spoke over each other, fanning the flames of fear and confusion into an inferno.

In seconds, the well-organized hive of industry that was a staple of the Xik'en mining bay became a riot.

Out of control mechanical arms, rock grinders spinning empty, and running mine workers were everywhere as confused reports spread through the massive bay.

Emergency lights flashed as equipment overheated and got overloaded with material with no one to remove it.

Sirens blared in various tones, which made Cassidy thankful that the helmet shielded her from the worst of them.

Countless Xik'en ran for the exits, though since dozens rushed within arms of her reach, they did not understand what they were running from.

One older female Xik'en reached down a taloned hand and hoisted Cassidy to her feet, shouting: "Get off the flight deck, miner. There's a rogue mammal here threatening to blow us all up!" With that, the good Samaritan mixed in with the flow of bodies, leaving Cassidy dazed and confused.

Forcing herself to move, Cassidy got herself under the hull of the mining pod that she had wanted to steal and placed a shaky hand on the open canopy. Pausing, Cassidy scanned the area, thinking she heard her name being called out.

She lifted the visor of her helmet, smoke and dust burning its way into her lungs. Over the din of a multitude of alarms, she heard her name called again.

"Cassidy Cane!"

Hordes of Xik'en were pushing and shoving their way to exit the vast mining bay. A few Xik'en tried to control and direct the flow of people, but their efforts were in vain. Cassidy saw that several clumps of Xik'en mine workers had turned the chaos into something more serious, and punches were being thrown.

Again Cassidy heard her name.

Out of the chaos of shoving bodies, a smaller than normal Xik'en pushed her way through the reptilian wall, and Cassidy could see it was Agnoix.

"Here Agnoix!" Cassidy yelled, and began waving her arms. She smashed her wrist against the side of the mining pod and stopped, but it had been enough motion for the youthful Xik'en girl to notice, and she changed direction to connect with Cassidy.

The joy of seeing a familiar and friendly face rushed through Cassidy and lifted the weight from her chest that adrenaline had been keeping aside.

Truth be known, Cassidy hadn't been very confident that she would have been able to fly the mining pod without some basic instructions. If the confusion held for a couple more minutes, Cassidy could get a crash course in written Xik'en. But before that, she moved out from under the mining pod and swallowed Agnoix in a big, clumsy hug, causing the young Xik'en to drop what she was carrying.

From her hands fell five pieces of Vao stones the size of an enormous egg, still embedded in asteroid stones. They tumbled and fell to the mining bay floor.

"I grabbed these for you, Cassidy. I thought, you

know, our deal? That you'd take me as far as this portal so I can see your world?" Agnoix said between gasping breaths.

Cassidy stared down at the Vao stones that had brought her to this strange place, and couldn't help but laugh all the harder now that they had fallen at her feet.

Squeezing Agnoix all the tighter until the younger woman hissed in discomfort, Cassidy said: "I think you've earned your glimpse of the portal that connects our two worlds, my friend." Releasing the young Xik'en, Cassidy waved her sore hand at the pod. "Plus, I could use a little help to figure out where the 'on switch' is with this thing."

"I'm sure between us, friend Cassidy, we can figure it out," Agnoix said, while thinking: *At least I hope we can. I may have slept through the classroom documentaries about mining now that I think about it...*

As the pair bent down to pick up the fallen Vao stones, Cassidy looked over Agnoix's shoulder and saw a small group of Xik'en off to one side. The speaker, as far as Cassidy could tell, was the same one who had discovered her. He was jumping up and down while pointing in their direction.

"Ah, Agnoix? I think it's time to leave, and I mean RIGHT NOW!" Grabbing the young Xik'en by the arm, Cassidy pulled her to her feet as the group of Xik'en ran towards them with make-shift weapons in their hands.

"Can I get a lift?" Cassidy asked, and gasped in surprise as Agnoix gripped her around the waist and hoisted her up into the bubble of the mining pod. *My goodness, these Xik'en are strong!* Cassidy thought to herself, even as she tried to make head and tails of the inside of the mining pod. She flinched when Agnoix pulled herself in like a gymnast. *Darn strong! I hope to never get on her nasty side.*

Standing on the bottom set of mechanical limbs of the mining pod, Cassidy looked over Agnoix's shoulder at the small group of angry Xik'en miners that were getting closer.

While Cassidy was no expert, their body language and the fact that they were holding make-shift weapons suggested to her that they didn't want to invite her to tea.

"I think NOW would be a marvellous time to get out of here, Agnoix," Cassidy said. "Do you think you could fly this thing?"

Agnoix looked over Cassidy's shoulder at the profusion of buttons and controllers that made her feel weak in the knees.

Perhaps Cassidy saw some dread pass through the young Xik'ens face, or could just sense it based on years of being exposed to different cultures.

"Now that's silly, Agnoix, we would need to switch places and we don't have time for that. I'm the pilot, you act as navigator, and my first command is that you get that hatch shut because our friends will be here any second."

Agnoix realized that Cassidy's suggestion was timely, and struggled to turn around in the cramped cockpit.

She turned, smacking Cassidy alongside her head with her tail just once, then hit the close button. The dome of the egg-shaped cockpit closed, and everything became quiet.

As Agnoix began the awkward process of trying to

turn around again, Cassidy asked: "Doesn't this thing have a seat or something? Do they fly standing up? This is the oddest setup I've ever seen."

Ha! This is something I can help with, Agnoix thought.

"We have little use for seats, Cassidy. Just lean into the centre groove. Your body shape being weird with those lumps and bumps will make it uncomfortable. Oh, and ignore the four hooks around the edges, those are for the harness so you don't get thrown around." Watching as Cassidy leaned into the body groove meant for a Xik'en, Agnoix almost jumped out of her scales as a bang rang in her ears. The mining pod vibrated. Putting out a hand to steady herself, she almost crushed Cassidy, who yelped in pain.

"Get out here, mammal. We'll show you what we do with your kind!" yelled a miner with a pry bar in his hand, having just smashed against the hatch not a hand's width from Agnoix's snout and about to swing again.

"I think we should leave now, Cassidy!" Agnoix said, turning away from the angry Xik'en.

"I'd love too, but I don't read Xik'en and I need your help, remember?" Cassidy said, her cheeks flushed.

"Oh, sorry." Agnoix jumped again as the pry bar smashed against the clear hatch.

I know they make the glass to withstand the abuse out in outer space; I hope it can survive a few more minutes.

"Agnoix, I need you now!" Cassidy yelled.

Smash!

"Sorry! Okay, there are two handles, one's up and to the side, the other is down to the other side. I'm sorry, I don't remember which is which, this looks so different from the videos I've seen."

"That's fine, Agnoix, I'll figure it out. But I need to know how to start the engine or whatever this thing uses to move," Cassidy shouted, just as several more bangs shook the mining pod as more mining bay personal directed their fear towards Cassidy and Agnoix. "Now would be good, Agnoix."

Leaning over her friend, Agnoix reached out her taloned left hand and smashed down on the yellow power button. That activated the thrusters and the whole mining pod vibrated as if it were an idling train on its tracks.

"Well, I have a 50/50 chance of getting this right," Cassidy said as she jerked the handle in her right hand back. The mining pod shot to the left and smashed into the mining bay wall, scattering the group of angry miners, tails and talons hurrying away.

"Okay, let's try this again." Cassidy eased the left handle backwards, and the pod went to the right until it was floating high above the largest set of cylindrical grinders in the whole mining bay. Each the size of a train car, Cassidy would have hated to think what they could have done to their stolen mining pod. Peering forward and looking down at the massive grinders that could swallow the mining pod in a second, Cassidy took a death breath.

"Let's see, if right back is left, and left back is right, what are the chances that left forward is up and right forward is down?" Cassidy said, looking over her shoulder at her friend crouched behind her. Agnoix's reptilian eyes were wide. "You know, they wired your brains kinda different. Has anyone ever told you Xik'ens that?"

Looking out the left side of the cockpit, Cassidy saw

that the miners who had attacked them were now running for their own mining pods. Pods that they would have had years of skill and experience to master against her crash course.

"Dang. Okay, Agnoix, I think I might have a handle on this. Now how do we go forward or reverse?"

"You grab this toggle with your tail and..." Agnoix's voice trailed off.

"Are you kidding me?" Cassidy yelled as she watched the first asteroid miner pop the hatch on one of the mining pods.

"I can do it, I know I can, Cassidy. Just trust me," Agnoix said as she stuck her tail into the shallow socket in the floor and gripped the toggle. With the finite control common with her race, the young Xik'en had forward and backward sorted out in seconds.

"Expert job, Agnoix," Cassidy said. "And now for the elephant in the room, how do you get out of here?" She thrust her chin at the apartment building-sized hole in the wall, with nothing between them but the naked void of space. "I've been trying my very best NOT to even look at it, but the time has come. Please tell me you know how to get through that, Agnoix."

I must show no sign of doubt. Cassidy is counting on me and she's afraid; this must be so foreign to her.

"That's easy, Cassidy," Agnoix said. "Just fly through it. They fit the pod with a shield key allowing it and anything attached to it to fly through. Everything else bounces off."

At least I'm pretty sure that's how it works, and assuming the key was turned on when the pod powered up, and assuming the damage taken hasn't broken it.

"You sure?"

"I have no doubt, Cassidy," Agnoix lied to her friend.

The angry miners lifted off the flight deck and gave chase, the pilots able to use the mechanical arms fitted with grips, lasers, and drills. Cassidy and Agnoix aimed for the stars twinkling between the asteroids, with their stolen mining pod like a stumbling drunkard charging through.

CHAPTER FOURTEEN

Well, maybe 'charging' wasn't the right word for how Cassidy and Agnoix left the mining bay.

In a move that resembled what stunt drivers would call 'drifting' around the corners on a track, the mining pod breached the environmental seal at an oblique angle, and no faster than a walk.

"Agnoix, we will need some speed if we want to get away from those miners back there," Cassidy shouted over the gong that sounded as the pod passed through the meter-thick shielding separating the dusty, yet breathable, mining bay and the void of space.

"I might give you more speed if you would point this thing in the direction you want to go. I'm scared we'll crash if we go any faster," Agnoix replied, her own fear and frustration coming through.

"Sorry, Agnoix, it's this blasted helmet. It's too big and the view port is all wrong for someone without a snout. Help me get it off would you?"

Taking her hands off the controls, Cassidy struggled to get the helmet off while laying down. Once Agnoix got her talons involved with a quick twist and a pop, the helmet floated free.

"That's much better. Thanks, Agnoix," Cassidy said as she gripped the flight handles and pulled herself back down into place. "I see why the miners had those harnesses. Every time I use the controls my body wants to follow along. At least I'm getting a good core workout."

Confused by what Cassidy meant, Agnoix realized that understanding the words differed from understanding their meaning, but still got the bare bones of what Cassidy was talking about.

"Yes, the mining pods are much too small to carry gravity generators, and they would likely make it harder in the long run. I've heard that the best miners are also the best swimmers; able to work in three dimensions and all that."

"That makes sense," Cassidy said, looking over her shoulder at her friend and getting her first look of the mining station from the outside. Her mouth fell open.

While grad school had been a while ago for Cassidy, and chemistry had never been her strong point, some tiny part of her mind whispered to her. The Xik'en mining station resembled a tetrahedral molecule, with a centre hub -- from which they had just escaped -- and four arms jutting out from it so it looked like a caltrop. No matter what way you looked at it, one 'point' was up.

Agnoix had told Cassidy all this, but she had never really believed it until now. Asteroids the size of human cities connected by tubes so Xik'en could travel.

"I just can't get over this... this complex, Agnoix. Humanity has nothing the size or complexity of this. There must be room for thousands of people there," Cassidy said, her voice a whisper as she tried to drink in as many details as possible of the marvel.

"Tens of thousands actually, though about a third of the people are short-term visitors passing through. My people don't normally like to move around a lot, but other races come here since the station sees so much traffic."

At the word 'traffic,' Cassidy's mind realized that the mountains and hills that she saw on the various asteroids were in fact dozens of space ships, each docked on the outside of the asteroids.

"Why didn't I bring my sketchbook or a camera with me," Cassidy scolded herself, just as the collision happened.

In their combined nervousness and excitement, the two had forgotten what brought them to this point. The thud of another mining pod striking theirs and throwing them forward against the dash of the pod brought their situation back to the present.

The other mining pods' mechanical limbs reached out with grips, lasers, and drills, none of which would be good for the two of them. Cassidy and Agnoix fought to untangle their limbs from each other and resume their make-shift driving setup.

"Give me forward now, Agnoix," Cassidy yelled, twisting the controllers so that the little mining pod corkscrewed away from the station. "A little more speed Agnoix. I assume he's still back there?"

Focusing all her attention on trying to not crush her friend in the cramped cockpit AND apply the right amount of speed, Agnoix thought she was doing a magnificent job for this being her first time driving. That was until she looked behind her.

"Scale rot!" Agnoix cursed. "He has hold of one of our limbs with a gripper and is dragging himself closer. Cassidy, what do we do?"

"I'm thinking!" Cassidy yelled, refocusing her attention on the view outside and trying to ignore the braid that kept floating in front of her face. "Flying through the magnetic shield that protects the station is the same as that in the mining bay, right?" Cassidy asked, her tone back to normal. "I mean, I don't have to do anything? Just fly through?"

I don't think I'm ready to be an adult, if knowing all the answers to questions people ask will continue, Agnoix thought as she stared back at the mining pod that had them in its grip and saw that a spinning drill attached to yet another arm was seeking them.

"Yes, absolutely, as you said," Agnoix babbled. "Just hurry, Cassidy, he's got a drill."

"Fudge nuggets," Cassidy swore as she shifted course towards the nearest shield emitters.

With only the barest idea of how the hundreds of metal spheres that formed the bubble of protection around the mining complex worked, Cassidy decided that it was time to show the Xik'en miners a thing or two about driving earth-style.

Seeing the apartment building-sized metal sphere getting closer and closer, Agnoix felt a little queasy and slowed them down. "Ah, Cassidy, what are you doing? I don't like this plan..."

"I will teach our friend back there about a little game we play back home called 'chicken', so pour on the speed again. I know what I'm doing," Cassidy said, as she leaned deeper into the pilot's position.

Seeing the drill skip along the metal hide of their pod, and the lights of at least three more chasers, Agnoix made the quick decision to trust her warm-blooded friend. Using her prehensile tail, Agnoix threw their pod into motion and prayed to her ancestors she'd made the right choice.

The surge in speed caught Cassidy by surprise. She wasn't sure that Agnoix would risk herself and put her trust in a being that she'd been told her whole life was their equivalent of the bogeyman. And if she was being honest with herself, she wouldn't have been angry if Agnoix had refused to go on. It would likely have meant a quick walk out an airlock for Cassidy, but at least Agnoix would have been safe.

This isn't the time for What if's. You can shake this fool, and make it home. I'm sure they'll go easy on Agnoix, she's just a kid, and I'll make sure she tells them I forced her into helping me.

Pushing down her doubts and worries, Cassidy poured all her attention at the metal sphere growing in front of her.

At first Cassidy thought the gleaming sphere was the size of a cargo van, then an apartment building, and now realized that it was bigger than a cargo ship and filled their view.

How bloody big is this thing? Cassidy thought to herself, before calling over her shoulder: "Is our buddy still with us?"

"He's still there, and I can feel the drill against our hull," Agnoix said. "I'm getting scared, Cassidy."

"Me too kiddo, this should be over in just a minute." Cassidy did her best to comfort her young friend as she aimed their pod for one of the antenna, streaks of blue fire outlining it like a Christmas tree.

As the crackling energy reached out and struck their

pod, the Xik'en miner decided that today wasn't his day to die. He pulled away in a hairpin turn, which broke off his drill, leaving it sticking out of their mining pod.

"He's gone!!! Cassidy, he left, turn, turn, TURN!!!" Agnoix shrieked, her fear allowing her to forget that she was in charge of their speed. Cassidy pulled their mining pod out of its suicidal run with a sharp twist of the controls. They passed by the menacing antenna without harm and breached the magnetic shielding around the mining station -- keeping it free from errant asteroids -- and made it to open space.

"Well, maybe not open space," Cassidy muttered as the wealth of the Xik'en was all around them; asteroids from the size of a chicken's egg to ones as big as an ocean liner, and their density increasing the farther in Cassidy could see.

"Ah Agnoix, maybe ease up on the speed? Things are kinda crowded in here."

"I don't think we should. There are three other pods behind us and they're getting closer," Agnoix replied.

"I just hate it when a date doesn't get the hint," Cassidy quipped. "Okay, I will see if I can lose them inside this shifting maze. You keep your hand, er... tail on the throttle, we might need to brake in a hurry."

Agnoix gripped her friend's shoulder and gave it a gentle squeeze of agreement, and the battered mining pod flew into the thickest part of the asteroid belt.

Later, when Cassidy thought back about that maddening flight within the Xik'en asteroid belt, she was only able to recall the barest of details. There were the near misses from asteroids that were almost invisible until they were right in front of them. The constant pursuit by the miners as they tried to flank them. The shouts of 'watch out, left, turn, and BRAKES!' that each of them yelled at the other, which echoed within in the small cockpit. Despite all that, it had still been good luck that saved them. Or rather, the bad luck of one miner chasing them.

"Something's happened, Cassidy," Agnoix shouted, easing up on their reckless speed. "One of the other pods either hit an asteroid or broke down. All I see is a trail of loose rock and venting atmosphere. The other two pods are moving to give it aid."

"I hope the miner is okay, but this is our chance for an escape. Give me some forward movement, okay, Agnoix?"

Looking back at the scene behind them, Agnoix hoped that the miner would get the attention he deserved.

He meant Cassidy harm, but I just can't wish him ill. He likely has a family waiting for him back home, Agnoix thought.

Home. A wave of homesickness rushed through Agnoix and the adventure of another world didn't hold the appeal it once did. Her previous plan of escaping to Cassidy's world no longer seemed like as much fun as before. Maybe there was a place for her in Xik'en society. Maybe not a traditional place, but a place nonetheless.

I just need to make sure Cassidy gets home okay first, then I'll have time to think.

"Agnoix?"

"Sorry Cassidy, I was just making sure the miner is okay. It looks like the other two are grabbing his pod and are towing it back towards the station." Using her tail on the controller, Agnoix started the pod forward again with Cassidy at the controls.

CHAPTER FIFTEEN

"There, I'm sure of it. The plane must be close, the flashes ARE getting faster," Cassidy said as she tapped the blinking red light strapped to her left wrist.

The hunt for Cassidy's plane had taken much longer than either of them had expected. Their flight from the miners was more important than noting their direction. With only the barest understanding of the secondary controls, they'd had a lot of backtracking to do to make their way back to the edge of the asteroid field.

Agnoix thought about mentioning how low they were getting on fuel, but since Cassidy wasn't aware, the young Xik'en didn't see the need to worry her friend.

"I agree Cassidy, the blinks are getting faster, but they have been for a while and I don't see this 'airplane' of yours floating around anywhere," Agnoix said. The lack of food, water and sleep had caught up with them both.

"Me either, but it must be around here someplace..." Cassidy said, scanning the crowded space around them through the cockpit window. "THERE! Down on that asteroid. The microgravity of that rock must have pulled it in."

Laying upside down with its missing canopy gone, Gamgee's experimental plane was a sight for sore eyes, even with a crushed wing and a buckled frame.

"It doesn't look like it will ever fly again. Not that I thought I would get that lucky. But since the homing beacon is still receiving, that means there's power, and that means the portal detector is likely okay. Gamgee reinforced it." Staring down at the only piece of familiar tech she'd seen since she flew into this dimension hit Cassidy hard. She hoped that Agnoix didn't see the moisture in her eyes.

"Okay, the easiest and safest way for me to get the portal beacon out of the plane is to figure out how these mechanical arms work. That's assuming they still work after the abuse they've been through," Cassidy said.

I've never been planet-side, but even if I was I doubt I would fly in anything so rudimentary. These humans do surprising things with few resources. I wonder if we Xik'en could learn a lesson or two from them, Agnoix mused as she looked at the craft which had brought her friend to this dimension.

"I think I can help with that, Cassidy," Agnoix said. "I may not feel up to the stunt flying that you seem to enjoy, but this thing," she pointed at the mechanical arms hanging on the outside of the pod like forgotten toys in a playground, "I have experience with stuff like this. It's not much different from the bubble gun I used to save you."

Cassidy only had the haziest idea how the emergency life saving equipment the Xik'en had created worked, and felt relief for the offer of help.

Good on you, Agnoix. I wonder if you would have been this forthcoming before we'd met. I get the impression you've grown a lot in such a brief span of time, Cassidy thought to herself, and chose not to give voice to her thoughts for fear of embarrassing Agnoix. "Sounds like a splendid plan. Let's get close, then you can take over and show me how it's done."

In a series of short controlled bursts, Cassidy and Agnoix got their stolen mining pod to within a few meters of Gamgee's experimental plane.

"Okay, your turn Agnoix," Cassidy said, and the two women switched places in the cramped confines of the cockpit. "I wonder how those circus clowns manage it?"

She received a confused look from Agnoix.

"Ah... never mind, it would take too much time to explain and it isn't that funny."

Once a Xik'en shaped body was laying in the body groove of the mining pod, the pair had much more room than before. Cassidy took the time for a good stretch to loosen her sore muscles before leaning over her friend's shoulder.

"Okay, Agnoix, show me how it's done." Cassidy patted her friend's shoulder before pointing. "I'd suggest using two grippers on the pontoon and rolling the plane towards us, being mindful of the wings." Seeing that her Earth-based words were giving the Branch of Languages a hard time, Cassidy used simpler language. "See the two long tubular things? Those are pontoons, they allow the plane to float atop of water."

"I thought you said this machine flew way up in the sky?" Agnoix interrupted.

"It does, ah... it can do both. I'll explain later, if there's time," Cassidy said, trying to get them back on track. "Just

grab one of the long tubes and lift the plane off the asteroid. We need to access the side against the rock."

Cassidy watched as Agnoix used the hand controllers
to grip the bottom of the plane with the long mechanical
limbs.

Once it was rolled towards the cockpit of the pod,
Cassidy saw that any thought of taking the plane back
through the portal would be a waste of time.

"Part of me hoped that I'd be able to use the plane
as a glider and slip back through the portal into Earth's
atmosphere. But that," she pointed at the crumpled tail
fins, "means that plan is out. I must risk the parachute and
hope the rescue boat is still nearby."

Seeing that she was upsetting Agnoix, Cassidy forced
a smile. "It was wishful thinking. I'll be fine, I promise.
The rescue boat had orders to stay in the area for a week;
I'm sure it will all work out. I do crazy stuff like this all
the time."

Brilliant job, Cassidy, dump more worry on the girl, Cassidy scolded herself, then set to distracting Agnoix.

"Okay, back to the job at hand, my friend. You see the
empty cockpit? Not that dissimilar to this one, though
we humans like to sit on our butts more than you Xik'ens
do." Cassidy attempted to lighten the mood, and Agnoix
rewarded her with a slight smile, her needle-sharp teeth
shining in the cabin light. "In the front cockpit, you see
that small square box bolted to the dash, right?" When
Agnoix nodded, Cassidy continued. "I need to see the
screen on the front of it. Do you feel up to playing with
a laser?"

The prospect of using the laser distracted Agnoix from

her worries, and she set herself to work.

She just needs a little self-confidence. I wasn't any different at her age, Cassidy thought.

Cassidy smiled as she watched Agnoix bring the robotic arm with the asteroid cutting laser on its tip up against the clasp holding the portal detector in place.

She's finding her own way and is stronger than she might think and just needs a little self confidence.

"Okay Cassidy, I think I have it lined up, through I can't be sure."

"I'm sure you have it bang on. Ah... you know I need the detector in one piece right?" Cassidy said, her tone soft.

"I understand. And if I'm understanding this laser right, I have it on the lowest setting and will just give it a quick burst."

"Then I say fire away, Captain Agnoix!"

Shaking her head at her weird human friend, Agnoix double checked her settings on the laser and tapped the thumb toggle.

One side of the metal band holding the portal detector glowed orange and popped away.

"Wow, I saw nothing, Agnoix."

"You can't see lasers in a vacuum, Cassidy."

"Ah yes... I probably learned that once, but that knowledge got pushed out by something else later."

"And you say Xik'en brains are wired weird..." Agnoix mumbled as she reset the mining laser. Within minutes, the portal detector was safely in the mechanical hands of the mining pod.

"It seems a little... ah, basic, Cassidy. Is all your world's technology like this?" Agnoix asked, unable to help herself as they looked at the blinking green arrow on the screen of the portal detector.

Cassidy chuckled. "No, not all. Gamgee knows that sometimes my adventures can be hard on gear, so he likes to make things simple. He believes that boys are smarter than girls and I don't correct him. I won't want to see him cry." Cassidy winked.

I will miss you Cassidy, I wish we could have had more time together, Agnoix thought, not trusting her voice to speak.

"Okay then, the portal is nearby. We should hurry; I assume your mother is looking for you. I'm sorry if I got you in trouble Agnoix. I have this habit of getting myself into trouble and dragging others along whether they want to go or not."

"Don't be foolish! It was my decision to rescue you and try to find a way off the mining complex. If I get into trouble because I helped a mammal, seeing the look on Axaik's face was worth it!"

Laughing, they hugged, and the laughter evaporated into sad looks as they made their way to the portal, each lost in their own thoughts.

"I can barely see it," Agnoix said as she leaned over Cassidy's shoulder. "If it wasn't for the glittering of the narrow funnel of rock dust around it, I would never have seen it."

"And that's likely why none of your people have come to my dimension," Cassidy replied, staring at the portal and her way home.

"Here, don't forget these," Agnoix said, handing Cassidy the five rough Vao stones that she'd stolen while in the mining bay.

"Why is it woman's clothing never has pockets?" Cassidy muttered to herself, as she tried to figure out a way to carry the stones. With an "Ah ha!" she pulled down the pilot suit far enough to stuff the stones into the empty tail section of her Xik'en spacesuit.

"I don't make a very good Xik'en, do I?" Cassidy asked with a grin.

"Maybe not, but you're a wonderful friend. I will miss you Cassidy." Agnoix's upper lip was quivering, exposing her needle-sharp teeth.

"I will miss you too. I won't make you any promises, but I may be back, and if I am, I'll be better prepared. Thank you for seeing me as more than a 'warm-blood'. Few of my people would accept the call to help an alien stranger."

They both paused and just stared at each other, neither wanting the parting to happen but knowing that it must.

"You're sure your mask and tank from the mining bay will let you breathe? I don't want to risk your life trying to get home," Cassidy asked, pointing to the equipment Agnoix took from the mining bay when she disguised herself as a worker.

"I'm sure, Cassidy. The masks and tanks are for more than the dust in the mining bay. They're there in case of a failure of the barrier shield. My people are pragmatic if nothing else. I'll be fine, trust me." The suppressed fear in the adolescent Xik'en voice was easy to hear, but Cassidy pretended not to.

"And you can pilot this home? Do you want me to go through it again?" Cassidy asked, leaning down towards the controls.

"Stop, Cassidy, I'll be fine, you showed me what to do, and I watched as you flew. I'm sure I can get back to the mining station with no problems. I promise to go slow and steady like you said," Agnoix repeated. They had already gone over all this once before, but now that the portal was right there and Cassidy's leaving had become real, they were both drawing it out.

"Here," Cassidy said, and reached up to remove the Branch of Languages that had been allowing the two to communicate.

"Wait, Cassidy," Agnoix said, holding her hands up. "You keep it. Maybe this doctor of yours can make use of it and make more. Consider it a gift."

Cassidy's hand paused as she considered, then gave her head a slight shake. "No, it's yours and it's too precious a gift to give away. Plus, if you're questioned when you get home you can say that you couldn't understand me, since no filthy mammal would give up such a beautiful piece."

It had taken some back and forth, but Cassidy and Agnoix agreed that Agnoix should tell a version of the truth, because as Cassidy put it: "The best lies are two-thirds truth." Agnoix was to admit to firing the bubble gun that saved her life, as any good Xik'en would do. It was not her fault that the life she saved was a warm-blood. It had been impossible to tell. Then she was to say that Cassidy had taken her hostage. As a helpless victim of a dangerous mammal, Agnoix had been dragged through the mining station, from which Cassidy had stolen a shuttle, and they had both escaped.

And when the 'noble and brave' Xik'en miners could not stop Cassidy and rescue the helpless Agnoix, she had

had to rescue herself.

Cassidy took them to the primitive craft and attempted to recover it using the mining pod. When she was distracted, Agnoix had opened the mining pod's hatch and blasted Cassidy out into the void of space.

While there were a couple holes in the story, the biggest one to Agnoix's mind was that Axaik and his drunken friends had seen Agnoix trying to hide and protect Cassidy. Still, she decided not to burden Cassidy with that concern.

Before Agnoix could object again, Cassidy peeled off the Branch of Languages.

The slight warmth and tingle she had felt while wearing the alien translation device faded, and with it, her ability to communicate to her friend.

"I know you can't understand me, Agnoix. I'll be forever thankful for you saving my life and showing a stranger your kindness. You've given me a lot to think about," Cassidy said. She placed the Branch of Languages in her friend's hand, closing Agnoix's talons around it.

Smiling, Cassidy picked up the discarded mining pilot helmet and struggled to put it on. Agnoix shoved the Branch of Languages into the pocket of her miner's suit and helped Cassidy connect the helmet, insuring that the air was flowing.

Once Agnoix had her own breathing mask on, they double checked each other's breathing equipment twice. Cassidy gave a double thumbs-up and Agnoix hit the hatch door and heard the pumps reclaim what air there was within the cockpit before opening the door.

The cold of the void flowed into the cockpit of the tiny mining pod. Agnoix could see the moisture that had been gathering on the inside of the windows. Unable to handle the hot breath of a mammal, it flash-froze into a beautiful but deadly web of ice.

Agnoix had a death grip on the side of the mining pod, and willed herself not to think of the cold seeping into her mining suit. How her life depended on a tank of air less than a third full. She hoped it would be enough. She watched as her friend Cassidy pushed off, floating towards the portal between dimensions.

It's beautiful, Cassidy thought as she pushed off from the mining pod and got her first proper look of outer space. *Even with so many asteroids, the light from the stars pokes through. Thanks to the headlights of the mining pod, I can see the minerals with the rocks reflecting the light.* Cassidy only had a few moments to enjoy the starry view before the portal dominated the scene. *Gamgee was right, this portal is invisible, but its effects are noticeable.* Cassidy watched as the minute dust particles swirled around the edges of the round portal, caught forever on the lip of the doorway.

Agnoix was right about the dust... and Cassidy remembered the youthful Xik'en woman who saved her life. Almost to the portal, Cassidy tried to turn around to see her friend one last time, but found it difficult in Zero G, and despaired. A memory of her ponytail hitting her in the face gave her an idea. Reaching behind her, Cassidy grabbed the tail of her spacesuit and the Vao stones within it and threw it away from her. That slight motion was enough to cause Cassidy to spin, and just as her back touched the open portal she saw Agnoix standing in the open cockpit. As she waved goodbye to Agnoix, Cassidy slipped back through the portal.

CHAPTER SIXTEEN

The abrupt transition from the weightlessness of space to the gravity of Earth hit Cassidy like a punch in the gut. Even encased in the Xik'en spacesuit, Cassidy could still hear the roar of her body falling through the atmosphere. Instinct and training kicked in. Before Cassidy knew what she was doing, she twisted herself around so that she was falling face first and spread her arms and legs wide to increase her drag. The tail of the Xik'en spacesuit even helped keep her level.

Okay, where the heck am I? Cassidy thought as she fell to the blue ocean below.

Looking at her left wrist without turning her head, for fear of getting whiplash, Cassidy saw that her beacon was still flashing a bright red.

That's good. Gamgee didn't think radio signals could pass through portals, so that means the rescue boat must be nearby. Sharing a common frequency was a smart move.

Without an altimeter, Cassidy didn't know how high she was above the water, and had to rely on her experience and looking at the curvature of the horizon and the setting.

Seeing as her spacesuit still had a quarter tank, Cassidy decided that she would rather spend her time in the sky than treading water in the bulky suit. Cassidy yanked on her parachute's ripcord and prayed it still worked.

As the leader shot and the lines trailing with it unfurled, Cassidy crossed her fingers and hoped that all the rough and tumble adventures of the past day hadn't damaged the parachute.

I'll know soon enough, she thought as the parachute unfurled, filled full of air, and snapped her head back and forth. She hit her forehead against the alien helmet.

"That will leave a nasty bump," Cassidy said, and risked the higher elevation and the dangers of lower oxygen by opening the helmet.

As the smell of Earth's air filled Cassidy's lungs, she smiled until her face hurt. She made long winding spirals through the sky to hunt for the rescue boat, using the beacon as a guide.

Good, clean air... I don't know how much longer I could have lasted in that muggy soup the Xik'ens called air without sprouting mushrooms.

Thinking of Xik'en and her experience there, Cassidy reflected on how the outcome would have been disastrous without Agnoix.

I hope her fellow people aren't too hard on her; I know she pretended it would all be okay to put my fears at ease, but I can't help feeling like I abandoned her. It sounds like only her father supports her freethinking ideas. He's rarely around and she has to deal with that brother of hers and a mother trying to make her conform to proper Xik'en society.

It's not all that different with me and my sisters. Ditch-

ing me to hang with their friends, teasing me for loving history books rather than those silly TV shows. Is what I did to Agnoix any different from what my sisters did to me?

With this thought rattling around in her mind, Cassidy vowed to contact her sisters when she got home and reforge their relationships.

With her mind settled, Cassidy noticed that her wrist beacon was flashing steadily. She saw the glint of the rescue boat as the setting sun reflected off its hull.

Using the D rings to steer her parachute towards the craft, her heart skipped a beat when she saw a flare reach skyward, signaling that they had seen her.

As Cassidy skimmed around the waves mere meters below, she closed the helmet on the spacesuit to keep the water out and splashed into the Atlantic Ocean.

She bobbed like a cork, even with her tail and its five pounds of rocks within it hanging below her. Cassidy floated on her back after the tricky task of releasing the chute with gloves made for Xik'en hands.

As the rescue boat came up beside her, its wake making her rise and fall like a message in a bottle, Cassidy opened her visor and shouted to the crew leaning over the railing ready to grab her.

"Hurry, would you guys? It's been a heck of a day and I'm starved. Does anyone have a sandwich handy?"

CHAPTER SEVENTEEN

"Easy there Agnoix, hold it together for a few minutes more," Agnoix said to herself as she guided the mining pod, with the remains of Cassidy's plane still in its grip, into the mining bay they had fled hours before.

She knew she shouldn't have done it. She should have closed the hatch of the mining pod as soon as Cassidy had exited the tiny craft. But Agnoix did not want to miss seeing her friend transition through the portal. There was no flash or anything: Cassidy just flowed through the portal, her waving hand the last thing to pass through into another dimension.

With cramped muscles that never warmed up after being exposed to the cold of space, Agnoix had started the trip back to her home on the mining station. It hadn't been as easy as Agnoix had led Cassidy to believe, but after some trial and error she figured out the instruments and activated the locator scanner. All Agnoix had had to do then was follow the path on the screen to exit the asteroid field, right into a swarm of mining pods and security barges, their powerful lasers aimed at her.

Agnoix's frantic and confused rambling over the radio had been enough to convince everyone that the "murderous mammal" was no longer on board.

Her 'escort' and its weapons watched as she flew into the mining bay, Cassidy's plane still gripped tight.

While no longer the madhouse it had been when she and Cassidy had left the mining bay, there were emergency crews putting out small fires and making equipment safe. When the work crews had fled the bay, they left a trail of jammed and overloaded equipment in their wake.

"Someone must have made some calls," Agnoix whispered in dread as she saw that her mother, Axaik, a dozen security personal, and hundreds of workers awaited her.

Not that anyone was noticing her landing, but without a bump, Agnoix landed the pod and lowered Cassidy's plane to the floor.

"I wonder if it's too late to follow Cassidy," Agnoix mumbled as she popped the cockpit hatch and tried not to struggle as two members of the security service marched her towards her fate.

Scale rot. Mom looks really mad, I wonder how much of the truth she knows? She looked at her brother, who appeared under the weather. *At least it appears Axaik is paying for his indulgence with the Grove juice -- serves him right.*

Orlol snapped at her daughter, cutting off Agnoix's thoughts. "Are you all right?"

Head hanging in shame and tail flicking, Agnoix replied: "Yes mother, I'm not hurt," and then almost fell over as she was enveloped into a massive hug, the first in recent memory from her mother.

"I was so worried when they told me that this mammal kidnapped you and made you its hostage. It did nothing 'unnatural' to you, did it dear?" Orlol asked, and started patting down her daughter as if to check for bite marks.

"I'm fine Mom, Cas... the Creature, the warm-blood didn't hurt me, it just scared me."

An elderly Xik'en walked up, ending the mother-daughter moment by slapping his tail against the floor for attention.

"Young one, my name is Xizik and I'm senior administrator for this mining station. I need you to tell me what happened. Take your time, tell me everything."

And with her mother's taloned hand on her shoulder for support, Agnoix told the story that she and Cassidy had came up, with a few addictions.

Agnoix told of how she rescued 'the mammal' not knowing what it was, only knowing that it was someone in danger and that she had done what any dutiful Xik'en citizen would do, which garnered her a nod from the senior administrator. She threw her brother a bone and covered her own tail, saying that Axaik had tried to save his younger sister from the warm-blood and that he had suffered an injury in the attempt. Any poor behaviour since then was likely because of the injury and the shock of not being able to rescue his sister.

I hope you realize what I'm doing for you, brother. I just saved your scales, so you keep your mouth shut about how friendly Cassidy and I were.

There was a surprised look on Axaik's face, which turned to puzzlement when Senior Administrator Xizik turned to him.

"Is this true young man?"

Axaik's puzzlement dawned into understanding, then he nodded. "Yes, yes, like she said. I tried to save her."

"My children are good Xik'en citizens, Senior Administrator. My husband and I raised them right." Orlol stood proudly and squeezed Agnoix's shoulder.

"Hmmm... yes, I see. Continue child."

Agnoix finished her tale as planned.

"And after that, Sir, I travelled back to the mining station with the alien's vessel in tow," Agnoix said to divert the conversation, and walked towards Cassidy's plane.

"Yes, yes. Splendid job, ah... Agnoix," Xizik said as he walked up to the plane. "Our scientists will have to study this craft, but to my untrained eye it looks rather primitive. These mammals care little for their lives or the lives of others. But I must prepare us for any future incursions..."

"I agree, Senior Administrator, and it's an excellent idea," Agnoix said, hijacking the politicians speech. "We must be vigilant and strong, and to do that we must know our enemy. We can no longer hide behind our walls and wait for the worlds to come to us. We must go out and seek them and study them for our own defense and the security of the great Xik'en Interstellar Empire," Agnoix finished in a shout.

I think I might have spent too much time with Cassidy; I didn't know I had that in me.

For the space of a couple heartbeats, the whole mining bay was quiet. Everyone stared at the young Xik'en woman, perplexed and confused by the unexpected speech, when Axaik thumped his tail against the floor in approval.

Orlol followed suit, then more and more of the onlookers.

Seizing the moment, Agnoix walked beside Senior Administrator Xizik, gripped his talons in hers, and raised them both to the sky, and the applause of Xik'en tails was thunderous.

EPILOGUE

Xizik stepped into the shadowed dark of the solitary confinement wing of the Xik'en penitentiary. It was a narrow room with cells on either side and floors covered with sawdust, with a single light hanging from overhead casting strange, oblong shadows on the walls all around.

"We had an interesting event today, Tallis," he said, stopping at a hand washing station in the center of the hall and scrubbing. He picked up a portable light from a dispensary beneath the station and flicked it on, its bright rectangle shimmering out into the void. He stepped past each cell, shining the light into each in turn along the way and examining the sorrow-filled faces within. "Had a visitor top side. Caused a lot of trouble... almost as much as you did."

He continued from one sad face to the next, finally landing on one that was not full of fear or anguish. Its lip was curled up into a rueful sneer. It was also human. He glared back out at Xizik, sitting at the far wall of his cage with his legs tucked up around him.

"I'd like you to tell me if you know anything about that, Tallis."

Tallis turned, running a finger along the dozens of tally marks that ran the length of his cell's stone wall, feeling the gouges of them absently. Despite his circumstance, he looked bored. There was a small, thin stress ball in his other hand that he rolled liberally between his fingers. "Why would I know anything about anything that happened outside these walls, Xizik?" he said, his voice somewhere in the realm between bemused and contemptuous.

"Because, Tallis. She was human."

Tallis turned and glared at Xizik, a light behind his eyes that had not been there in months. Even though he tried to hide it, he started to smile.

FROM THE DIARY OF CASSIDY CANE

Someone once told me I adapted too quickly. They said that it robbed the people around me of the chance to adapt as well, to be in the moment. They said they always felt like they were playing catch-up. I suppose in some ways I've always lived my life the way an improv actor lives a performance: I "Yes, and" and then move on from there. Accept and adapt, because those seconds that your mind spends sputtering to grasp hold of reality could mean the difference between destiny and disaster.

I wonder what he would have thought of all this.

I've thought about that analysis of me a lot lately, because I feel like I did adapt quickly to the portals. They went, very swiftly, from something new and dangerous to a tool that could be used. I wonder if those around for the invention of the automobile felt the same way – that at one moment they were new and frightening, and at the next they were everywhere. Commonplace.

And now, it occurs to me, I could find a world that has yet to experience automobiles and see firsthand if that was the experience.

Nothing seems out of my grasp anymore, and that

is both exciting and disturbing at the same time. Infinite worlds, with infinite possibilities... what could be on some of them?

I find myself thinking of Jordae a lot. That sort of idyllic, lovely place that – on the few times I picture retirement – I might retire to. Everything seemed lush and sweet and wonderful... and yet when I arrived there, my "Yes, and" took over, and trouble soon followed. I adapt too quickly, but not just to danger. I adapt too quickly to peace as well, and make it less so. It occurs to me now that I could have left Jordae without consequence.

In a dozen years, will they view visitors from other worlds the same way the denizens of that first one did? With fear and immediate suspicion, persecution?

But then I remember Agnoix; how she trusted right away. She adapted quickly, but it didn't end badly. Even in a world that had engineered itself to push back against outsiders, she did not. I'm trying hard to remind myself that that's the way it can be. That adapting quickly doesn't have to always mean getting bored – that it can be just the good bits, and not the rest.

I'm going to spend more time with my sisters. Being with Agnoix and visiting Jordae has made me realize the importance of peace, and of family. In travelling farther away from home than I ever have before, I've realized how much I treasure the things I love most about this world.

But I can't help but think about what would happen if someone learned the opposite lessons. What if that other part of me, the bored part, ever takes hold... and just goes looking for trouble? Family helps with that.

Cassidy, out.

SUPERHERO FANTASY FROM ENGEN BOOKS!

infinity

The world is changing, and we have to change with it. That was the one thing that Victor was really sure of when he started looking for special people: people who could change the possibilities of the future from something certainly grim... to something *infinitely* positive.

Now four unsuspecting people from different backgrounds and walks of life have been thrown into the mix together, and nothing will ever be the same. But there's a difference between hoping for a better world and actually having one, and there will always be resistance to change.

Book One: Infinity (October 2010)
Book Two: The Tourniquet Reprisal (October 2012)
Book Three: Exodus of Angels (April 2016)
Book Four: Garden of the 8th Circle (August 2020)

Related Books:
              light|dark (April 2012)
              Roulette (October 2009)
              The Long Road (May 2014)
              Touch Your Nose (May 2018)

Written by the superstar team of Ellen Curtis (*Compendium*) and Matthew LeDrew (the *Xander Drew* series).

Destiny doesn't wait for anyone.

MORE SCI-FI FROM ENGEN

COMING SOON FROM ENGEN BOOKS

BIFOCAL: CURIOUS TALES & THEIR REFLECTIONS
Engen Books is proud and honored to announce our first 2021 reveal: 'Bifocal: Curious Tales & Their Reflections' by Andrew Peacock, with art by the astonishing Kaleigh Middelkoop.

Kaleigh Middelkoop is an amazing artist and photographer who primarily uses self portraiture as a means to tell stories and express ideas with the aid of costumes and props she makes by hand. Heavily influenced by fairy tales and the slightly strange, her work has surreal and magical elements woven throughout. Kaleigh is a featured artist at Bellazo in downtown Wabash, IN as well as Ocean View Art Gallery in Carbonear, NL.

'Bifocal: Curious Tales & Their Reflections' is a collection of short fiction by Peacock, with accompanying images by Middelkoop. It examines the human condition and imagination, and is a must have for any collection.

"I'm thrilled to be working with Kaleigh Middelkoop and Engen Books on the illustrated short story collection "Bifocal". Kaleigh and I have been working for a number of years on this project and we can't wait for everyone to see our pictures about stories and stories about pictures." -- Andrew Peacock

JD Ryot is the reclusive creator of the *Slipstreamers* series from Engen Books. JD is an avid fan of young adult literature and adventure serials. When asked if they had come to this world through a portal themselves, JD Ryot refused to answer. No record of their birth has ever been found... on this world.

Matthew LeDrew holds an Honours Degree in English from the Memorial University of Newfoundland with a minor in Anthropology. He has served as a jury member for both the 2018 NLBA awards and the 2020 Arts and Letters Awards. He lives in St. John's, Newfoundland.

Ali House is an Award-Winning, Bestselling author, a Newfoundlander, a playwright, a traveler, and a reader. House is a graduate of the Fine Arts program at Sir Wilfred Grenfell College and currently resides in Halifax, Nova Scotia, where she works in arts administration and spends more time than a person should in and around theaters.

Peter J. Foote is a bestselling speculative fiction writer from Nova Scotia, Canada. He runs the FictionFirst Used Books, specializing in fantasy & sci-fi titles. Peter's stories are a reflection of his personal life, as he is a firm believer in the adage that a writer should write what they know.

He is the founder of the Genre Writers of Atlantic Canada group.

www.ingramcontent.com/pod-product-compliance
Lightning Source LLC
Chambersburg PA
CBHW020544020726
47494CB00006B/1907